HEARING VOICES

HEARING VOICES

A. N. WILSON

W. W. NORTON & COMPANY
New York London

Copyright © 1996 by A. N. Wilson

Printed in the United States of America
First Edition

For information about permission to reproduce selections of this book, write to
Permissions, W. W. Norton & Company, Inc. 500 Fifth Avenue, New York, NY 10110.

Manufacturing by Courier Companies, Inc.

Library of Congress Cataloging-in-Publication Data

Wilson, A. N., 1950–
Hearing voices / A. N. Wilson
p.   cm.
1. Manuscripts—Collectors and collecting—New York (N.Y.)—Fiction.
2. Murder—New York (N.Y.)—Fiction.   3. Forgery of manuscripts—Fiction.
4. Biographers—Fiction.   I. Title.
PR6073.I439H44   1996
823'.914—dc20   95-25869
CIP

ISBN 0-393-03875-0

W. W. Norton & Company, Inc., 500 Fifth Avenue, New York, NY 10110
http://web.wwnorton.com
W. W. Norton & Company Ltd., 10 Coptic Street, London WC1A 1PU

1 2 3 4 5 6 7 8 9 0

TO
Selina

There are in history no beginnings and endings. History books begin and end, but events do not . . .

So long as the past and the present are outside one another, knowledge of the past is not of much use in the problems of the present. But suppose the past lives on in the present; suppose, though encapsulated in it, and at first sight hidden beneath the present's contradictory and more prominent features, it is still alive and active; then the historian may very well be related to the non-historian as the trained woodsman is to the ignorant traveller. 'Nothing here but grass and trees,' thinks the traveller, and marches on. 'Look,' says the woodsman, 'there is a tiger in that grass.'

R. G. Collingwood: *An Autobiography* (1939)

Acknowledgement

The quotations at the beginning of each cha[
from A *Catechism of Christian Doctrine, Approv*
bishops and Bishops of England and Wales and
Used in All their Dioceses, revised edition, 198[
the Catholic Truth Society.

A list of characters mentioned in the story, [
have previously appeared in earlier volumes [
Papers, is to be found at the back of this boo[

ONE
(October 1968)

Where will they go who die in mortal sin?
They who die in mortal sin will go to hell for all eternity.

'You!'

The old man was about to die, and he knew it.

His hams teetered and wobbled these days, so that he never seemed to stand upright. His lips drooped; slobbered and dribbled with whisky and with the brown juices which always bubbled between his noxious teeth when the cigar was removed. His cheeks sagged, melancholic and self-pitying, beneath the blue spectacles. In the face of Virgil D. Everett, Jnr there had always been an element of self-importance. Now, there was fear.

He stared at his adversary. He should not have been puzzled; there was motive enough for wishing him dead. Nevertheless, his features asked the question – Why? Why now? Why me? There was, at that precise second, no more vulnerable being in the whole of Manhattan, for all his millions of dollars.

Virgil D.'s whims could influence the rise and fall of prices on the Stock Exchanges, not only of Wall Street, but of the world. If Virgil D. bought gold, a dollar or two was automatically added to the world price of an ounce of gold; currencies wavered slightly, wondering what he was up to. Then, if he sold his gold, the currencies recovered. The handful of people who watched Virgil D., and what he did with his money, felt confident once more; and they spread their confidence to

1

the hundred or so people who watched them, and the thousands who watched that hundred reassured their investors that, for the time being, they could leave their money where it was. The world was safe again. And yet, the man who had his large, banana-like finger on so much financial power was about to be eliminated, with the same ease with which you might kill a monkey in a laboratory.

In a few seconds' time all that money and all that power would cease to belong to Virgil D. Everett, Jnr. Much of it would belong to his son (by a marriage which had long since dissolved, and of which few knew the existence). Much would be distributed amid the various trusts which he and his legal colleagues enjoyed setting up. A legal wrangle would ensue (nothing to do with this story) about that cheque, signed the morning before his death, but not sent, diverting two million dollars to the Democratic Party. Did the death stop the cheque?

This was a man about whom rumour had circulated freely on the lips of the *cognoscenti*. Nothing had ever reached the pages of the Press – perhaps not surprisingly since he owned some of it. Some said he owned a large house in Saigon, inherited from a relation who, in the early years of the century, had married into a French family. Some said that Virgil D. had threatened to withdraw his funds from the party unless the President continued to bomb Hanoi, continued to be hawkish at the Paris peace talks. Who could say whether this were true? Like most rich men, Virgil D. Everett, Jnr was hard to classify. He was no liberal. When Bobbie Kennedy had been shot earlier in the year, he had slowly and humourlessly remarked that this was 'one less thing for the President to worry about'. (That *had* been reported in the paper; reported, and subsequently withdrawn; lawyers had seen to that; the journalist who wrote the story had possessed a promising future until it went into print; after two years of unemployment he was abjectly grateful to do baseball commentaries for a small local radio station in Idaho.)

Perhaps Virgil D. Everett, like others in that strange year, was a victim of the Fates – doomed before the autumn had turned to winter, to join the Czechs who had died during the invasion of Prague that summer, the students who died during *les événements* in Paris during the spring; to join the shades of Bobbie Kennedy and Dr Martin

2

Luther King. It was certainly the worst of times; Virgil D. had never much liked those optimists who thought it was the best of times.

Maybe he knew too much. In his collector's zeal, maybe he had accumulated just one treasure too many; one painting, one house, one stuffed animal, one literary document, one secret too many. The ownership of Virgil D.'s vast collections was, in one violent stroke, about to change hands. Someone other than Virgil D. (in fact, the trustees of the Everett Literary Trust, presided over by the biographer Raphael Hunter) would discover themselves the owner of one of the biggest assemblages of Decadent Art in the world – hundreds of Beardsley drawings, for instance. The Ann-Louise Everett Collection named 'for' Virgil D.'s mother, was a considerable library of literary manuscripts. When Alfred Douglas's diaries had so surprisingly come to light, Virgil D. had paid twice the auctioneers' 'estimate'. He possessed the largest collection of Pater manuscripts. Holograph poems with interesting variants from their published form, by Baudelaire, Mallarmé, Swinburne and Ernest Dowson, were all housed in the Ann-Louise Everett Collection.

And then, again, as Lord Lampitt once remarked to the author of these pages, 'Don't forget the Everett Dalis'. He could have added, 'Don't forget the Lampitt Papers' – more accurately, the archive of the late James Petworth Lampitt, the belletrist historian – a collection which consisted chiefly of letters to Lampitt from figures as various as Gide, Henry James, Frank Harris and Lawrence of Arabia.

Of the Lampitt Papers themselves, rumours circulated, little scurries of rumour, it is true, gusts unworthy to be compared with the hurricanes and tornadoes in the political and financial world which Virgil D. could call up or could still, like the miraculous calming of Galilee. Such little storms as ruffled the Lampitt Papers with their breezes were, however, not without their interest. His library was a fortress to which only the privileged were admitted. The public were barely aware of its existence – only booksellers and collectors knew of it, and even they had the haziest idea of its contents, since no catalogue of it was ever published for general reading.

When Mr Everett fell to his death, this was the end of the Ann-Louise Everett Collection. No one had any interest in keeping it together, and it was dispersed. The secret of the Lampitt Papers could be deemed to have died with the old man. The letters written by

Henry James to young Lampitt went to Boston. A collector in Paris bought the few letters from Canon Gray and Robbie Ross. All the 'evidence' which had been utilised to substantiate Raphael Hunter's two-volume biography of James Petworth Lampitt had been scattered. Almost no one, after Virgil D. Everett's demise, could prove one way or the other whether Hunter's book had contained any elements of truth or whether it was riddled with lies from beginning to end. Almost no one knew, almost no one cared.

Only very few scholars had ever been allowed to work in the Ann-Louise Everett Library. It was not strictly a research library since unless the visiting scholar knew what he or she was looking for they would never find it there. Julian Ramsey had spent the better part of two months, dotted here and there, trying to read through the Lampitt Papers and his readings were necessarily haphazard. Raphael Hunter, by contrast, a rival Lampitt biographer, possessed unlimited access to the archive, and this perhaps explained why he was able to produce those two substantial volumes of James Petworth Lampitt's biography.

Some said that Hunter had invented the sexual adventures of Lampitt for his own perverse purpose. What if, however, there was someone in a position not to suspect Hunter of fraudulence, but to discover him at it? What if, in the midst of all his other activities, Virgil D. had taken the trouble to read the Lampitt Papers, or at least to get a sense of them? What if he knew that they contained no such adventures as Hunter hints at in his book? What if someone in a position to know such things had told Mr Everett that Hunter was a fraud? He had only bought the Lampitt archive on Hunter's advice! What if he had confronted Hunter with this; or, what if Virgil D. had found out something discreditable about Mr Hunter, something which would damage this literary man's career? Powerful man, Everett; powerful, that is, until his sagging frame was pushed to its destruction.

As he faced his murderer now, he did not look so powerful. Ever pallid, he looked like a corpse already, in the dim electric haze of that cold autumnal light, as he stood facing his assailant.

It would be fanciful to believe that his last thoughts were of the Lampitt Papers. He had many other concerns. In addition to the oil wells, and the financial conglomerates, there was his partnership in the law firm of Everett, Everett, Klein, Ahrlich and Kavanagh, one of the biggest on the East Coast, the firm of which he was still notionally, since the death of his uncle, the head. The tongues which wagged after Virgil D.'s death had plenty to say about that; lawyers are talkative people. Which law firm was one of the greatest rivals to Everett, Everett, Klein, Ahrlich and Kavanagh? Was it not Nixon, Mudge, Rose, Guthrie, Alexander and Mitchell? The latter five of those gentlemen are totally blameless. But there had been rumours, as the general election approached, that Virgil D. Everett knew a little something about the first of them – Richard M. Nixon. It was said that Virgil D. was privy to information which could have been fatally damaging to Richard M. Nixon at that late stage of a closely-fought election campaign. No one for a second implicated Mudge, or Rose, or Guthrie; as for Alexander and Mitchell, they were pure as the driven snow. But supposing – just supposing – that some Republican zealot, or perhaps some enthusiast for Governor Wallace, believed that Virgil D. Everett, Jnr had it in his power to put Hubert Humphrey, rather than Richard M. Nixon, into the White House? Would it not, from such an enthusiast's point of view, have been in the national interest for Virgil D. Everett to step just a little beyond his balcony on that cold October night?

Other rumourmongers could see it differently. There were all those stories of strange preferences and practices. The young people themselves who were cajoled by threats, or lured by financial inducement, into his sordid and voyeuristic pastimes, cannot have been sorry that he was dead. Any one of them might have been in a position, when the 'fun' was over for an evening, to bring that cycle of sexual degradations to an end. Has it not all been written in the extraordinary biography by Raphael Hunter – *The Everett Story* – serialised in newspapers on both sides of the Atlantic and published in book form in 1985?

Equally, in that murky world, blackmail and threat must have been exchanged. His immediate circle contained those who could not afford to be tainted by the stories of his sexual predilections, nor by his allegedly hawkish attitude towards the War. Men like Congressman Newt Ahrlich, a partner in Virgil D.'s law firm, had done much for the Democratic Party before that disastrous Chicago convention less than a month before Virgil D. died. Newt had worked hard in all the previous three years, to make sure that his brother-in-law, Atlas Birk, was going to become the John F. Kennedy of the 1970s. Birk was a young Congressman, but Ahrlich was determined that his protégé should be talked about at that convention. Birk was to be the voice and the mind of young, Democratic America; the America which would rebuild itself after the War – not on the neo-Christian claptrap of Eugene McCarthy, but on simple and wholesome patriotism, and homey American values like hard work and thrift and fondness for ball games. This was the well-scrubbed image of At Birk which Ahrlich had been busy promoting. Neither of them would be well-served if the public ever associated At Birk with Virgil D., or heard the rumours – about the orgies, the criminal violence, the drugs.

It will probably never be known how far Virgil D. Everett knew of his personal financial involvement in the purchase and sale of illegal narcotics. The greatest of the hauls – the stuffed water-buffalo whose head was filled with cocaine ('no wonder his horns were curling,' remarked the officer who made the discovery) – happened after the old man's death. Perhaps he had no idea how many drug barons he was doing out of business by his exchange and purchase of stuffed animals, nor by his patronage of the old Hungarian taxidermist in E. 14th Street.

However you regarded the matter, there were plenty of people who wanted the old man dead, and there were plenty of people who rejoiced when they saw the front page of the newspaper the next morning, and learnt that someone had accomplished what they themselves had been too cowardly to perform.

Before he flies – let us savour the moment. Let us imagine him looking at his assassin. The self-satisfaction which normally lit up his face is rapidly ebbing away, as he realises that his killer means business. His face has begun to wear its puzzled-scholar look, an expression which it would sometimes assume at dinner-tables when he was just sober enough to know that he was boring people, but not sober enough to stop. His grin reveals those cigar-brown teeth which make it so unimaginable that anyone had ever voluntarily kissed Virgil D. Everett. Hope is still playing there in those features, hope that he might have misread the outright malevolence of the face into which he is looking.

'I mean – ' his voice is not merely maddeningly slow, as ever, but slurred and hesitant at the same time – 'if this is something we can maybe talk over. If maybe you'd like some whisky . . .'

As was by now his wont, he has already drunk a lot of whisky. He carelessly turns his head and looks out at the night sky. The hair – seen from the front, a convincing slab of well-coiffed silver – is thinning at the back. The skin of the scalp is soft, vulnerable as a baby's.

'It's a mistake,' he says, 'to be hasty.'

It was never a mistake which, conversationally, he appeared to make himself. In the hour of his death, the incurable slowness of speech even possessed its own bizarre heroism.

He wanders through the french windows and on to the roof garden. 'I hope you're not going to use that thing?'

Beneath, like ten thousand discarded cigarettes spangling with the last sparks of life, Manhattan flickers. Sirens sound. It is too high up to hear specific traffic noise, but the generalised hum of the city in all its overpopulated motorised roar ascends through the darkness to the roof shrubs.

'I'd like to think,' says Virgil D. Everett, 'I'd like to think, that . . .'

He says it nice and slowly, with the consequence that the world will never know what he would have liked to think, for he has been pushed, very hard, against the balustrade which edges the roof garden. Fierce fingers have been pressed against his face. His weak, trousered hams have been lifted up and his screams, if heard, are unheeded. In his last seconds of existence, Virgil D. Everett flies. An unlikely Icarus, down, down, he hurtles, towards E. 63rd Street.

The body did not hit the pavement; it fell on to a moving yellow cab, badly dented the roof and caused the car to screech sideways across the street, colliding with an oncoming Ford. There were some nasty injuries. The cab-driver, a Puerto Rican, needed fourteen stitches in his face. In subsequent years, he (unsuccessfully) tried to sue the Everett Foundation for an alleged diminution of his sexual prowess, following a period of depressive convalescence from the accident. At least no one was killed in the accident – no one, that is, except Virgil D. Everett, Jnr.

TWO
(October 2000)

After your night prayers, what should you do?
After my night prayers I should observe due modesty in going to bed;
occupy myself with thoughts of death . . .

Fifth Avenue might seem an improbable venue for a visionary experience. Even more improbable might be the notion that one could have such an experience and that it could vanish from the mind totally – but this is the case, and only on a return visit to New York, more than thirty years after the 'vision', has it come back to my mind. I can remember the most trivial conversations of thirty or forty years ago. But memory has played this strange trick and cancelled out the vision. (Perhaps, like that part of our brain which edits our waking recollections of dreams, the memory is better than our conscious mind at deciding what is important or significant. Just because it was paranormal does not mean it was important. Funny to have forgotten it, though.)

I am in one of those huge, impersonal, and, by my very English and very middle-class standards, absurdly opulent hotel rooms. The large double bed is almost the size of the dining-table at Mallington Hall. It feels very empty with one, lonely, skinny old man in it. Can I really be sixty-five? The huge colour television set could, at the flick of a button, bring me CNN News, or advertisements, or revivalist meetings or soft pornography or sporting events. The Frigidaire is stuffed with chocolates, cheese, peanuts, drinks of every description.

8

I am sitting here, however, without any such stimulants, gazing down on this city, which I have not visited since I was in my early thirties, and where I am a stranger. I can't quite see St Patrick's Cathedral but I hardly need to do so. That afternoon in the spring of '66 has revisited me. I am not sure that I am much able to distinguish any more between memory and an experience which is really like repetition – I don't need to recall the past or to summon it up artificially; the difficulty is getting *out* of the past. Ever since this afternoon, (when I remembered the vision) the rest of New York has been in the new millennium, and I have been stuck in 1966; I am hoping to get back to the present before this evening's performance.

Perhaps, when one finds oneself thus caught up in the past, this is a glimpse of 'eternity', a dimension in which time has either ceased to matter, or to move lineally. If this is the case, then the two beings with whom I have not been able to live my life, but who preoccupy me on various planes for much of my waking life (my child and my mother), have not perhaps been lost to me. I am quite uninterested in theology and I do not want an explanation to justify this feeling of mine. I am perfectly content to be told by the cleverer philosophers that such feelings as mine are without rational foundation; that *they are nonsense*. I shouldn't wish to argue with that, except to say, as Dr Johnson said of ghosts, that 'all argument is against it; but all belief is for it'. Ghost stories are the crude expression of an almost universal belief, a belief which has a multitude of expressions – in the activities of spirit mediums, in voodoo, in Chinese ancestor-worship, in chantry chapels and requiem Masses, in Days of the Dead and Armistice parades – that the Dead are not wholly dead, but that they are in some mysterious way *revenants*, either reborn as figures in the material world, or as memories which haunt our psyche at some usually forgotten and best left impenetrable level; or as the 'souls' in Purgatory, Limbo, Heaven and Hell. Imaginations as different as Plato, Virgil and Dante have all posited not merely the survival of the dead but also the possibility that we might, on this side of the divide, reach out and make contact with those on another shore.

Idle by temperament and naturally sceptical, I have never pursued this idea, preferring to bask in the imaginative expressions of those three writers, and in the great Requiems of Mozart and Fauré and Brahms, rather than taking my own steps to the point where I was

9

forced to say what I think or what I believe about the dead. So, although I yearn to see my lost mother (who was killed in an air raid in the Second World War when I was a child, she and my father both together), I have never consulted a 'medium' and although I have never ceased, periodically, to be haunted by my lost child, I have never taken refuge in the formal practice of 'religion'. How different from that child's mother!

It was in St Patrick's Cathedral, which I had supposed we were viewing merely as tourists, that she suddenly told me to wait for her by the door. Persy invariably seemed cross, and her voice was always on the verge of being inaudible.

'Are you feeling all right?' A crass question on my part. I did not actually fear that she was ill. Her round face with its waxy little nose (the feature which more than any other had made me fall for her initially) gave off those generalised expressions of discontent which she appeared to feel constantly. I have often enough had reason to believe, egocentrically no doubt, that I have 'made' another person unhappy. Out of habit, such beliefs, cognate with those of guilt but morally void, lingered. I knew, however, that Persy Nolan had not been happy to start with. Her happiness had not been noticeably enhanced by allowing me to hang around, but it was always hard to know how far her smouldering bad temper was real, and how much it was part of an act. Since student days, apparently, she had made a 'thing' of being 'difficult'. If there were a competition for 'difficulty', used in this sense, I do not know who, among all the people I have known, would win. Persy would certainly stand a very good chance of being short-listed, though whether she would wrest the prize from Sargent Lampitt would be a nice question for the panel of judges. Certainly she was as 'difficult' as her brother and sister-in-law, Fergus and M.M., were 'easy', though I must confess that I speak with prejudice, being one of those many people in the world who fell in love with M.M. and remained in this condition for some years.

The Newnham Norns, the singing group in which Persy was so conspicuously toneless a vocalist had, astonishingly enough, been able to organise a little American tour. I never did decide whether Persy thought she had a good voice; nor could I decide whether the other Norns allowed her to sing as some elaborate joke; nor, if this was the case, whether this was a cruel joke, perpetrated to humiliate Persy, or

10

a surreal prank played on their enthusiastic audiences. I was still notionally writing the official history of the Lampitt Family, and so arranged that a necessary month in the Ann-Louise Everett Library should coincide with the week or so which the Newnham Norns were spending in New York. Ever since the Norns had hit town, my work had suffered, but we had had some fun, seen some sights, looked up old acquaintances. Having been lonely for the best part of a fortnight, I suddenly found that I knew more people than I had time for; I had made arrangements to move out of the Chelsea (where the Norns were staying) as soon as the band moved on to the West Coast, and to take one of the rooms over the old Hungarian taxidermist's in E. 14th Street, lately vacated by a friend of Wilmie Birk's.

Persy and I had been getting on as badly as we always did from the very first second of our meeting. We were gratingly at odds from the moment that our incompatible personalities had first collided. Certainly I lusted after her (to the end of our association and beyond it), and I can't believe such feelings were completely absent on her part. But even in this area there was a quality of strife – even in the act itself. I remember during one session, in a hotel on the outskirts of Birmingham, that as we writhed and moaned and tore and fought, I thought of Matthew Arnold's line about ignorant armies which clash by night. (I reckon that it was during that episode that the baby was conceived.)

In any event, here we were, a Newnham Norn and I, in New York with half a day to spare, and we both thought that we should see some sights; so, we had eaten bagels and looked at the Rodins in the Met. and gone from one end of the island to another by bus, and taken the Staten Island ferry, and enjoyed very little of any of it because of Persy's vinaigrous inability to enjoy *anything*. The English concept of being a good sport or pretending, out of good manners, to like a thing even when you didn't, had been left out of Persy's temperament and upbringing. Hardly surprising since there was no English blood in her veins. When we found ourselves on foot once more, and half inclined to slog up to the Museum of Modern Art and see *Les Demoiselles d'Avignon* she suddenly announced that she wanted to see St Patrick's. You will have gathered already that Persy was a Catholic. I had no idea of this when our affair began, and took no more interest in her religious allegiance than if her parents had

11

happened to be Methodists or Jews. Only when I came to know her family in Birmingham quite well did I realise how strong, how overpoweringly strong, this form of Roman Catholicism was (perhaps all forms?) and how different it was from the rather mild High Anglicanism in which I had been brought up by Uncle Roy and Aunt Deirdre.

I was particularly aware of it because of the obsession felt in that Church with the birth control question. You could not very well get away from it in Wiseman Road, where Fergus and M.M. lived, since Fergus was one of the Catholic scientists being called upon to advise the Pope about the moral admissibility of oral contraception. Of course, Fergus was very discreet and never told us what was being discussed by the Pontifical Commission itself, but the subject had threatened the tranquillity of many a Sunday lunch at M.M.'s table.

For me, religion was, as a child – still is, I suppose – a mixture of human responses to the world of phenomena and superphenomena. Its great proponents – William Blake, Albion Pugh, even Mr Pilbright in his odd way – were those who have been able to lift the veil between one layer of consciousness and another, or at the least to suggest that it made sense to speak of such a veil. The Catholics, I discovered, merely assumed the existence of the supernatural world, and took for granted concepts about which the rest of us might be extremely tentative. At first, when I got to know them and their strange ways of expressing themselves, I felt that they were rather like the old British Imperialists, who had planted Union Jacks in the most inaccessible places and established that rocks in the Antarctic wastes or tracts of inaccessible forest in Canada were 'British'. The RCs, similarly, seemed to have taken heaven by storm. Monsignor Ronald Knox – a hero to many of the Nolans' guests at those luncheons – had actually announced that all the identity discs in heaven were labelled RC, prompting one (silently of course) to wonder what the old inhabitants of heaven – such as the Almighty and the Angels – had done before there *were* any RCs.

Their belief in their Church was something which took me entirely off guard. I had been singing since I could remember that 'The Church's One foundation/Is Jesus Christ Her Lord'. They actually believed this! When I thought of the Church, I thought of an actual, physical building where, as a boy, I had first come into contact with

12

Christianity – and with Christianity, the whole of Europe's past: the parish church at Timplingham. Anglicanism was not the only possible way of confronting the unknowable, the unseen, any more than this fifteenth-century Perpendicular was the only form of architecture. The Church, for me, was merely the expression of a collective human experience, not necessarily even an experience of God (though we did not rule Him out), but a sense of the past, a feeling for the dead, a generalised sense of the numinous which we had wished to enshrine and which we sometimes felt more able to do in stone and glass and music than we did in words.

The Catholics had much clearer ideas about this divine society, or what Uncle Roy's liturgy called 'the blessed company of all faithful people'. They thought the Church had a specific teaching authority, given it by Christ himself and enshrined in the teaching *magisterium*, particularly though not exclusively in the Papacy. This was the reason for all the hullabaloo in '68 when the Pope finally published *Humanae Vitae* outlawing the use of any contraceptives, even the Pill. It was not that the Catholics were *per se* more interested in birth control than the rest of the human race but that they found themselves members of a society where human beings were not, like the rest of us, struggling for light to guide them; rather, they were being told the will of the Almighty because of a particular relationship enjoyed between God and the Pope. This was what caused the row – the conservatives insisting on the Divine Guidance promised by Christ to the Church, and the liberals taking the view that the Church was only a human institution which might pray for illumination, but which *might get it wrong*.

Until getting into bed with Persy it had never occurred to me that any intelligent person could actually believe in Catholicism. In fact, this central teaching of Catholicism, that the Church can know and teach God's will, even in quite specific matters of sexual conduct, was something which I had never directly encountered, although one had heard quarrels about it in pubs.

Why Persy believed in it, beyond the fact that it was in her blood, and she had been taught to believe it, I could not fathom then, and I have never understood since. I remain the most invincibly ignorant of Protestants. But believe it she – and her clever brother Fergus (though he in a much more agonised way, poor man) and her sister-

13

in-law M.M. (ah!) and all M.M.'s family, and all Persy's huge brood of relations – most indubitably did. I think I can understand the religious point of view. Nor do I wish to cut myself off from the imaginative experience of my ancestors who built, and worshipped in, the parish churches of England and who punctuated their lives with the liturgy of *The Book of Common Prayer*. Since I grew up, I have been perfectly at ease with this position, being neither clever nor curious enough to map out my own metaphysical opinions but feeling no embarrassment at occasional attendance at Anglican worship.

For the Catholics, however, this is pure heresy and isn't a religious point of view at all. Not content to revere our ancestors, they wish to ape the ancestral mind-set, as if a contemporary painter would only consent to work in the manner of thirteenth-century fresco artists. Certainly what troubled Persy was that she had transgressed the laws of the Church. It was the Church which had the power to leave her wallowing in her sins; and since these were 'mortal' sins, she was in danger, should she die in this state, of going to hell. This was why she needed to wipe those sins away with the Church's gift of absolution, and it was of this gift, in St Patrick's Cathedral, that she was availing herself. Only, of course, being Persy, she did not explain what she was doing, she simply wandered off, muttering rather crossly that she would find me by the door.

Ideas of the beautiful are obviously subjective, but the interior of St Patrick's struck me as of quite staggering ugliness and brashness, bearing as much relationship to the mysteriousness of a true Gothic cathedral, such as Chartres or Salisbury, as a cheap hamburger might to the most perfectly prepared sirloin. With its twinkling night-lights burning by every statue in its overcrowded aisles, and with its shiny flooring, it was about as numinous in my eyes as a shopping mall or Disney World.

Like New York itself, however, the cathedral fizzed with vulgar energy; one had a sense of hundreds of thousands of men and women coming to this place, as Day Muckley, my dear old friend, would have said (keen churchgoer and Catholic he) 'to lay down their burdens for Christ's sakes'. As I stood at the back of the cathedral watching people of every age and race come and go, and thinking of all the guilty, worried thoughts which people had suffered in that spot, I

14

found the consciousness of these burdens oppressive; each flickering, garish night-light represented some unconquerable life-destroying habit, or some anguished sorrow for a loved one in pain, or some superstitious belief that in the case of the one who lit the light, the irreversible and callous processes of Nature might be reversed. As I stood there, with the consciousness of the general unhappiness of so many people, I had a telepathic knowledge of Persy Nolan's unhappiness. She was so habitually disgruntled that I knew that I could not be the cause of it (or not the only cause) and so I had lost my capacity to sympathise with her. Indeed, her anger had become, in my mind, if not a joke, then something a little like a joke, so that I was able to blot out consciousness of her unhappiness. Now, however, I felt it, not merely as something imagined but as something which I actually felt myself; so intense was the pain that I was shocked by it, knowing for the first time that her churlishness was the manifestation of a profound inner disgust with existence itself. To this was added a grief which I felt telepathically and understood with perfect clarity.

She had never discussed the matter with me. I had not known (we had a fairly on–off relationship, and never lived in the same town for more than a few days at a time) and I had never guessed, until that peculiarly gloomy éclaircissement in St Patrick's, that she had been pregnant; but I wasn't allowed a single, split-second of joy at this knowledge because even as I realised its truth, I knew too what she was doing in the cathedral: she was confessing to an abortion. I mention this strange phenomenon because I had not at that stage taken any hallucinogenic substances, nor had I gone mad, nor had I undergone the treatment for madness which all came eighteen months or so later. Completely sane and completely sober, I was *given* this knowledge about Persy. Such an enlightenment or telepathy is perhaps not surprising, since we had both been close to one another at least some of the time, and since we were both the parents of the child. It was what followed which is so extraordinary. To call it a vision – as I have already done – suggests that I 'saw' something external, like the miraculous apparitions at Lourdes or Llanthony. My vision lacked any such 'photographic' clarity, but it *was* a vision, for I saw not just with my eyes but also with my imagination, our child – Persy's and my child – hovering over the heads of the people who came and went in St Patrick's.

15

I must crave the reader's indulgence! This is a recollection at third remove! (That is, I am writing these words about a memory which came back to me a few months ago; and the memory was of an experience which took place in 1966.) I know that I must try to disentangle the clarity of the original vision from the nonsense and oddity which it accumulated when it repeated itself in my brain at intervals during the next couple of years. It does not seem difficult to find a reason that I had forgotten the vision, until recently returning to New York. So much of that period, for my feeble constitution and my poor brain, is simply intolerable to recall, and I have therefore blotted it out. 'The remembrance of them is grievous unto us; the burden of them is intolerable.'

In my wilder moments, during that bad period, I would become unable to distinguish between the vision of my unborn child, and the Christ Child in various manifestations (as the Infant of Prague, as the Infant in the arms of St Joseph or of St Christopher). Agennetos, my unborn one, became a representative at times of Unborn Humanity, a representative of those beings whom (as I supposed) the Pope was trying to protect. Nobody in that excitable decade, except the Catholics, seemed to advance an articulate case for believing that human life is going on in the womb, and that a life is still human, before as well as after the experience of being born. Later, in the poor old century to which we have all said 'good riddance!' the idea of Life Before Birth was politicised. In the United States it became the property of the Protestant Right. But I was not aware of aligning myself either with Catholics or Protestants while the vision was in progress. As I recollect the vision, I also remember all these reinterpretations which I made of it, and all the madness and anguish and poetry which I brought to it. In order to 'make sense' of the story, I suppose my mind had had a thousand visions and revisions, until the original vision had been lost, and discarded. Presumably all these things have been quiescent in my skull for thirty years because I did not really need them.

At the time – which comes back to me now, sharp and luminous – when the Child appeared, I thought how like it was to photos of myself as a baby, proudly held up in the arms of Daddy or Mummy or Mrs Webb, either on some beach in Norfolk or on the South Coast or in our little back garden in Alderville Road. My vision-baby, however, was more than simply a photographic memory of myself. I'll attempt a phrase which might be too Blakean, but this is how it felt – *He shone with humanity*. As well as knowing that this was my baby, I knew that this was *echt* Humanity, human nature incorrupt, with all its potential for wisdom and laughter and goodness unscarred.

Even as I saw this child – a fact which I discovered about three years later in conversation with his mother – Persy was praying to him, asking his forgiveness, and imploring that his frustrated Guardian Angel might intercede for her poor childless brother Fergus and make Margaret Mary pregnant.

For me, the Child was only a child but, in the few split seconds of the vision, he hovered over the heads of the people in St Patrick's, large and brooding, as large as one of the roof-choristers at Timplingham. The poet whose words best describe what I saw at the moment is the sixteenth-century Jesuit Robert Southwell; not so much in his most famous visionary poem in which –

> A pretty Babe all Burning bright,
> Did in the air appear

as in his strange poem, 'Look home', in which he states –

> Man's soul of endless beauties image is
> Drawn by the work of endless skill and might.

My vision-baby was an embodiment, an image, of such 'endless beauties'. What gave the vision its intolerable poignancy was my simultaneous knowledge, even as I saw the child, that I was not to be a father in the ordinary sense of the word, that the abortion had already happened. (Incidentally, although I have called the Child Agennetos, and likened it to myself when young or to Christ, I at no time sexed this strange being, thinking of *her* or of *him* indiscriminately; though more often I said *him*, I did not think of the child as specifically male.)

'There you are!' Persy Nolan's quiet fury suggested that I had been hiding, rather than standing at exactly the agreed spot by the west door of the cathedral. I was still standing gazing upwards and did not exactly hear her, or even at that moment recognise her because the

17

vision was not completely over. If I were St Bernadette I should probably 'rationalise' my vision and say that it 'spoke' to me. This would certainly be the simplest thing to say since I was under the impression that I 'heard' the Child speak. If there are any hardened rationalists who have come with me thus far in the narrative without flinging the book down in disgust, let us say that I had so focused my entire attention on the Baby that I could not distinguish between its powers of speech and words which had come into my head. When Agennetos spoke, he said, '*I am the Resurrection and the Life.*'

That I 'added' to the vision afterwards, by thinking about, embellishing and trying to explain it to myself, I would freely admit; but these strange words which, by a straightforward train of association I link less with their source in the Fourth Gospel, than with funerals, above all Mummy's and Daddy's funeral, when the tear-choked words were said by my daddy's brother, Uncle Roy, these words were certainly part of the original vision. I did not add them later.

'Shall we go, or do you still want to hang about?'

(This furiously whispered by the Newnham Norn.)

You might think that, having barely descended from a visionary experience, I should have been in a holy 'glow', but I snapped back at her in a combination of fury and grief over which I had no control. In the healing years which have followed, of course, I understand and forgive what it was not in my nature, at that moment, to comprehend. Persy was in a real 'jam'. She got on very badly with me, and even if she had not done so, I was penniless and not in the best position to 'start a family'. She could have no notion (I did not realise it myself until I came so close to it) how much I wanted a child. At that moment, though, I felt sore and enraged and grief-stricken and was utterly unable to support her in her own desolation. Almost as soon as we were out of the cathedral we had started a row about religion.

One never says the right thing at the right time; otherwise we might, during that conversation, have tried to exercise a little kindness. I had been given a telepathic knowledge of her predicament, and I was in a position to be sympathetic to her. Instead, I was out of my trance immediately and saying,

'You think you can just treat this as your problem – what about me, what about the baby?'

'I don't have to consult you. Do you know what I was doing in

18

there? I was going to confession. Not that that would mean anything to you!'

As it happened, though brought up High, I had never been to confession. (Uncle Roy used to go, to an old priest at St John Maddermarket. What can he possibly have had to confess, dear old innocent?)

'So, you just go to confession and think that absolves you of any responsibility for your actions?'

'O, you're not just the bastard who got me into this whole mess, you're also God, are you? You're going to pass judgement. And damn and blast you, fuck you, when I've just been to confession – you're making me so angry.'

'That doesn't matter – you can go back in and confess to that as well.'

And, so on, pointlessly and cruelly for an hour or so. And all the good times – which there must have been – which we had had together just evaporated in this bad atmosphere. And an act of love-making in which a child had been conceived, had become, for the purposes of the argument, an occasion when an absolute bastard got a complete bitch into trouble. We were both in far too bad a mood to go to that party. Equally, we were getting on so badly that we should not have wished to spend the next couple of hours together in that bleak room at the Chelsea. At one time, I used to wonder how much my illness had chemical origins. If my mind had not been full of grief for a lost child at the time of my first 'bad trip', might I have avoided having to spend more than a year in a mental hospital? I shall never know. I just wish I had not started to think about it all *now* as an old man, as I stand at my hotel window in E. 52nd Street. I am in my underpants, my socks and my shirt, and I am wondering whether to change the shirt before they come for me.

For this 'One Man Show' (my reason for being in New York) I hardly need a 'costume'. In fact, I've decided to wear an old summer double-breasted suit of Uncle Roy's with one of his gold watch chains. (The suit looks purely Edwardian, though actually I can remember Uncle Roy having it made in Cambridge to take his mind off the South India crisis in 1956.) Props? Well, this silver-knobbed cane did actually belong to the man whom I am portraying – his brother gave

19

it me – and the large black fedora is the sort which I know he used to wear towards the close of his life.

Half past five. They are coming for me at half past six. I am feeling sick, as I always do before a stage performance. The success at the Oracle – that dear little Edwardian theatre just off Shaftesbury Avenue – of *Jimbo* – was gratifyingly unexpected. A young man entirely unknown to me had 'got keen' on the works of James Petworth Lampitt, the belletrist, essayist and anecdotalist. Though Jimbo, as he was always known in the family, survived until 1947 (he was seventy-something when he fell from his fire escape) it was this young man's genius to see that the essential 'Lampitt Years' were those of the Edwardian era. This stage monologue represented Jimbo in old age. This young man had relied heavily on Jimbo's wonderful letters to Cecily, which only came to light after Hunter had gone to press with his final volume of biography. (Their publication, with myself as editor, had largely exploded the myth of Jimbo as a promiscuous homosexual in his youth, though he was still regarded, perhaps rightly, as a highly 'camp' taste.) Using these letters, and interlacing them with paragraphs from Lampitt's journalism, essays and reviews, this young man had succeeded in producing something of a story. Agents and directors had been approached. It started life as a radio play. Since I had been a radio actor all my adult life (for most radio listeners I am only known as Jason Grainger on 'The Mulberrys') it is not surprising that they approached me for the part, not least because I had also edited Jimbo's letters and, though I had never met him, I had known many of his relations.

The radio show was a *succès d'estime* – and it led on to the successful little run at the Oracle. Now – a two-week run in a small theatre in Greenwich Village.

There is so much left out of this play! I wonder if that is why (to discard false modesty) my performance has been so much better than anything I've ever done before, why it has held audiences, and moved them? Because they sense behind the bland comedy of much of this stuff the strange story of Jimbo which I did come to know and which, for a whole set of muddled reasons, I never made known at the time? Does it matter, any of it, now that they are all dead, and I myself have become an antique? I do not know.

I stand in shirt tails and socks, a cadaverous figure according to the looking-glass, brushing his hair. I remember Sargie Lampitt, Jimbo's young brother, attired in just such a way on the morning of Jimbo's funeral, when Uncle Roy and I went up to Timplingham Place to fetch him. Sargie's panic attack on that occasion, lubricated but not allayed by gin, was something with which I vividly empathise, as I recall it. Sargie on that morning must have been the age that I am now, on this evening more than half a century later. I should dearly like, at this moment, to be relieved of the torment of going on stage tonight. Jimbo was a distinguished writer, a figure on the literary scene. No one except the Lampitts themselves, and my Uncle Roy, were aware of the dramas of Sargie's reclusive life. In so many ways I should prefer to be enacting the part of Sargie.

The telephone rings.

'Yes?'

I am so frightened that I contemplate saying 'no' or pretending in an assumed voice that the desk clerk, announcing the arrival of my minder and my limo, has got the wrong number. I have all but given up alcohol, and I make it a rule never to drink before work; but on this occasion, while I finish dressing, I mix myself an unwonted dry martini from the mini-bar and drink it in memory of Sargie.

Sargie, dear! I see you now, half-dressed, stroking your cat, Joynson-Hicks. 'Let's do a bunk, eh? I don't want to go to this bloody funeral and you don't want to go to your bloody school.' Oh, as I knock back that drink, how I miss you. Are you with me, helping with my performance tonight? Is that why it takes the form it does? For, now I am on the stage – it is an hour later. I am *being* James Petworth Lampitt. What *would* Uncle Roy have thought?! The obsession of his life being dramatised before an audience of New Yorkers!

Impossible for me to judge, but I suspect that almost all Englishmen sound, to American ears, faintly camp if not flagrantly homosexualist. I mean – and of course, it is impossible to know how one's voice might sound in another's ear – my guess is that when an American hears the voice of, let us say, Quentin Crisp or the Duke of Edinburgh or Sir Laurence Olivier, they would just sound like three, more or less indistinguishable old faggots – just as we can't really tell the difference between the voices of J. K. Galbraith and Sergeant Bilko. Another factor in the evening was the composition of the audience. In London, the audiences had been mixed. Since the success of

21

Hunter's television series 'Petworth Lampitt's People', there had been a preparedness on the part of the English public to take Jimbo seriously. In any event, 'style' had come back into vogue in England years ago (though too late for Jimbo to bask in glory in his own lifetime). Modernism was over. Stern critics like Dr Leavis (in whose estimation, Jimbo's work had been mannered, effete, decorative) had long ago sunk into oblivion. Since then – the orchidaceous blooms which flourished in Edwardian hothouses had enjoyed such a very popular revival that a fondness for the old stylists no longer implied a taste for the decadent. When I was a young man, who could ever have predicted that serious or 'highbrow' people might have taken an interest in the architecture of our great country houses or the choral music of Elgar? I am not quite sure that this shift in sensibilities ever took place on the western side of the Atlantic. To judge from the whoops of laughter from the audience, there are more men out there than women. Of course, I have been imitating Lampitt voices all my life. You could say it had been my life's calling. Though I never met Jimbo, I have heard recordings of his sound broadcasts – his tones were a slightly squeakier version of his brother Sargie's. In this, the first performance before an American audience, I am almost shocked by how funny they find it. This is a quiet little show which is designed to bring smiles to the faces of the middle-aged, the middle-class and the middlebrow. It never produced belly-laughs in England. But, finding that the Americans roar, I start to overplay. The audience is in my palm and I can manipulate them – the most extraordinary feeling.

'Mr Proust' – I am quoting one of the pieces which Jimbo wrote for the *Saturday Evening Post*, 'is not a man whom I have yet had the privilege of meeting . . .'

Jimbo could not have conceivably have meant this sentence to be amusing. Even I did not mean it to be funny, and it certainly does not look funny on the page. Indeed, as I speak the line on stage, I want to hold back the audience's laughter if I can, because if they continue bellowing at this rate they are going to miss the poignancy of the piece as a whole – its elegiac mood, its underlying English melancholy. But they are guffawing and hooting, and the power of the thing is going to my head. I am ashamed of myself, but I am going to exploit that audience as much as I can.

'Ah! Those evenings of rapture with Mr Irving . . .'

One man near the back of the auditorium is sobbing with laughter, letting out high-pitched moans; I begin to fear that he will have to be carried out.

'. . . those alchemical moments when Mr Forbes-Robertson ceased to be himself and was possessed by the spirit of Shylock, or of Cassius . . .'

Well said, old Mole!

'Is it any wonder that all my available spare time, and money, were spent, during that marvellous era' – Jimbo pronounced the word 'ay-rah!' – 'in the environs of Shaftesbury Avenue and the Haymarket; for what can equal its magic when the transformation has occurred, when the actor or actress is lost in the part and the audience is collectively in the thrall of theatre? Alas – it did not always happen thus . . .'

When Jimbo tried to be funny, he did not always succeed; but the English audiences had laughed at his recollection of two theatrical 'disasters' – a spearman missing his cue and forgetting his one line in the whole play; and an old chestnut about Charles Hawtrey. In these intentionally droll accounts of human misfortunes, the American audience quietens down – perhaps Americans are less satirical by temperament than the English.

I can remember a retired priest, not higher than Uncle Roy, but more Romanist, called Father Delmar, a strange whimsical creature, who came to live in the district and whom we all mocked. On one occasion, he asked my uncle if he could use Timplingham Church for a service of his own one weekday afternoon.

'You see, dear Father,' – he always intoned, rather than speaking in normal inflexions – 'when I left my last parish in Barking, I started a Confraternity of the Blessed Sacrament and each year we hold a Solemn Vespers and Benediction – so, if you were to let us use your church . . .'

Timplingham Parish Church is enormous; before the Reformation it was a priory and it could easily seat two hundred people. My uncle did not hold with post-Reformation Catholicism, so that the idea of Benediction, or of calling clergymen 'Father' was little to his taste. Since, however, it was impossible to dislike Father Delmar, and the church was always empty during the afternoons, it presumably seemed churlish to refuse. Nevertheless, as the day of the ceremony

23

approached, both my uncle and aunt became anxious about the party from Barking – not the most salubrious region of outer London. What if they were expecting refreshment?

'We couldn't have them in the house, not a whole charabanc party,' Aunt Deirdre said, in appearance more than ever the cross boy scout. I entirely shared her resentment at the idea of the invasion of our quiet Norfolk village by a bus-load of cockneyfied hooligans.

'I'm sure they'll bring their own sandwiches and Delmar won't allow any litterbugs.'

'And what will they do when they've had their tea and sandwiches?'

The cross boy scout had her mind on the practicalities; her determined expression told the world she was jolly well not going to dig latrines; Uncle Roy, however, as airy in his way as Father Delmar, had not given his mind to the question of whether, after a journey of three hours, the Confraternity might require what Sargie called the Topos.

The Gents, as we all called the downstairs loo at the Rectory, flushed quite adequately, but it required a particular knack – not unlike that required for bellringing – of pulling the chain with just the right degree of vigour, while keeping the chain taut. One could not believe that Father Delmar's Confraternity would master such a trick. Though none of us would spell it out verbally, we all inwardly foresaw a unpleasing prospect: days of horrible odours, or quarrels with the plumber who was always trying to persuade my aunt to replace the fine old Victorian cistern with a handle-flush of more contemporary design which she deemed flimsy.

'Please ask Mr Delmar how many are coming,' was my aunt's daily request.

I happened to be with my uncle when he bumped into his fellow clergyman – in the post office buying St Bruno tobacco – and plucked up the courage to put the question.

'Good morning, Delmar – it's Thursday week, isn't it that you're having . . .'

'Ah! dear Father!' sang that priest. 'How kind, how kind, dear Father! Our little Confraternity . . .'

'A thought which occurred to me . . . that is, I wondered how many would be coming exactly?'

Delmar, who had thick spectacles and a black Homburg hat, smiled broadly so as to reveal cheap dentures thickly coated with bits of fish pie.

'Dear Father, so kind! But none of them will be coming! Didn't I say – they are all in Barking?'

Once a year – until he died – Father Delmar was allowed to sing a Solemn Vespers at Timplingham, entirely alone in the vast airy church. *They are all in Barking* became a catchphrase in the family. Like so many things which one considers completely ridiculous as a child, it seems less mad to an aged brain. All the people I love, and all those who have been most important to me, have a teeming life inside my head. It makes little difference whether they are dead or alive; nor does it make much difference whether they are old acquaintances or whether like William Blake or Jimbo Lampitt I never even had the chance to meet them. *They are all in Barking.*

And I am not in Barking but New York – *being* Jimbo, or rather, being a parody Jimbo, camping it up for the New York queens. Nevertheless, there must have been more substance to Jimbo than his critics would have allowed in his lifetime. More than half a century after his mysterious demise, his words – some of them casually written paragraphs for the newspapers – have the power to move an audience.

The first part of the show is a series of unconnected reminiscences. How to end the second part – that did cause problems to the young man who put the piece together; it caused particular personal problems for me when I discussed it with him and with the producer at the BBC before I decided to take the part. One hopes that the first part makes up in humour what it lacks in drama or pace.

As I have already suggested, the show leaves out much more than it puts in. It omits Jimbo's relations with his family. (Uncle Roy would certainly have found this incomprehensible, since for him the most important thing about Jimbo was not that he was a famous writer, but that he was a Lampitt.) It omits the relationship with Cecily. Since there's no need to make this into a mystery story, I might as well set down roughly what that relationship was.

In the course of 1917, when Sargent Lampitt (then in his twenties) had 'a nervous breakdown', his young wife Cecily fell in love with her (considerably older) brother-in-law, Jimbo Lampitt. They remained close companions for the next thirty years. Until I read

25

through Jimbo's letters to Cecily, when they were housed, after her death, at Mallington Hall, I had not been able to envisage their relationship. Letters, of course, do not prove anything, but some were of a candour which made its character obvious. At some period when Sargie had been in the asylum, and before he went back to Timplingham Place to live with his mother, Cecily and Jimbo developed an intimacy. This is not a coy synonym for sex. I have been unable to make up my mind whether Cecily and Jimbo were lovers. After a period in which they exchanged love letters, they settled down – so I should infer from the correspondence – into a gentler, easier friendship. Cecily managed to take out an injunction forbidding Hunter to mention her by name in his second volume of *James Petworth Lampitt*. For those of us who know anything about Jimbo, this makes the final volume – covering the thirty years of Jimbo's and Cecily's close association – of limited value as an historical source. Nonetheless, Hunter's suggestion that there were those 'close to Petworth' (as he always called Jimbo) 'who resented his fondness for young men' probably contained seeds of truth. Jimbo undoubtedly did 'take up' young men, favouritise them, take them (if they were sufficiently presentable) to lunch at the Travellers' or (if they were not) invite them to tea in his flat. He liked lending them books and talking about what they had read; I never found any corroboration of Hunter's assertion that there was anything explicitly sexual in Jimbo's dealings with the young men.

All this meant that the second half of my 'Jimbo' stage performance needed some careful thinking. The whole monologue is to be imagined as spoken to a new young visitor to the flat in Hinde Street – one who did not necessarily know who Beerbohm Tree or Arthur Machen were, but who will quickly pick up, from his store of anecdotage, that Jimbo is a survivor from a lost age. But our young author was surely right to avoid melodrama, and not to have Jimbo's death enacted on the stage. (James Petworth Lampitt died in the spring of 1947, just after the snows thawed, by falling from a fire escape outside his London flat, near Manchester Square. The fact that he was not alone at the time of his death – but entertaining a young man called Raphael Hunter – meant that Hunter's evidence at the inquest was of the greatest importance.)

It was Albion Pugh (aka Rice Robey) who, in the early 1960s, first raised the possibility that the coroner's verdict might have been wrong, and that the death was not 'through misadventure'. Jimbo was not a large man. The railings on the fire escape would have reached almost to his chest. Cecily Lampitt was insistent, when she gave evidence in the libel trial (*Hunter v. Pugh*) that Jimbo would not have taken his own life wilfully. Albion Pugh accused Hunter more or less openly of having murdered Jimbo and Hunter won the ensuing libel trial with substantial damages. Even if the law of the land permitted the repetition of a libel on the stage, it would have ruined my monologue to have alluded to this in any way.

My own obsession with the manner of Jimbo's death would have made it impossible for me to weave such a charming 'One Man Show' out of his life. Returning to New York has woken up many unacted tragedies and comedies inside my skull. I am forced once more to contemplate my personal preoccupation with Jimbo's demise – it developed into a mania, all mixed up with my uncontrollable dislike of Hunter. And there was my involvement with the Nolans – my lost Nolan baby, my furious Persy, her charming brother Fergus, his beautiful wife Margaret Mary. That was the period, after the abortion, when I first became 'ill', an experience which it is difficult to recall, since memory is a gentle companion, blotting out much which is painful. All these things coalesce – Uncle Roy and his Lampitt-mania, Jimbo's death, my love for M.M., my loss of Mummy, Persy's loss of the baby – and none of them has much to do perhaps with the 'real Jimbo' whom I have been trying to resurrect in this stage performance. If you saw the London show, where there was more of a 'set' than in New York, you will remember that about halfway through the second half I move centre stage, and then back stage – further and further away from the audience. In London there was an elaborately constructed french window and a simulated 'skyline'. In New York there is simply an effect of light on the back wall of the stage to suggest an open window at twilight. I am gazing down now at the Wallace Collection in Manchester Square, a building which always reminds me of Italy. I speak a sentence or two from *Lagoon Loungings* (Jimbo's Venice book, his comments on the quality of dying light behind San Giorgio Maggiore) and then some remarks on death from the Tennyson biography. The lights go quietly down, and the thing ends on a dying note of quiet nostalgia as I am left, standing, an obsolete silhouette against the alien, modern London sky.

A pregnant silence – then that noise which every actor thrives on, and which explains why we should endure the ignominy, the poverty, the boredom of the profession – a burst of applause. I am not really an experienced stage actor, so it probably thrills me excessively. The applause at the end of a one man show is even more exciting than at the end of a play where you have to share the glory.

And now, I have returned to my dressing-room, and I have showered, cleaned my face – 'freshened up' in Virgil D. Everett's vulgar phrase – and I am ready for the *vin d'honneur* which has been arranged not far away in a beautiful old club in Gramercy Park. That mahogany, polished opulence of old New York reminds me that underneath the modern surface of things this is a Victorian city, dotted with warehouses, churches, clubs, houses, whole streets, which would still be recognisable to Edith Wharton and Henry James.

I am in that condition where one has just come off stage, a condition close to madness. (I know; I have been in both states.) One is simultaneously high and confused. Faces press up, perhaps they are total strangers, perhaps they are my oldest friends. They are all in Barking. I should find it hard to name them. I grin. I want to relive every second of the last two hours, every laugh, every round of applause, every successful effect. At the same time, I am shot through with melancholy, with the most overpowering sense of futility. What, after all, have I been doing – a grown man, and an old man now, standing on a stage in front of strangers, pretending to be someone else? Could anything be more insane?

'Hi Julian – how yer doin'?'

I stare at a funny little old woman in a bright green trouser-suit. She has blue hair and the frames of her specs are green to match her pants.

'You haven't forgotten De Sett have you?'

'I'm sorry, I . . .'

But now, another person has pressed forward and the little green leprechaun, De Sett, has vanished in the crush.

'Did Lampitt model his style, you know, like on Henry James at all?'

'Good evening, good evening. His prose style? Good Lord, no.'

28

'I was thinking, more like his personal style, you know, like maybe the way he tied his neckties . . .'

But my minder is leading me through more grinning faces, so that the question of Jimbo's neckties goes unanswered.

'Wonderful. Just wonderful.'

'I thought that thing about Tennyson was just so funny.'

'Swinburne.'

'Excuse me?'

'Swinburne was the funny one. The Tennyson thing was surely rather touching . . .'

De Sett. Dorset. Oh, *hell*. Hell and damn. That old crone was *Dorset* . . . She will be thinking how stuck up I am, now I'm acting on the stage, and how ungrateful I am, and how unfriendly. I turn around, looking for her in the room, but she is not there.

'Excuse me, Mr Ramsay, but is your book about Jimbo available in the United States?'

'To my shame, I never wrote one.'

'I thought you'd written. Now let me get this clear, 'cause sure as hell someone wrote Lampitt's autobiography, I'm just sure of that.'

'May I butt in here and say, Mr Ramsay, that I think it was just wonderful.'

'Thank you, thank you.'

'Hallo, Julian.'

For a moment or two, I am shocked. It is not that I do not recognise her – it is a face which has haunted my dreams for years. It is the incongruity which silences me – the surprise of seeing her *here*. But though I am old and dotty enough to have forgotten Dorset, I am hardly going to forget Margaret Mary Nolan! The novelty of the well-spoken, quiet English tones penetrates the nasal whine of American voices like a clear silver bell rung in a room alive with the noise of electric drills. A very well-groomed head of hair bows towards me to perform that ritual – mmwah!, mmwah! – the double kiss in which miraculously little physical contact is made between the participants.

Margaret Mary Nolan has not changed as other women change. For example, she is not wrinkled. The features which in youth were so haunting are still recognisable; the eyes are still as bright as stars.

What, then, has happened? M.M. was a goddess on a pedestal to me, not (exactly) an object of sexual desire so much as of *une grande passion*. So I am not making ungallant comments about whether she is as alluring as she once was. (I'm no picture!) But M.M., my darling, you have become hard-edged. You were always so clean, you always seemed, in a suburb of Birmingham, as if you were in the middle of the country, the young wife of a farmer, perhaps, rather than the spouse of a research scientist and medic. Your hair when young was light and fluffy – now it is so sharply cut! And you have powdered over that luminous skin. Everything about you now is neat to the point of being almost tidied away.

'Dominic's grown a bit since you last saw him,' she says, bringing forward a very tall, extremely handsome man of about thirty whose voice and manner resemble one of his pompous uncles, the Mount-Smiths.

'Hallo, Julian.' His smiling, familiar use of my first name is very slightly surprising from the career diplomat, posted by the Foreign Office, as subsequent conversation reveals, at the UN.

'I'd no *idea* that Lampitt was such a funny man,' M.M. is saying. 'I know you used to keep us all in fits with stories about his brother Sargent, but you evidently kept all your Jimbo stories up your sleeve.'

Had I? Kept them in fits? My memory of those years – when I was, first, Persy's boyfriend, then an *ami de la maison* of Fergus and M.M. – was that (even before my spell in the bin) I was melancholy to the point of madness. When those long Sunday luncheons return to my memory, I see myself as a figure of pathos, one of M.M.'s 'lame ducks', like those ghastly priests she used to entertain, and the seemingly unending supply of lonely unmarried women who worshipped at the Oratory.

'Anyway, well done!' It is very 'embassy', the way she says this. It is one hundred per cent Mount-Smith. That is what has happened in the thirty years since I fell in love with you, my dear. You've reverted to type. Blood will out. You seem to be glowing with pleasure to be out with this young companion.

'Margaret Mary, don't slip away – let's see one another. Come and have lunch at my hotel.'

'I'm going back in two days. Honestly. It was Dominic who cleverly spotted that this play was "on", didn't you, darling?'

'We're very lucky, we can usually get seats.' In this context, I take 'we' to mean, 'we diplomats'. 'You were sold out tonight as you probably know, but I rang the director of the theatre, explained that I was at the UN, and that Mummy and I were old friends of yours. He very kindly asked us to this party.'

'We've been down in Washington staying with the Birks,' M.M. stated.

'Well, they really are voices from the past. He never became President, after all.'

'There was a chance of his becoming Secretary of State,' says Dominic, whose self-assured tones half imply that he might have something to do with advising the White House on political appointments.

'Anyway, it was nice to see him,' simpered M.M. 'And his second wife!' (Why is this worth smirking about? Simply because At Birk has married again? Or is there something funny about the wife? These knowing smiles of the Mount-Smiths and their kind – how they used to intimidate me!) 'At's miles better – you know he had open heart surgery last year?'

'I never kept up with them. How's Fergus?'

The inquiry after her husband provokes a smile which is not knowing, but callous. (And your smiles used to make me weak with love! Have they changed, or have I?)

'He retired last year as Vice Chancellor' – she names the northern University where he had worked for over a decade. 'We dragged him away from Brum at last, didn't we, darling? It's been lovely being nearer the rest of my family in Yorkshire. We're quite close to Ample-forth – where one of my brothers is a monk – I think you knew? Fergus still needs the fast train to London. He spends as much time on committees as ever! And for the last three years there has been his work in the Lords.'

'Yes, yes. Congratulations!'

More peals of silver bells. Is it self-mockery, to think of herself as 'Lady Nolan' – or are we all meant to think there is something slightly amusing, pitiable even, about Fergus's life peerage, given not for his work as a scientist but for tireless endeavours on the University Grants Committee?

'We always listen to you on "The Mulberrys",' says M.M.

Oh dear – am I really such a vain silly old man? I melt at this praise of the radio 'soap' in which I play a small rôle. We are looking

31

at one another, and the telepathy of love tells me quite clearly that we both see everything so clearly. If I allowed this conversation to go on for ten more minutes, I should be as much in love with M.M. as I ever was; and I would still mean as little to her as I ever did, and she would find my adoration cloying, and be obliged to shake me off. Both of us see this, don't we, my dear? We are 'free among the dead, like unto them that are wounded and lie in the grave'. Both of us know that if we wanted to risk the pain of becoming acquainted we should have done it years ago. The past is a land whose inhabitants are all in Barking – and that includes you, my dearest M.M. You can come to the Solemn Vespers which plays inside my head whenever I think about you, but we have nothing to say to one another in life. I spent so long being in love with you. And I do not deceive myself – the important relationships in your life have been those of blood – with your parents and your brothers and your son; you never loved me. You never even fancied me, as you did the biographer of James Petworth Lampitt! It seems strange that you should have come to hear me 'do' Jimbo now, and here in New York rather than in London. Perhaps your overbearing puppy of a son insisted, and brought you against your better judgement?

When Dominic Nolan takes my hands and smiles at me with his lordly smile, I no longer see the Mount-Smith relations whom he so predominantly resembles. Nor, however, do I see the face of Fergus Nolan either. In the soft feminine beguilingness of the smile, I see the man whom I have always taken to be his real father, Raphael Hunter. How strange, given the relations between Hunter and James Petworth Lampitt, that Hunter's son should have come to witness me in this performance! Does Dominic Nolan know that he is Hunter's son? As I squeeze his paw and smile politely at him, it seems inconceivable that he should not know. He has almost become Hunter's double! Does he know how inappropriate, or appropriate, it is that he should be here?

Does he know what tortuous discussions went on between the author of the piece and myself about the ending of the script? Does he know that we even wondered whether to include a bit part for a young actor to portray Raphael Hunter? In one version of the show, I suggested to the director that Jimbo should stand by the open window and, turning to meet Hunter, his carefully controlled features would suddenly display alarm. 'You!' he would exclaim before falling backwards; but the director rejected this as too melodramatic.

M.M., the love of my life, the object of my concentrated and religious devotion for a decade, is lightly tapping my elbow.

'The real thing. Shakespeare's *Sonnets*, *Tristan und Isolde*, *La Prison-nière*, the whole horror story. Has it ever happened to you?'

William Bloom, publisher of these words, do you remember saying them to me in a pub in Brentwood, about a thousand years ago, while we were doing our National Service together?

Well, in this richly polished New York room, where waitresses are 'circulating' with delicious little bits to eat and I wish someone would refill my glass of Bourbon, here she is – the young man of Shakespeare's Sonnets, Isolde, Albertine. Here is the unattainable fantasy, the angel of God, the goddess, passion for whom destroyed all capacity for happiness, contemplation of whom was my religion. And what do you see, folks, you nice arty Americans milling about at this party?

'Would you like more mineral water?'

'I shouldn't mind more Bourbon if you've got some.'

'Excuse me?'

What do you see, nice ones? Two English oldies? The tall woman touching the balding actor's elbow. Why aren't the skies opening? Why are not doves descending on us at this moment? They would if Mr Pilbright were painting it.

'We must be going, Julian.'

'It was so kind of you to come, my dears.'

The touch of her fingers and the smile of her eyes have begun to resurrect memories which are almost intolerably painful. I am glad when my minder leads me up to a Mrs Jolene Belringo to discuss that evening's performance. And the party goes on, and I drink my mineral water out of nervousness, and then another, until I am asking for the men's room. (And when I get there, oh dear, here we go again. In spite of a full bladder, I can't 'go'; when this run of *Jimbo* is over I'm going to have to have that prostate seen to; but before that, I shall find Dorset, and apologise for being so vague, and have a real talk.)

And now I come back into the room and someone has kindly set a table, and the director of the theatre, and my English director and a number of well-wishers and I have been very kindly provided with cold chicken and some salad. My appetite has returned, and I

33

wash the crunchy iceberg lettuce with ice-cold fizzy water in my gums. But no Dorset, I have not seen her. And the evening is over, finished, and I am back in this luxurious box, this hotel room, alone again.

Tout le malheur des hommes vient d'une seule chose, qui est de ne savoir pas demeurer en repos dans une chambre. Nowhere is this old saw, to which I ardently respond, more amply demonstrated than in an American hotel room. I used to feel less restless than this in the asylum. I have been up and down to the lavatory twice. Discontented with my own company, I have flicked through the TV channels. Then exhaustion overcomes me and I fall asleep; but too soon, too soon. It is a sleep induced by hypertension and alcohol from the mini-bar, not by real fatigue, and, having sunk to the depths of black oblivion, I bob up again out of dream-consciousness into waking bleariness in about an hour. Waking in the dark, my body does not know what hour, or day, or year it is. I am transported out of time. The electronic clock by the bedside says 2:14 in bright green, as vividly emerald as Dorset's trouser-suit. How could I forget her? And how will she be feeling right now? Oh hell.

Outside, sirens squeal. The darkness is dotted all over with shop lights, with lighted apartment buildings, with the headlights of cars and trucks which never seem to stop driving up and down the island. All those people in Barking are enacting their *danse macabre* in the shadows round the television and the mini-bar, and in the shadows of my brain – my parents on the beach near Mallington; Mummy, waving goodbye three years later, as my train pulls out of Platform One on Paddington Station – the last time I ever saw her – and M.M.! Who was it, at one of those lunches, who had show-offishly quoted a sonnet of Michelangelo and said that 'Lampitt's translations of those sonnets are not widely-enough known?' One of the awful priests – the really snobbish Jesuit? Linus Quarles, SJ, that was it! Or was it Fr Reilly, OP, the fatty? I can even remember the lines –

> I' fu', già son molt'anni, mille volte
> ferito e morto, non che vinto e stanco,
> da te, mia colpa; e or col capo bianco,
> riprenderò le tue promesse stolte?

34

Oh, darling M.M., not again! I am feeling just as painfully in love with you as I did thirty years ago. How absurd!

And – in that sea of faces – of you, Margaret Mary, and your Lame Ducks, of whom I was one, I see those whom you knew, and those you did not know. I see Sargie, Cecily, Uncle Roy, and sad Persy Nolan. I see our baby who was never born; and earnest Fergus, Persy's brother, the Birmingham doctor; your husband, M.M., I see; oh darling, whenever I think of you, I see beside you smiling, smiling, smiling, the face of Raphael Hunter.

THREE
(April 1966)

How can you prove that there is a purgatory?
I can prove that there is a purgatory from the constant teaching of the
Church.

It was, that night in New York, a changing-point for all of them –
for Julian Ramsay, for Persy, for her brother Fergus, for his wife
Margaret Mary, for Father Bonaventure Reilly, OP, perhaps, too, for
the Americans who, with Virgil D. Everett and Raphael Hunter,
found themselves at the dinner in the Club. In Julian Ramsey's
memory it was by no means clear who, even, had been the host of
the dinner, or how this miscellaneous assemblage of persons had been
contrived, some from the deepest past, some from the unknown future.
Father Bonaventure, for example – what was he doing there? Some
lectureship at Fordham took him to New York. He was Fergus Nolan's
oldest school and university friend; so he had been dragged into the
party. The Birks had been known, but fleetingly known, to Ramsay
in his teens, but they were old diplomatic friends of Margaret Mary's
people, the Mount-Smiths. But how all these connections were
formed, and how the dinner itself was arranged, was long lost to
Julian's memory. When the evening returned to his mind as, in its
disconnected fashion it quite often did, he would imagine that it
contained 'clues'; and had life, as in an old-fashioned murder story,
been a puzzle capable of solution, perhaps some of its clues were, in
Ramsay's case (perhaps too in the case of the others), buried in this

36

assembly. But the evening came before him not as a carefully-drafted mystery-story; more like that most puzzling of things, an old photograph album in which no contemporary of the subjects has troubled to append any names. Faces, frozen by the developer's fluid into some pictorial shape, stare out of the page at us, like patients in a mental ward condemned to everlasting amnesia.

That they had looked in at a party, Persy Nolan and Julian Ramsay, a couple of hours before the dinner was due to begin, probably explained the confused patterns of faces and incidents which afterwards lodged themselves in both their brains; but they both, in their emotional post-mortems of what had gone wrong – why, how, when – in their affair, often found themselves reverting to that night in New York.

'So far,' Julian Ramsay was saying, 'no effects whatsoever.' He addressed himself to Christopher, a new friend met that minute, introduced by Wilmie as bearing an amazing resemblance to Jimi Hendrix, whoever that was.

'You only taken half a tab, man. But wait a bit. You wanna go easy with that stuff.'

As Christopher made this remark, and fixed on the Englishman a charming smile, Julian had the momentary sensation of seeing all the pores on the Hendrix lookalike's face expand. It was like watching someone's skin transform itself in an instant into a well-toasted and well-buttered crumpet. The pores were huge holes. Their moisture dripped.

'So, you got woman trouble, man?'

Julian laughed in agreement. At that precise moment this was an understatement. After a dreadful bust-up outside St Patrick's Cathedral, when they had unwisely got on to the subject of religion, Persy Nolan and Julian Ramsay had repaired to their hotel. They were staying at the Chelsea and, by the time they had got down to W. 23rd Street on the bus, they were barely on speaking terms. The afternoon nap which both their bodies craved could all too easily have turned into Round Two of the conversational warfare in which they seemed doomed to engage, always at slightly cross purposes from one another. It was a relief to both of them to find, lolling on a black leather sofa in the lobby under some unsparingly orange abstracts, Wilmington Birk and the remaining Norns, and various young Ameri-

cans. They were going to this party in the Village if Julian and –
what was your name again – Persy? – would care to join them. This
spontaneous arrangement would nicely fill that awkward couple of
hours before Persy and Julian need be on parade at the Club for
dinner.

'I don't understand,' said Wilmie Birk, 'when you say you're doing
research, is that scientific, right?'

The young Englishman had not been long at the party – less a
party, in fact, than a casual group of fifteen or twenty people sitting
around in someone's room playing some Dylan records. A high proportion of those present had already noted his tendency to talk about
his research, which was, perhaps, why he found himself sitting with
Wilmie (who took the responsibility for bringing him to the party in
the first place) and Christopher, whose expression suggested a cheerful
indifference to his company. The others used body language – the
slightly swaying shoulders of T-shirts were decidedly turned away
from Ramsay as they rocked to Mr Tambourine Man – to emphasise
unwillingness to hear any more about the Ann-Louise Everett Collection, and the difficulty of using it as a research library since the
librarian only brought you one leaf of paper at a time. Most of
the letters he had managed to read – and he had spent a whole week
there and concentrated on the letters to James Petworth Lampitt from
Henry James – were concerned with the times of trains from London
to Rye when young Lampitt went down, at intervals during the years
1901–1914, to the Master at Lamb's House.

'You wanna watch yourself with that guy,' Christopher said, 'he's a
dangerous guy.'

'Henry James?'

Christopher grinned, then laughed.

'Not old Henry, no. We all love him, don't we, Wilmie. I mean
Virgil D. Everett. You goin' to meet him tonight? That's something.
He doesn't often go out, man. Usually waits for the business to come
to him.'

'I had heard he was something of a hobbit,' said Julian Ramsay
carefully.

'Excuse me?'

'Herbalist. Hermit.'

'Hey, Christopher, what have you given this guy?'

Julian was laughing at his inability to say the word *hermit*. Persy, from the other side of the room, had no doubt been taking her own stimulant – probably only alcohol – for she found the voice to shout out – 'Take no notice of him; he's drunk already.'

In private this would have been a signal for all-out war. In such benign company, it was merely a joke. Everyone laughed.

'Y'know,' said Wilmie, 'it's real funny. Julian and I and my brother and sister were all together, right, when we were kids, we had this vacation together. I hadn't seen him since – and then he wrote and said he was going to be in New York, and how 'bout meeting, an' stuff. You know what At said – At's my brother – when I told him we were all going to have this dinner tonight? "Wilmie," he said, "I don't remember this guy! Do you think we really, really knew him?" Isn't he funny?'

'At's had a much busier life than I have,' said Ramsay, 'he's had more to forget.'

Wedged behind Wilmie's head, a man in a yellow pigtail, who had already made close friends with a Newnham Norn (not Persy), was impressing her by asking, 'So, where do they get their money for the G-boys? All out of federal funds? Forget it. Dirty-tricks departments need funding and that's where a man like Everett comes in useful.'

'You better listen t'this,' said Christopher, gently prodding Ramsay's shoulder, 'they're talking about your friend.'

'Why did they need a red-neck President in the Democratic Party to promote the War? Why did they need Dallas?'

Wilmie, her dander up, half turned and said to Pigtail, 'Are you saying my brother murdered the President of the United States?'

'I don't even know who your brother is, sweetheart.'

Everyone chorused that it was Congressman Atlas Birk.

'I didn't know, Wilmie, I'm sorry. But Atlas Birk's a very, very ambitious man, no doubt about it; he was one of the youngest Congressmen this century; for all we know, he wants to be the President. And we know that Virgil D. Everett is a very, very powerful man. Everyone knows that this War is tearing the Democratic party apart.'

'It's tearing the country apart.'

'It's tearing *our* country? What do you think it's doing to the Vietnamese country?'

Christopher began to explain how and why he'd burnt his draft

39

card. Pigtail spoke through his words, outlining the right-wing back-lash, since J. F. Kennedy was assassinated, every bit as extreme as that of the 1950s. Amphetamines speeding up his speech allowed him to race forward with statistics, anecdotes, names and figures. Ramsay's brains, softened by substances of a different order, allowed Pigtail's words – hard-edged, political and fast – to become colours, floating, gentle and hilarious.

'This isn't funny, I'm telling you.'

For the previous ten minutes or so, Ramsay had been rootling around in the back of his mind for the title of his favourite Henry James novel. He wanted to bore his new friends with his belief, not yet based on certain research, that Henry James's normal amanuensis had fallen ill during the dictation of this work, and that her place has been taken, for a crucial fortnight of the novel's composition, by Jimbo Lampitt. It was hardly worth interrupting them, however, if the name of the novel in question continued to elude him.

'So,' Christopher was in the middle of relating a horribly violent anecdote. 'I go 'cross the corridor and I call out – you all right? What's all that screaming in there? We never knew whether she was a hooker or what she was. Melanie, the kid was called. And she's kicking and screaming with this guy, this English guy he was. Kinda – I dunno – sinister, you'd say. He was trying to drag her out of the house and I say, hey man, you stop that or I'll call the police. So he says to me, we'll shut that nigger mouth of yours, nigger – that's right man, he said that. Anyways. I make some coffee. Get Melanie calmed down. I don't ask her nothing she doesn't want to say, man, but we get talking, an' she says she's met this guy a couple of times in a bar, right. He works for someone real important – he's a chauffeur, right, only he goes out in the evenings for a little bit of fun. So he meets Melanie in this bar and okay, so she had him back to her room – jus' right over there – that room opposite on the landing.'

'Julian, this just isn't funny.'

'You said you didn't know she was a hooker – but you must have known she was one if she had this guy back to her room.' This from Pigtail.

'So,' – Wilmie, belligerent – 'a girl asks a guy home for a cup o' coffee and she's a hooker?'

40

'What's all this got to do with Virgil D. Everett anyway; and Julian, we should go.' Persy had appeared in the group.

'What it had to do with Mr Everett,' said Christopher, 'is that this guy, this English guy – the chauffeur guy – was asking Melanie to go back with him to his apartment, or to Everett's apartment at the top of the Everett Building in E. 63rd Street – and perform for the old man. That's what he likes.'

'He named Virgil D. Everett, this guy?'

'Sure. When I said I'd go to the police, he came at me like all Mr Big, you know, and said, you lay one finger on me, boy, and I'll have you in deep shit.'

'That's hardly the same as naming Mr Everett. Julian, we really must . . . the time.' Persy took her boyfriend's elbow. He showed himself unwilling to break away from the story; in fact, he appeared transfixed by it, and, even though he could not stop himself grinning as the extraordinary tale began to unfold, he stared as if he were gazing at a vision.

'It was all hearsay,' said Persy Nolan in the taxi. 'Sordid hearsay. That's just the sort of thing people do invent about the very rich; that they use their money to make other people their slaves – making the chauffeur perform with the prostitute. It might be true, but then again.'

'*The Ambivalents.*'

'What?'

'*The Ambivalents.* I've been trying to remember the name of that book for the last hour.'

'Oh, Julian. You've told me so many times about *The* bloody *Ambassadors.*'

'You see, if I'm right, and I think I am, it's the most crucial bit of the whole book where Strether tells young Chad Newsome that he should "live all he can"; though you see, even that's ambivalent and double-edged – coming from Stetson.'

'Strether. Oh, hell, Julian, you *are* drunk.'

'I suppose it's ironic when you think of it. I mean Jimbo was a bit of a Strether in his way. He never really lived – not in the sense of letting go, letting rip.'

'Julian.'

'What?'

'Before we go in. Look at me, Julian – oh God, your pupils are so dilated you look like a bush-baby. Look at me, bush-baby – and it's not funny.'

His bush-baby eyes looked at her pale serious face, its snub nose and its glasses. He felt terribly fond of this face, much fonder than he had done during their quarrel of four hours previous; and then he realised that it had changed from being Persy Nolan's face to being that of the art mistress at his preparatory school.

(To extend the Barking metaphor – do we ever get beyond, each of us, more than a skullful of friends from Barking? When we meet 'new' people, new friends, new lovers, are we doing anything more than recycling old scripts? My loss of Mummy was the first calamity but also perhaps the last; just as Miss Beach could be seen not as my first calf-love but as the same old love affair which I was doomed to repeat again and again. Persy was important, of course she was, because of the baby, because of my emotional involvement with her family. But I have had dozens of crushes and 'disturbed' fortnights because of women who, either because of their bobbed hair or their snub-noses or their 'artistic' attitude to life, recalled, as Persy did, Miss Beach. Love is a virus; at times quiescent in the body but impossible to eliminate without the destruction of the whole system.)

'I know I hurt you, Julian,' Miss Beach was saying. 'I'm sorry, Julian. I just had to do it. You understand that, don't you? It would have been terrible to *be* that child with us as the parents; and yet I think I'm going to regret what I've done for the rest of my life.'

With tenderness he leaned forward and kissed those pale lips, and rubbed his cheeks against that frail, freckled brow. He loved the smell of her hair, always.

'I'm sorry sir – sir!'

A figure in a tailcoat, an individual who might have felt more at home in the New York of Henry James than that of Jimi Hendrix was advancing with anxiety.

'I'm afraid that you cannot come into the club without a tie.'

'Julian, where's your tie?'

'In the hotel – can we go back?'

'It's half an hour away and we are late already.'

'It's all right, sir, we keep a supply here for visitors who have come – er – without them.'

Having satisfied himself that Persy and Julian were *bona fide* visitors, the Jamesian butler ushered them upstairs to the dining-room where white Corinthian columns swoop to a splendid ceiling, suspended with huge crystal electroliers. It is said that the Vanderbilts built this club, and leased it to the university, under the impression that the humble graduates would tire of it after a year. It was not intended for University men, but for Vanderbilts – this profusion of pilasters, this swooping of banisters, this finery of plaster and ironwork. The architectural splendour produced if not awe, then a certain dignified hush even at the most convivial of tables. The two ragamuffins who had lately entered would have seemed conspicuous in any setting, but in this, their untidy clothes, their glazed unwashed faces and the air of bewilderment with which they stared about them seemed to shake a fist at the setting into which they had blundered. Though both of them in their different ways had believed, before setting foot in this country, that they were embodiments of old Europe, slumming it in an urban jungle, they would nevertheless have conjured up to a dispassionate observer images, less of a patrician race among their rude colonists and more those of the lumpen barbarian tramping into the well-marbled forum several centuries before the fall of Rome.

'And you sir – you are dining tonight?'

Another Jamesian figure in a frock-coat checked their progress across the dining-room.

The male ragamuffin was giggling.

The female one said, '*Julian!*' and then, to the waiter, 'I'm terribly sorry. We are dining with Mr Everett.'

Margaret Mary Nolan's giggles were not, like Julian's, embarrassing or uncontrollable. Her silvery laugh preceded her and – there she was! Tall, with a face that so many had called 'elfin' that we have to begin with that word to convey it; high cheek-bones and thin cheeks; penetrating, mischievous green eyes and a determined mouth. Seen from some angles not beautiful at all, but then, from a certain three-quarters profile, such a face that the masters of the trecento might have given to the Mother of God. She began at once to speak animatedly about a recent episode of 'The Mulberrys', in which Jason Grainger had made a pass at the vicar's daughter.

When they were settled at the table, Mrs Ahrlich asked them, 'What've you done with my sister?'

43

She was Wilmie's sister, Coral, now married to Congressman Newton Ahrlich. 'At's real sorry he couldn't be with us tonight; he doesn't often see Wilmie these days and I reckon that's because neither of them want to meet; they do belong to different worlds, you might say.'

'I'm so sorry – I had no idea we were meant to bring your sister,' Persy said.

Mrs Ahrlich shook a bangled wrist to signify the unimportance of Wilmie's absence, the looseness of the arrangements. 'My husband couldn't make it tonight either,' she said. 'At and he work closely together as you may know, and they're both still in Washington tonight.'

Wilmie Birk had been more or less as Julian had remembered her from the old days at Les Mouettes – nearly twenty years fatter, but recognisably the same old Wilm. Coral, now Mrs Newton Ahrlich, was completely unrecognisable, with her slightly beehived blonde hair, her carefully painted lips and eyes and a voice which seemed half an octave deeper than Julian had remembered it. The exquisite cut of her clothes – she was ludicrously well-dressed for what was described as an informal supper party – and the fact that even an untutored eye could not fail to value the brilliants in her ear lobes alone as the cash equivalent of a small flat in London – had somehow aged her. She was nearing forty, but she would now look like this more or less for ever – always perfectly attired and groomed – pampered skin stretched, tucked and lifted into an expression of perfect amiability and painted to look healthy, even when age had withered and the years condemned her European contemporaries. Even in death, probably, Mrs Arhlich would look a little like this if the mortician did his work.

With an amiability which combined formality and complete naturalness, she was politely making sure that everyone around the table knew one another: Fergus Nolan, Persy's brother; his best friend Father Bonaventure Reilly, OP, who was by a very happy chance over in the United States on an academic placement at Fordham University; Mr Hunter – but she was sure that they were bound to know Mr Hunter? And, of course, Mr Everett.

Fergus Nolan, his mouth filled with some particularly delicious crab,

44

rose from the table as the new members of the party arrived. He had never understood his younger sister Persy, so he made no particular effort to understand her boyfriend, the apparently quite ineffectual Julian Ramsay. Fergus found it difficult to sympathise with a dabbler; and Ramsay had *dabbled*: a little of this, a little of that, a novel (apparently very bad), a bit of acting, now this research into the Lampitts.

Temperamentally one-track and obsessive, Fergus Nolan found this impossible to understand. The child of petty bourgeois parents in Birmingham, the first member of his family to attend a university, or to aspire, properly speaking, to a professional career (his father was a pharmacist), Fergus Nolan placed a high value on success and effort. He had met – or *seen* would be more accurate – feckless upper-class people when he was a student at Oxford. Presumably, there would always be such drones in the world. But Julian Ramsay, who stood on the same rung of the social ladder as Fergus did himself (his father had been a manager in a shirt factory), had no idle aristocrat's excuse for wasting his life. As far as Fergus was concerned, the so-called Protestant work-ethic was not in the least Protestant. It was a class thing. The Parable of the Talents applied to Catholics and Protestants alike, but perhaps only those born with some social advantages realised its sacred truth.

Fergus did not, however, feel threatened by Ramsay as he did by the rest of his company, by Coral Ahrlich, by the old man Virgil D. Everett and by Mr Hunter, the Man of Letters. Ever since agreeing to serve on the Pontifical Commission, Fergus had felt himself 'got at', either by official pressure groups of one persuasion or another, or by individuals wishing to assert their point of view. It had reached the point where a certain paranoia had set in and he suspected even innocent individuals of wishing to approach him or to speak to him at social gatherings, with the sole function of nobbling him about the birth control question.

Such feelings might on the surface have seemed far-fetched when faced with Raphael Hunter – television highbrow, and Sunday newspaper reviewer. Yet Fergus, from the first, felt threatened by Hunter, disliked his easy manner, particularly the ease of his manner with Margaret Mary, never met before this evening, but already touching her elbow and drawing her into his metropolitan way of regarding all

45

matters discussed. (Not jokes exactly – Hunter did not appear to go in for jokes – but a lot of quiet laughter which implied, no, insisted upon, Hunter's superiority to the rest of the world. Forced to such a distinction, Fergus would have wished to line up with the Rest of the World.)

Nolan felt threatened by Hunter, and wondered if he were the first to sense something appropriate about the surname. That he moved among this group as a predator there could be no doubt. With his fashionably flared velvet trousers, his *coiffure* from a London 'hair-dresser', his wide kipper-tie of psychedelic design, Mr Hunter was a man, clearly, with conquests in mind. The outfit just stopped short, even in a man of Hunter's forty-odd years, of ridiculousness, and asserted, rather, a complete kinship between the wearer and the spirit of the age.

Fergus Nolan's own appearance, by its refusal to enter any such sartorial compact, presumably made its own kind of statement. The suit, a dark green lovat castigated by Margaret Mary, with one of her silvery tolerant laughs, as 'awful', had been bought off the peg (January sales) some years before in Rackhams. Fergus was of the view that a man had dark grey flannels and a sports jacket for work, a suit for smarter occasions and a dark suit for funerals. Beyond that, he had no wardrobe. Similarly, he had never given any thought to the question of whether he should have a 'hairstyle', and did not even believe that such a word had entered his vocabulary until it was, as it were, too late and he had lost half his hair. A short back and sides man, he, with the straggling hair receding further from a bony forehead as year succeeded to year. He had the sunken-cheeked, long-jawed (as opposed to the chubby or 'potato-faced') type of Irish physiognomy.

Fergus had spotted at once, over the drinks before the meal, that Hunter had a more than literary interest in Virgil D. Everett and his concerns. Fergus had once (years ago, and before hormones took over as the overriding interest) considered doing some research into the warning signals which (to speak loosely) it would seem as if the brain of mammals sent to the body in times of danger. The butterflies in the stomach, the sweating palms before a time of trial, these interested him; so, too, did the apparently inexplicable early-warning signal which is given to the lower species: the hackles rising on the beast's back before the predator is seen or heard. Some thing or some sense warns the wildebeest that a ravenous lion is in the savannah. Some such feeling – a prickle in his own short back and sides – gave Fergus Nolan a bad feeling in the presence of Hunter the television celebrity.

As for Virgil D. Everett – he was known to have a finger in many pies. He was a big lawyer, a businessman, a collector, a politician, or at any rate a political activist. Only during this visit to New York had Fergus discovered quite what a big fish Virgil D. was in Lixabrite, the huge pharmaceuticals company, which Everett's other company – PJKA – had taken over three years before. Already, scores of millions of dollars had been made by this company on the Wall Street market since the contraceptive pill for women had been pioneered.

It seemed as if this single invention would revolutionise the world, change the position of women in society, alter the very fabric of family life itself. The argument which was raging in the Catholic Church about it had been churning in Fergus's brain for slightly longer. It was an argument which rent in two the Pontifical Commission which had been set up to investigate the whole question and of which Fergus was a member. On the one hand it could be said that this pill did no more than neutralise the activity of nature. The body itself discarded almost all the eggs produced by a woman, almost all the seed produced by a man. The odds on an average man and an average woman achieving conception after one act of coition were actually quite small. If they did it, say, three times a month, even if they were not carefully waiting for the 'safe period', they would probably not conceive a child for several months, if not years. Surely the Pill did no more than to make such couples 'safe' for as long as they wished to be safe? From the viewpoint of theology, according to nearly all the experts on the Pontifical Commission, the Pill was therefore different in kind, both from the sin of abortion and from other sorts of artificial contraception such as French letters, the Dutch cap and so forth, all of which did involve either the deliberate spillage of seed which might, had it met the right egg, have fertilised it; or the flushing away of such eggs.

From the non-theological point of view, it seemed that the benefits which would be brought to the human race by the new pharmaceutical product were only starting to be calculable. If the women of the poorer parts of South and Central America could be persuaded to take it, the Pill would bring about a revolution within a generation,

47

which would be a true revolution, unlike the Marxist disturbances and right-wing *putsches* which went by that name. For if the Pill reached the shanty-town it would bring an end to that poverty and degradation which was the cause of social unrest and the seed-bed of Marxist revolt against the order of things. No wonder men like Virgil D. Everett were obsessed by the possibility of selling this pill of theirs to the relief agencies and to the Governments of South America and Africa! If the world were filled with small, well-regulated families on a Protestant suburban pattern, the CIA would have almost no more work to do in the world. It was over-population which made Communists of the Chinese, of the North Koreans and of the Vietnamese. This disastrous war could be attributed quite directly to the evil of over-population.

As for the social implications in the United States and Europe – why, when women decided how few babies they wished to nurture, society itself would be overturned. At present, the tiny minority of women who enjoyed equality with men in the professional classes or in industry were from the same privileged and educated backgrounds. The Pill would change all that. In this respect, Fergus could tell that the Pill was an extraordinary enabler which would release untold talents. Instead of only a handful of women engineers, women doctors, women judges and scientists – there could be as many as there were men!

For well over eight years, as a medic and a research scientist, Fergus had been at the forefront of those explorations which had made possible the evolution of the Pill. There were probably few people in England, or the world, who knew more about this matter than he did or who had made a more intimate study of all its implications, psychological and spiritual as well as physical. It was hardly surprising that he was in demand as an adviser to the leading pharmaceutical companies in England, and he had been approached by one of them – a subsidiary of Lixabrite, as it happened. He had not been tempted. A genuine love of knowledge and a slightly puritanical fear of filthy lucre made him disdain their offers to employ him and take him away from the Queen Elizabeth Hospital and the University at Birmingham. He regarded himself as an academic and a medic and he did not wish to become a mere tool in a commercial empire. He had not, however, been above allowing this pharmaceuticals company – Blaby Kohn –

48

to endow some demonstratorships and research fellowships at Birmingham University and to be generous in their support, replacing expensive lab equipment which could never have been bought with existing moneys and government grants, generous as these now were. In short, though Fergus had not been bought his department had already enjoyed the benefits of the Pill. This fact was borne in on him this evening before the meal when Mr Everett had squeezed Fergus's hand in his large, warm, soft paw and murmured, 'We – that is, we at Lixabrite – feel honoured, Mr Nolan, to think that in some small way we have managed – to help you, sir – in your endeavours.'

Mr Everett, whose appearance produced in Fergus's optic nerves a first impression of broad brushstrokes of pale silver – silvery hair, pale grey suiting hanging somewhat loosely in its beautifully-cut double-breasted silk from sagging shoulders – Mr Everett, this giant, spoke extremely slowly. He was beginning to show signs not merely of age but of decrepitude, and Fergus was surprised, having heard that this man was a figure of such power and influence, to be so painfully aware of his physical vulnerability – a quivering of jowl and scrawny neck, a slight gibbering of the lower lip as though incipient Parkinson's might be around the corner. But the assertion, in his very first sentence, that he, Virgil D. Everett, Jnr, was responsible for the purchase of Fergus's Birmingham laboratories established at once where the power was meant to lie. It had been the first time that naïf Fergus bothered to draw together the numerous connections – Blaby Kohn and Lixabrite, Lixabrite and Virgil D. and their obvious interest in nobbling a member of the Pontifical Commission.

'I hope you're having a real nice time in New York.' This sentence, with its tremendously long pauses between epithets, felt as if it took the old man about five minutes to enunciate. It gave Fergus the chance to decide not to be led; nor to mention his meetings over the last few days – at the UN, with the Cardinal, and with several other of his Pontifical Conferands.

'And – have you left – your children behind in England?'

A raw nerve here, so that he was able to change the subject somewhat.

'It is very good to meet you, Mr Everett. No,' – what he was denying was not made syntactically very clear – 'no, what's been so nice has been to catch up with my friend Bonaventure Reilly' – and

49

he had led Mr Everett by the hand to meet the huge, sweating Bon Reilly – an incongruous sight in such a palatial setting, and in such company as Coral Ahrlich's with her jewels and her tailored costumes. Though a Dominican friar who normally wore his religious habit, Bon on this occasion was wearing a badly-made black suit several sizes too small, and, if the heat and moisture of his face were reliable indicators, it seemed as if he might, quite literally, burst out of it at any moment.

'I'm at Fordham for this semester.'

'Indeed? Well I'm very pleased to meet you, Father. So you're a Jesuit?'

'I'm a Dominican actually, so I feel I'm in a strange land in at least two senses of the word.'

Reilly had been at the Oratory Grammar School in Hagley Road with Fergus Nolan and then they had gone on to Oxford together, both provincial boys of Irish ancestry. Fergus was not much aware of whether he himself spoke with any sort of intonation, but it seemed to him that with the years Jim Reilly (Fergus never thought of his friend by his name in religion) had actually exaggerated the slightly Brummy vowels and the firm deviation from southern Standard English. In the United States, of course, such linguistic signals were either undetectable by the majority of speakers or they created impressions in American ears which were not quite the same as those which would be received at home. In short, in spite of his ungainly girth and his being slightly unwashed, Bonaventure Reilly, OP, seemed, in the transatlantic context, less consciously an exile from the system. His claim to be doubly a stranger at Fordham required from Everett some ponderous explanation. Reilly was surprised that an *homme d'affaires* as famously worldly as Mr Everett should have been able to distinguish between Jesuits and Dominicans, and asked if the old gentleman were a Roman Catholic.

The ums and aws which this superficially simple question produced suggested that Mr Everett might have been considering such a step, might even, by the end of the sentence, have taken it. But the conclusion was negative.

'I have a certain – interest – in – the Nineties,' said the collector Everett.

'The converts of that time tended to have a particular decadence,' said Bon Reilly. Father Reilly's sentences always sounded as if they

50

might be addressed to a seminar- or lecture-audience less well-informed, if not actually less intelligent, than himself. His total lack of diffidence, his preparedness to show off, made him a popular teacher and he clearly saw no reason to discard at the dinner-table techniques which had served him well in the class-room. 'It's scarcely an original remark, I know; but when you think that this was precisely the time when the Church was condemning the modernists, and hounding intellectuals in France and Britain, it is curious that other sorts of intellectuals, Wilde and so on, if he could be called an intellectual, should have been drawn to the Church; drawn, I suspect, by the very things which caused such difficulty to Loisy or Von Hugel. Chesterton of course said that alone on earth the Church makes reason supreme; but it does not always seem that way to the outsider.'

These sentences by Father Bon – as his students knew him – were literally spat out, with some drops of wine and fragments ·of well-chewed olive flying into the air as the priest warmed to his theme. Feeling unable to respond to any part of the paragraph, and perhaps having failed to understand any part of it, Mr Everett had turned away and momentarily left the two old friends, Fergus and Jim, standing side by side.

Before he left New York, Fergus longed for a really long talk with Jim about the professional matter which was agitating him so painfully. For, before he was a scientist, Fergus Nolan was a Catholic. When it became known that the Holy Father was sounding out Catholic opinion on the question of contraception it was inevitable that Fergus should have been co-opted on to the Pontifical Commission. There were few scientists with his religious conviction, and few with his convictions who knew so much from a scientific angle about the particular matters under discussion.

It was an open secret in the Catholic Church that such a Commission existed but for reasons which he chose not to articulate Fergus preferred to keep his membership of it a secret from colleagues and even from quite close friends. It seemed self-important to allow it to be known that the Magisterium of the Church, and ultimately the Pope himself, should be seeking guidance from, among others, 'just a medical student from Birmingham'.

Isn't that how his mother-in-law, Mrs Mount-Smith, had described him when trying, twelve years before, to justify her objections to the

51

marriage? (She judged him on his entertainment value, which was not high, and, knowing nothing of the interesting things inside his head, she was moved to dislike his dullness and what she regarded as his commonness.) She had spoken in private to M.M. and M.M. had repeated her mother's words, angrily, to her love; but he had often wished in the subsequent years that his fiancée – as she was then – had not done so. Just a medical student from Birmingham. Fergus knew perfectly well that Mrs Mount-Smith would not object to M.M. marrying a doctor with a distinguished Harley Street practice in London, who worshipped at Farm Street or Spanish Place, or one who had been educated, like her brothers, at Downside. It was the Birmingham Irish to which she objected, the fact that, while Fergus was quite as intelligent as his father-in-law and his brothers-in-law, he came from a family which had eaten tea instead of dinner.

Fergus had a confessor (purely as a matter of discipline, he used the university chaplain even though he did not find him sympathetic), but in this matter on his mind, the contraceptive question, he wanted to talk to a friend, and he had missed Jim Reilly during his term away!

The whole matter had caused in Fergus Nolan not merely a personal agony but the certainty that this discovery would spell disaster for the Catholic Church – hence, for the human race. There was no doubt that the Pope would have to say *something* about the Pill – and about the whole question of sex, the family, the regulation of birth. There was growing a positive clamour for him to speak out not just in the wilder parts of Holland or the United States, but within the solid ranks of the Council Fathers in Rome, and in the mainstream Catholic churches throughout the world. Nearly all Fergus's Catholic colleagues, for example, were of the view that the Pill constituted a breakthrough which would allow Catholics to be true to their old convictions while not appearing obscurantist to their fellow-citizens, nor cruel and heartless in the face of terrible suffering in an over-populated world. Moreover, nearly all his colleagues on the consultative Commission – this was what he had confided in Jim, swearing him to secrecy – believed that the Pill was compatible with Catholic teaching. There were even rumours that Montini himself, an obvious liberal, was in favour of changing the party line and in his encyclical letter, *Populorum Progressio*, he had said that 'too frequently an accelerated increase in population adds its own difficulties to the problem of development; the size of the population increases more rapidly than available resources and things are found to have reached apparently an impasse'. This was a clear hint that the Pope was sympathetic to the idea of controlling the population explosion.

When Fergus was away from home in America, in Italy, in Scandinavia, conferring with all these medics and theologues, the belief was growing that the Pope would issue an encyclical which would reassert the value of family life; which would condemn abortion outright and the easy use of contraception among fornicators; but that the Pope would say that there were certain circumstances, within the context of a Catholic marriage, in which developed medical helps might be acceptable. If he could issue such an encyclical, which would allow Catholics to take the Pill, everyone would be happy, or so it seemed. Honour would be satisfied among those conservatives who were afraid of the Holy Father condoning what people called the permissive society. Liberals, equally, would be happy that the onus of deciding this question had been taken away from the Pope, away from the clergy and left where it belonged, with those immediately concerned, the married couples themselves. But this, precisely, was where Fergus's difficulties began.

Educated as he was at the school next to Newman's Oratory, taking his first steps in science, maths, theology and Latin only yards from the house where the great man had lived for nearly half of the last century – how could Fergus Nolan fail to see the great importance of Conscience in religion? Newman, an abject failure in his own lifetime, was already being hailed as the Father of the Second Vatican Council. His remark that he would drink a toast to the Pope, but to Conscience first and to the Pope afterwards – was quoted *ad nauseam* in the liberal Catholic papers, but Fergus Nolan had read *The Grammar of Assent* and he knew that John Henry Newman meant much more by the word *conscience* than the slight hunch that it might be okay to use contraceptives. (Indeed, in so far as he would have been prepared to give his fastidious mind to such an idea, one could be perfectly certain that Newman, like most Victorians, Protestant or Catholic, would have thoroughly disapproved of contraception.) *Conscience*, in Newman's vocabulary, meant the human capacity to know not merely Good from Evil, but to know even as we are known – that is, to

53

perceive God. Newman would not have given up a comfortable and highly-respected position in the Church of England if he did not believe that personal judgement must sometimes be submitted to the wisdom of the wider church, to tradition and to the hierarchy.

That was the burden which Fergus and the Pontifical Commission, together with the bishops of the entire church, wished to place on the shoulders of Pope Paul VI. They were not being blind, nineteenth-century Ultramontanes, submitting to a monarchical pontiff; they believed, with the fathers of the Second Vatican Council, that the Holy Spirit would guide the people of God into all truth and it was ultimately the Chief Shepherd's task to articulate the truth for them on so important a matter.

The modern assumption was that freedom of judgement in all areas was a good thing. The result was the breakdown of western society. Fergus was a liberal in most social matters and a Socialist in politics; but in matters of sexual ethics he was deeply conservative. When he saw the way that students had started to dress and to behave on their own campus at Brum, he recognised that nothing but chaos would come of it – the easy availability of recreational narcotics, the promiscuity and the increased acceptance of homosexuality as an equivalent, both morally and socially, to heterosexuality (Fergus had always felt it to be a deplorable, pitiable aberration from what was natural). Birmingham students, with their long hair and Ringo Starr moustaches, were innocents when compared with their opposite numbers in Berkeley. What sort of a society would this generation produce, with their make-it-up-as-you-go-along morality, their abortions and illegitimate babies? Was private judgement such a sacred thing if the judgement was being formed in brains as undisciplined as these?

Human beings, Fergus believed, were not capable of making up morality as they went along.

The crab was finished. Superb roast beef was being served. The ethical questions which were never far from Fergus's mind were now being aired by Bonaventure Reilly, OP and Persy. Fergus – no good in company and not a conversationalist except one-to-one with old and trusted friends, was jealous that Persy should have drawn out of Jim precisely the sort of talk he needed.

'No – but have you read Aristotle?' boomed the friar; and with the *tot* syllable of the old philosopher's name a piece of half-chewed potato flew from his lip and touched Persy's cheek. Either she did not notice or she did not mind.

'We did the *Ethics* for our Tragedy paper in Part One, but . . .'

'Well, anyone who's read the *Ethics* knows that Morality cannot be a private thing. Whether you believe that the rules which govern our lives have been devised for good Benthamite reasons of social convenience or whether like the great majority of Muslims, Jews and Christians you believe it to be a given thing, it is visibly obvious that chaos comes when you try to organise a society without it or when you think that there is no need to organise a society.'

'But it is a matter of private judgement – it's a woman's right to make that judgement, Bon. Whether she has a baby or not – you can't get more private.'

In her eagerness, Persy, not normally a demonstrative person, had with her two tiny and slightly pudgy hands taken hold of Father Reilly's upper arm.

'Yes, but, Persy, you must see, that if the Pill became universal that it would quickly become the excuse, in the poorer countries of the world especially, for the State rather than the Church being the body who determined what was moral. The one way, a hard way, a poverty-stricken way, but a sure one – as sure as grass breaking the paving stones – for the apparently weak individual to break the strong system in this world is to have families.'

'You're not serious.'

'I'm not saying that contraception is necessarily evil, or even the worst evil . . .'

'Thank God for that.'

'I'm saying that the real subversives here are the babies, the kids, actually being born in spite of what the social pundits and the capitalists tell them.'

At another end of the table, Mrs Ahrlich, Mr Everett and Mr Hunter were finding it difficult to discuss the current political situation in the United States since the English radio actor, Ramsay, was determined, every few seconds, to interrupt with a monologue about the arrangement of manuscripts in the Ann-Louise Everett Foundation.

'I'm sure,' said Hunter with reference to the library clerks, 'that Dorset or Mr Leegrober will allow you access to . . .'

55

'I can't write my book about the Lombardies! Lumpy-Lompies.' Ramsay found his own failure to catch the word 'Lampitt' riotously amusing and, whenever Hunter attempted to smooth things over, Ramsay began to speak more loudly.

'Julian is just talking about the Library, Virgil.'

'Of all my . . .' A pause lasting about a year and a half during which Ramsay yelped, 'Here we go Lampy-Loo!'

'. . . various . . .' Virgil D. Everett paused and smiled as if surveying the great extent of his oil wells and his newspaper empire, '. . . interests, I'd say my . . .'

'LAMPREYS!'

'. . . my – er little collection there, which I've named for . . .'

'The Limpies!'

'Ann-Louise Everett, my, my, my er . . .'

'The Lampitts are going out all over Uruguay,' said Ramsay.

'. . . my mother – '

'Mother of God Free among the dead like them that are wounded.'

'Is he often as drunk as this?' Fergus crossly asked his kid sister, Persy.

'I'd say,' proceeded Virgil D., for by patience he was determined to reach the end of his slow, steam-operated sentence while the others whirred past on their verbal speed-boats, 'that my, my er collection is my greatest joy; and among all those literary eye-dums, I'd say I valued the – er, er, Lampitt papers as highly as any of them. And of course I'd never have gotten hold of 'em without the help of Rafflhuntr.'

Coy as a woman complimented on her pretty little hat or legs, or her dandy way of cooking pecan pie, Hunter blushed and directed his smile not at his patron but at the gaudiness of his own psychedelic kipper-tie.

'All murdered!' declaimed Ramsay, 'For within the hollow crown,

That rounds the mortal temps of Nat King Cole,

Keeps Death his court . . .'

By the time this recitation was in progress the party had left the table and were standing at the far end of the splendid room. Heads were inevitably turning in their direction. Some of the diners, no doubt, turned because of the fame of the old man who with one hand held the banister and with another the arm of the kindly, slightly

56

womanish Englishman in the pale grey suit. Others watched the entertaining spectacle of the other Englishman making a donkey of himself.

'Is he often like this?' repeated the Irish doctor.

'Oh, Fergus,' said his sister, 'I'm just so sorry.'

'Don't be sorry,' said Dr Nolan. 'I just wondered if he had taken a bit too much to drink.'

'Let's go along with them. The walk will do us good,' said the fat priest.

I was aware that I was being discussed but only partially aware that I constituted a problem. I was not really capable of making any reasonable contribution to the debate. The party had split up. Mr Everett and Mrs Ahrlich and Mr Hunter were no longer there; and what I could describe as the Birmingham Five were standing outside the Club on the sidewalk. I was in such a state of mind I could have fallen in with any suggestions made by the rest of the party. Hindsight makes it obvious that they would all in their different ways have liked to tuck me up in my hotel room and then either go to bed themselves, or pass a few more waking hours in company more stimulating than my own. Fergus had not seen Bonaventure Reilly for several months and would probably have valued a few hours with him in a bar *à deux*. Persy, by now thoroughly obsessed with Catholic talk, was no fit companion for me, and seemed unwilling to allow her brother the privilege of a *tête-à-tête* with his old friend. The Friar's proposal that we all walk a few blocks would seem to have met with general approval, for we had all set off southerly. The daddy-long-legs effect had very much reached my legs. On occasion my legs were the expected length and walking posed no difficulties. Then, quite suddenly, I would feel as if I were balancing on stilts, and it helped to have Margaret Mary at my side. She was perfectly biddable, and allowed me to take her arm. When I did so I was aware of her breast touching my upper sleeve. When I laid my head near her shoulder she asked, 'Are you all right?'

I wanted to explain, succinctly and in a manner which was devoid of mawkishness, that I was far from all right; that I had never quite come to terms with Mummy's death nearly thirty years before; I wanted, but did not want, to say that her kind, beautiful, spiritual

57

face very nearly consoled me for this death; indeed, that as we went along, sometimes at normal height, sometimes precariously at twelve feet high, she *was* Mummy. Am I saying that I thought she was my mother come back to life? No – I did not need any such magical consolations. It was that my mother's kind smiles seemed to shine out of M.M.'s kind smiles; the two faces blended together, so that, in remembering Mummy, I saw M.M. and in seeing M.M. I remembered Mummy. The two acts, seeing and recalling, were inseparable, free among the dead like them that are wounded.

'The Birks are rather hard going, aren't they?' she said. The fact that she was quite censorious, very far from bland in her assessment of other people, made it all the more exciting that she appeared tolerant of me. 'My father knew theirs in Geneva before I was born. He always says that they were a bit too grand for the likes of us.'

Her silvery laugh suggested that this was a direct inversion of the truth, but that the word 'grand' could usefully explain why such a woman as Coral should dress and speak as she did, and why Atlas should at the last minute have called off his attendance at the dinner.

'I'd like to see Wilmington again though,' she said. 'Oops.' She laughed gently as I swayed about.

'I'm sure we could find the party again. It was near E. 14th Street. There was this shop selling stuffed animals. It was above that. Our friends got rooms to let there because of the name above the shop. A. LOUER. But that was his name, Arnie Louer. It did not mean there were rooms to let at all.'

'Persy will know,' said M.M. 'We'll ask her when we can get a word in. Never saw her so talkative.' Again, quite a satirical touch in the laugh, but no unkindness.

We caught the words 'Thomas lived six hundred years before modern medicine had got off the ground' – this from Father Bon, and Persy was astonishing me, if by nothing else then by her audibility, when she said, 'No, hush, Fergus, I want to get this straight with Bon.'

'Are you a Catholic?' asked Margaret Mary; she must by then have known the answer but I suppose the question was a way of explaining that there was no point in explaining the intensity of the conversation between the three. It was a remark, given the way the day had gone, which could have angered me, or excluded me from their charmed circle. No, I decidedly was not a Catholic; and yet I was the one in this company who was grieving for a lost child while the woman who had just had the abortion was holding an animated theological discussion with the priest, and I had no one to talk to about my lost child, nor about the vision in St Patrick's Cathedral.

'Do you believe in visions?' I asked her.

I was aware of her cheek very close to mine and she did not seem to mind me holding her hand as well as leaning against her as we walked; and yet there was no particular sexual come-on in all this. Would there have been – if I had pressed on for an advantage at this early stage? Perhaps. I think she managed to transform me from admirer to Lame Duck in the space of a couple of hours, probably. I cannot remember – my brain is too hazy, how we came to divide, or when the parting of the ways occurred. Persy and her brother took Father Bon off to a bar. Margaret Mary and I, presumably armed with the correct address and telephone number supplied by Persy, returned to the party which I had left some four hours before. Yellow Pigtail, nice Christopher, a handful of Newnham Norns and Wilmie in her cheesecloth blouse did not appear to have noticed that I had left. I tried to reconstruct for M.M. the allegations which had been made earlier in the evening concerning Mr Everett's strange habits and preferences. Having just eaten a meal with the old codger it seemed less probable, somehow, that he liked to spend his evenings in sessions of quite such voyeuristic depravity. I do not know whether this was merely a case of 'how exceedingly seldom the unseemly or unforesee-able rears its head' – to use a phrase from a favourite writer – or whether I felt that the witness of the young people was obviously tainted by political prejudice. Mr Everett had his own reasons for supporting the War, perhaps. I had no doubt that he was anti-Com-munist. Did this mean that he was guilty of all the other sins as well?

'Julian's quite a well-known actor now, you know,' M.M. was telling Wilmie over my head. We had left the room, apparently. Hours and hours had passed and we were sitting on the doorstep, as greyness of dawn began. More than half ashamed of my rôle in 'The Mulberrys', I took each mention of it, in those days, as a reminder that I had failed to do anything 'serious' with my life; and that I was reaching the point where I probably never would. M.M.'s claim that, because I was in a popular radio show, I was 'a well-known actor' belonged to the same confusing semantic territory as that in which the Birks, with their moneyed self-confidence, could be labelled grand.

'You're kidding.'

'There's a wireless programme called "The Mulberrys".'

'You're kidding?'

'He plays this absolute bounder – spiv sort of person; the charming con-man. I get the feeling he will turn out to be rather a marvellous person as he grows older.'

'Who, Julian?'

M.M. was laughing at the very idea. 'That too, no doubt. I meant Jason Grainger – the character he plays in this – well, I suppose you would call it a soap opera. Do you think he's going to be okay?'

'I think he dropped a little acid earlier, that's all.'

'He dropped what?'

'Excuse me?'

Having conducted a conversation over my head or across my face for about an hour they finally reached impasse; the American and the Englishwoman actually did not know what the other was talking about; might, indeed, have been conversing in different tongues for all the sense they were making.

The effects of the evening – alcohol, over-excitement, and whatever it was that Christopher had given me – began to wear off and night was turning to morning. When the skies above E. 14th Street became tinged with pink and I had decided that my head had cleared once and for all, the funny stuff took one final possession of my brain.

Pssw! Pfffff! From the brown dry street, steam sent up a sudden ejaculation and I saw in it each particle of light, saw all its constituent parts, vibrant, more alive than anything I had ever seen. I watched this cloud, gravity-defying, soar upwards and dissolve into tendrils of mist, up, up into the sky, beyond brick and brownstone façades, treetops and the dusty-windowed towers beyond, each window of which caught refractions of multi-coloured brilliance. The sun was up, and street cleaners were driving a monster truck along the kerbs, spraying roads and sidewalks with water.

'I'm going to be wrecked today,' said Margaret Mary, 'and I'd meant to go to the Frick.'

'You're kidding.'

'Mr Hunter promised to take me. He does seem extraordinarily charming.'

'Poor Julian.'

'He's not going to be sick, is he? Shall we get him back to his hotel?'

'To the Chelsea?'

'If you just take the other arm.'

'Just relax, baby, you're okay, you're okay,' said Wilmie. 'I'll put him in my bed here; let him sleep it off.'

But inside my head it was Mrs Nolan who had taken up residence. It was hard, at that moment, as she pulled me to my feet, to distinguish her from Mummy. Maybe they were the same person? Where was Persy – my supposed lover? With the fat priest? I did not care. As the pinkish smudge of dawn light brightened into a perfect summer day I recognised all the painful symptoms. I was in love with Persy's sister-in-law, Margaret Mary.

FOUR
(Summer 1966)

Can the Church err in what she teaches?
The Church cannot err in what she teaches as to faith or morals.

'The little Michelangelo book isn't nearly widely-enough known.'
This remark was shouted across the table, against the noise of all the
children, by Father Bon. He seemed as if he had come to the lunch,
armed with this crumb of Lampitt-information which would somehow
trump the two known Lampitt-experts present – Raphael Hunter and
Julian Ramsay.

Ramsay looked very displeased, particularly when the priest went
on to quote one of Michelangelo's sonnets in Italian; but Raphael
Hunter smiled at all his company. His face suggested that he took
positive pleasure in being exposed as an ignoramus by this large,
lumpy, innocent friar whose mediaeval rig made such a striking figure
in a modern Birmingham kitchen – the black scapular, the flowing
creamy-white habit, the belt jangling with rosary beads, the somewhat
smelly white socks, the black sandals. Hunter, in his crimson open-
necked shirt, smiled.

'Now I've looked up Belloc in the index of your book,' boomed
Father Bon.

'I only mention Belloc very briefly,' said Hunter. The amiability of
his expression did not alter, in spite of his sudden display of some
orange, rat-like teeth.

'The rumpus over the Porta Latina?' the Dominican insisted eagerly.

62

In this company there were so many children yelling that his loud voice, heavily inflected with a Birmingham accent, was useful to make itself heard; but as was notorious, he always shouted, whether or not it was necessary. 'I remember what you say about them meeting in London when Belloc was an MP and I think you are quite wrong about that, incidentally – but it's quite interesting, because it was one of the few times Belloc was flummoxed by having one of his mistakes pointed out to him. Lampitt, you'll recall, in his travel book – oh, what's the name of the thing?'

'*Lagoon Loungings,*' said Ramsay.

'No, the Roman one.'

'Oh, that one. *On Tiber's Bank.*'

The interruption and the momentary quieting of the childish din allowed the other priest, Father Linus Quarles, SJ, to reintroduce a note of general (at any rate, not Lampitt-obsessed) conversation. Few, after all, can really have been interested in the minutiae of James Petworth Lampitt's life; it really seemed as if it were the only subject on which Mr Ramsay could converse.

'I loved *On Tiber's Bank,*' said Father Quarles. 'I had the old Nelson edition printed on India paper and I always kept it in my pocket during my two years as a scholastic in Rome. I think my superiors were under the impression that it was the Little Hours of Our Lady, I consulted it so often.' He quaffed the last of his claret, and held his glass out for more, confident that, from some of the company – from Margaret Mary, and her brother, and his mousey wife Chantal, and from poor shy Miss Dare – he would get a sycophantic laugh. The belief that he was a wit, and that everything he said was slightly droll, had been cultivated in the various religious houses where Father Quarles had lived. The truth was that few other Jesuits liked him, but they had found that it was easier to endure his conversation at meals if they treated this essentially dull man as possessed of a turn of phrase and a spontaneity of humour which would have been the envy of Voltaire. It had not been difficult to convince Father Quarles himself that this was the true state of things, and the consequence was that he uttered nearly all his sentences, however tedious, as if they were *bons mots.* An example of Father Quarles's 'wit' was to speak of the different ends of the Nolans' kitchen as if it were Duke Humfrey's library at Oxford. The kitchen part with the sink and oven was the Selden End, whereas the sitting area, where he often reclined on a sofa, was the Arts End. A large refectory table ran between the two 'ends'.

Father Linus Quarles, SJ, was as neat, and as genteel, in his punctilious dark suit, as Father Bonaventure Reilly, OP, was coarse. Father Quarles, SJ, so much aspired to the status of a gentleman, that it was quite a surprise to some of those who met him for the first time that he was a Roman Catholic clergyman rather than an Anglican, even though his bony, sallow face had an almost Hispanic or Levantine complexion. Had El Greco painted drawing-rooms, this Jesuit would have made an apt subject for his brush. His presentable clothes, his fondness for the table, his general air of worldliness, would have made him a fish out of water in many Catholic parishes; perhaps this was why he had chosen to limit his apostolate to a few personal friends, and to those in the academic world who shared his interest in an obscure recusant martyr, Blessed Richard Bedesman, about whom he was supposed to be compiling a book, who had spent several exciting years spying for the King of Spain before his incarceration. In Newgate his piety (making rosaries out of hazel-nut shells) impressed even his gaolers. Father Quarles seldom spoke of Blessed Richard, whose heroic death in the year of the Armada (he was stretched on a rack, then squashed in a press before being disembowelled) hardly made suitable table-talk. Instead, the Jesuit preferred to demonstrate his wide aesthetic range by discoursing on other topics.

'Lampitt had an extraordinary eye; I commend to anyone his chapter on the Pantheon; it is truly remarkable. I always tell people to take *On Tiber's Bank* if they are going to Rome for the first time. After all, Rome never changes. Not in its fundamentals.'

This again was followed by a curious pursing of the lips and a pause for the laughter of the fans.

It was ungallant, perhaps, of Mr Hunter to reply, 'That's not what we read in the newspapers.'

Fergus Nolan surveyed the miscellaneous assembly of human souls there assembled. There were his two sisters – Persy and Joyce (Joyce had brought three of her brood with her, leaving the older ones with a neighbour). There were the two priests. There was Miss Dare, a neurotic convert who worshipped at the Oratory. There was his brother-in-law Henry Mount-Smith, Henry's Mousey Wife, Chantal, and – though they had only been married for five years – their three children, Magdalen, Kitty and Patrick. And there was the largely silent, chain-smoking Julian Ramsay, a radio actor who had lately battened on to the household; and Mr Hunter from London. Smiling gently in the midst was his wife Margaret Mary who regularly cooked a huge meal for an average of twenty people.

Every Sunday was like this. Fergus dutifully supposed that this was the way things 'should be'. He was an extremely lucky man, that was what he kept telling himself. Where else in Edgbaston would you get a meal like this? Though Elizabeth David's books had been in print for some time, their impact was not yet universal. M.M.'s absorption of their simple messages made her kitchen in Wiseman Road a refuge for gastronomes as well as for the intellectual and emotional inadequates which it had always been her destiny to accumulate (M.M.'s 'lame ducks'). She never went in for elaborate dishes, but the regulars at her table belonged to an English generation who had never tasted, in their own shores, a perfect and simply made *risotto Milanese*, or salad made with good, thick green virgin olive oil. M.M.'s fish soups, her *tartes à l'oignon*, her *faisans normandes* (pheasants shot in Yorkshire by her father and brothers), her taramasalata, her roast spring lamb, all added to the magic of those Sundays in Wiseman Road.

Thanks to a Mount-Smith legacy, he and his wife had a much larger house than other professional couples of their age. As a young grammar-school boy in Edgbaston it would never have crossed Fergus Nolan's mind that he would one day occupy one of the Edwardian, half-timbered Arts and Crafts mansions in Wiseman Road. He knew that he was privileged in every way, except the way he most wanted (with fatherhood). He knew that everyone spoke lovingly of these Nolan Sundays and that, particularly since his parents had died, it was 'nice' for his own siblings (two sisters, four brothers, one of them a monk in Ireland) to feel that this was 'home'.

Like all who live the life of the mind, however, Fergus Nolan could not banish the feeling that social life such as this was a waste of time and the last few years had seen so many encroachments on his time. Though he had trained as a medic and was a qualified doctor, Fergus Nolan was primarily a scientist. His early work as a young researcher had been on hormonal regulation and a comparison between the endocrine system of human beings and other comparable vertebrates. In his twenties, still at Oxford, he had become sidetracked into helping Professor Shipley for two years, on the causes of rapid growth in adolescent males. (This was when he met Margaret Mary, he a research fellow of Linacre, she an undergraduate at St Anne's – they'd met at the Catholic chaplaincy.) In his early married life he had worked on testosterone and again, by a series of accidents, and the offer of a senior research post at Birmingham, he had worked on the inter-relationship between male and female sex hormones.

In 1960, he was at work on the ovulation of cats and rabbits compared with that of human beings, and with the secretion of progesterone, noting the curious phenomenon that, when it is secreted in conjunction with oestrogen, it suppresses ovulation. By the most roundabout of routes, therefore, Fergus Nolan had found himself in the forefront of a branch of research which led to the development of the contraceptive pill.

Fergus Nolan was a thoroughly decent, amiable individual, but human beings, outside the immediate context of family, had very little interest for him except as physical phenomena. He was more at home with the secretion of progesterone than with the expression of feeling. He was glad to be a research medic, rather than having to sit on the ends of hospital beds and put people at their ease. He had been slow to recognise the human, or theological, implications of his work. He was not employed by a pharmaceutical company, and his work only touched glancingly on the development of what was now known as the Pill. But he was a loyal son of the Church, an unquestioning Catholic, who – unlike his best friend from student days, Jim Reilly, now Father Bonaventure – had never experienced the slightest 'difficulties with the faith'. To this extent, he had been an obvious, and ideal, candidate to serve on the Pontifical Com-mission which had been set up by Pope Paul VI to look into the whole question of the Church's teaching on artificial contraception. He did not pretend to have any ideas; he was not an amateur theo-logian, still less an amateur moralist. He accepted the Church's teach-ing, and her claim to teach. He just wanted to get on with his work. He would probably have been happy, given any scientific problem to solve or to investigate. The suppression of ovulation was just one of the hormonal 'problems' which he had enjoyed examining in his lab. Given the extreme literalness of Fergus's mind, its luminous humility in the presence of information, its patience, its willingness to sift evidence and draw logical conclusions therefrom, he was proud to have been recruited by the Commission. He felt, as a loyal Catholic, that he could not very well refuse membership of this important body. But it had been a devastating experience. Before it all began he had not envisaged how much time, and work, membership of this august body would entail. He had imagined that he would simply be asked to submit factual, scientific information, and that the theologians and bishops would decide among themselves what to do with this information. Meanwhile, he supposed, he would continue to be a scientist, constantly at work in the laboratory, apart from the unwelcome interruptions of the Commission.

It had not turned out like this. For a start, he had to travel so much – something he loathed. It had never occurred to him that the Commission would meet so often; nor that, when it was not meeting, it should have broken up into sub-committees, demanding his presence (when the discussions were at their unsavoury height) several times a month, often in quite different locations. He hated being away from his lab; he hated being apart from Margaret Mary, with whom he remained very much in love; and he hated what he was doing; for it had soon become apparent that the Pontifical Commission saw it as its duty to change the very nature of the Catholic Church's teaching about birth control; and the justification which most of his fellow-committee-members found for this was precisely the scientific research into hormones which Fergus, and others like him, had been making. For if some organisms interrupted ovulation as it were 'naturally', and if it were possible to pioneer a pill which would prevent ovulation simply by reproducing these 'natural' circumstances, would this not alter the Church's age-old objection to birth control? After all, even Pius XII, no modern trendy he, had allowed the use of the 'safe period' as a means of controlling birth. If you admitted the principle of allowing sexual intercourse which could not lead to the fertilisation of an egg, then you had presumably allowed the possibility of some form of 'natural' birth control, using the terms 'natural' and 'unnatural' as St Thomas Aquinas would have used them, to refer to the in-built laws of nature made by Almighty God.

This was precisely the area of discourse which Fergus had avoided all his adult life. He detested it, and he was no good at it. He knew

67

that there would be those who accused him of childish unwillingness to examine his faith; so be it! He did not care. He was perfectly happy to be childish about his faith, as his parents and grandparents, all highly intelligent and articulate people in their different ways, had been. The members of the Pontifical Commission were all Catholics; some of them were theologians and some were medics and others were 'concerned' individuals, such as social workers. Fergus said as little as possible at the meetings, and had made it a personal rule that he would never contribute a personal opinion for as long as he sat on the Commission. He would only correct some of the wilder assertions made (even by the medics) about matters of fact. For the truth was that he did not believe that Catholic doctrine was altered, or needed to be altered one iota as a result of his research. He hated the work of serving on the Commission with men and women of different academic disciplines because he knew that he had the wrong sort of intelligence for dealing with them. He knew that if he had received a training in philosophy, or even one in psychology, he might be in a stronger position to justify a certain hunch he had about nearly all of them: and that was that they were not primarily interested in the subject under discussion. Fergus could not explain his hunch – he certainly could not prove it; but he felt that even the decent ones were determined to undermine traditional Catholicism and that they were just using the birth control question as an excuse to do so. He could not begin to imagine why any priest, or Catholic doctor, should wish to rock the boat in this way; it was simply beyond his comprehension, and he wished that he had never consented to serve on the Commission.

There was a difficulty for him, however. As he saw to what use these people were all putting his research, picking up the most garbled layman's version of quite complicated (and often speculative) matters, he found an extraordinary change had taken place within him. He had come to distrust the one thing which had previously given him unalloyed joy – the pursuit of knowledge. He had reached a crisis. He no longer wished to return to the lab and absorb himself in examining the hormonal life of cats, dogs and human beings. He had a sense, as he flew from one conference to the next, and attended more and more meetings, that the human race was not really to be trusted with knowledge. The myth of Adam and Eve being forbidden to eat from the tree of knowledge now made perfectly good sense to Fergus. He came to believe that most people are too stupid and morally too vague to be in a position to make decisions based on data. He therefore suffered a crisis of faith – not of religious faith but of faith in his entire professional *raison d'être*. The excitement in science which he had felt, since schooldays, had now died on him, and he felt it to be a personal tragedy. Not, however, being the sort of man who could find the words to discuss such matters, even had he possessed a confidant who would have understood him if he had tried, he was left brooding silently on his sorrow. Whenever he heard Bon Reilly talk of the subject of the Church and birth control he flinched, being in a condition where he did not wish his friend to expose what seemed to Fergus like a blindness, a blustering bullishness which he had started to find repulsive.

It was an added source of bitterness that he, of all the Catholic doctors in the world, should have been called upon to supply evidence to the Pontifical Commission on this painful subject when he (and, he assumed, Margaret Mary) yearned for a baby. They had been married for twelve years. In the eyes of both their families, and of their friends, they were the perfect couple. Fergus Nolan was now forty-one years old. His wife was thirty-four. But, as Nolans and Mount-Smiths on both sides of the family increased and multiplied (Joyce, who lived quite near them, had seven and another on the way), Fergus and Margaret Mary were unable to breed. He knew that this would make it easy for anyone to find motives for his rigid view about the Catholic birth control question; which was why he chose not to discuss it ever, with anyone, in public. The fact that it was now aired regularly in the Sunday newspapers, such as the one for which Raphael Hunter wrote reviews, was a sign to Fergus that there was no chance of sanity prevailing – unless (which seemed desperately unlikely) this modernising Pope had the guts to reassert the traditional Catholic teaching on the matter.

Fergus was a reasonable Catholic, one who prided himself that the use of reason was one of the gifts of the Holy Spirit. Nevertheless, like all human beings, Fergus was not wholly consistent and there was a part of his nature which was profoundly superstitious.

When he realised that he was in such a minority in the Pontifical Commission and that nearly all his colleagues were determined to rush the Pope into stating that birth control was permissible in some circumstances, Fergus Nolan had gone to Mass and made a private contract with God.

'Oh Lord,' he had prayed, 'if my view of this matter is the right one, have mercy on us all; have mercy on the whole Church and deliver her from evil; and if I remain faithful to the truth, Lord, then will you in turn give Margaret Mary a child?'

This prayer had been made about a year ago. (As it happens, it had been made during Mass in Toronto on the feast of St Vincent de Paul.) Margaret Mary was still without a baby. As he stared at them all – some paying attention to what was said, some not, Fergus wished that they would all go, and he rather cursed the suave, worldly Raphael Hunter for having raised the subject of the changes in the Church, because it would certainly mean that they were all there for another half hour at least.

Margaret Mary Nolan was famously 'good' with her lame ducks. Father Linus Quarles (an *old* family friend but washed up, like her, in poor old Birmingham!) sometimes wondered whether it did not, in the mysterious Providence of God, have something to do with her failure to have babies. A Mount-Smith unable to conceive! (When Father Quarles, SJ, thought of the Mount-Smiths he had baptised! Flora, Clare, Richard, Louis – no, he told a lie! Louis had indeed been 'done' at Farm Street, but on an occasion when Father Quarles was abroad – Sebastian, John, Ronnie, little Magdalen and Kitty who were skipping about the room today – the list was almost endless!) Margaret Mary herself was the fifth child in a family of nine. They had all been a little worried when she married her clever husband at Oxford, and of course it was a thousand pities that the marriage had led her to being 'stuck in Brum'. But in spite of the disadvantages of birth (which Father Quarles had, at the time of the courtship, privately advised her parents made the marriage unthinkable) Fergus had turned out to be very clever and so forth; and now he was sitting on the Pontifical Commission, no less. Now that Father Quarles found himself 'stuck in Brum' – and thereby hung a tale which need not worry readers of these pages – he considered it a further working of the mercy of Providence that Margaret Mary was here! Where else could he spend his Sundays? As he often thought, watching the hundreds stream out of church when he was persuaded to say a public Marce, there were so few *people* in Birmingham.

By people, Father Quarles, SJ meant a category of being that was fairly easy to define; he meant either famous people; or socially elevated people; or Roman Catholics who aspired to belong to either of these categories; or, failing that, Roman Catholics who had educated their children at one of about half a dozen schools, and who pronounced the word 'mass' as 'marce'. Oddly enough, in Father Quarles's scale of value, the Mount-Smiths only just qualified as 'people' in this sense. During his seven fat years in Farm Street (Dear God! They wouldn't, would they, insist on his spending seven years in Brum?) his diary would have been just a little too full to fit in many Mount-Smiths. But, in the wasteland of Birmingham, the large house in Wiseman Road was a wonderful refuge; and, as he guilelessly remarked to anyone who was interested (even to those who weren't), Margaret Mary could never have afforded such a house if they were to live in London.

In Margaret Mary Nolan's features the invincibly ignorant would see only a pleasant, well-scrubbed country sort of face. But ah! Those who saw what Father Quarles, SJ, could at that moment see! It was a glimpse of the eternal in that sad girl's expression. He would have had difficulty in explaining what it was about Margaret Mary's sad expressive mouth and eyes which summoned up such powerful feelings.

She appeared to be in a perpetual state of slightly low spirits – had been since childhood – and this gave to that perfect oval of a face and those hooded eyes – and to her whole frame, though clothed in twentieth-century styles (today a jumper and pleated skirt), and to her long white hands, which might have been depicted by Duccio – the tragic air of some trecento Madonna trapped in the alien world of the 1960s. Those who liked to place the word 'poor' before her name – almost automatically, as one would before the word 'Clares' – considered that poor Margaret Mary, or even at thirty-four, poor old Margaret Mary, might be as virginal as her appearance suggested. Father Quarles was not quite so extreme a fantasist as this; he wished he were. He could see that, as couples went, the Nolans were ideally suited. He was dispassionate and intelligent enough to guess that Margaret Mary was happily married, and he even went so far as to attribute this to the fact that, unlike most other Catholic women he knew, M.M. had put the baby question out of her mind. That M.M. and her husband had deliberately chosen not to have babies did not even cross the priest's mind; but he considered it possible that both the husband and the wife were quite pleased that Divine Providence had not sent them nine sets of dirty nappies, nine sets of school fees at St Mary's, Ascot, and nine sets of all the expenses which fell to most Catholic parents. (By 'most' – but by now it will be clear what Father Quarles meant by 'most'.)

'Linus!' said M.M. 'The most extraordinary thing! Julian here stayed with our old friend Mme de Normandin at Les Mouettes, when he was a teenager; and he just missed meeting James and Francis by a whisker. They were going to have their holiday there at the same time . . .'

'It was where I met the Birks, too – our American friends,' said Mr Ramsay.

The priest looked blank. These arrangements could not be of interest. It was true that Mr Ramsay was an actor and might have qualified as interesting had he been introduced by a real *friend*, such as Alec Guinness, or Ralph Richardson, both of whom had attended Father Quarles's Marces in London. Father Quarles did not listen to 'The Mulberrys', however, a programme which was broadcast, as far as he was concerned, three nights of the week, when 'people' in London were attending publishers' parties or *vins d'honneurs* at embass-ies or small gatherings of other 'people' before it was time to attend dinner parties. The only other opportunity presented in the course of the week to hear 'The Mulberrys' was on Sunday mornings when people were at Marce. So, anyone who had anything to do with 'The Mulberrys' was, *ipso facto*, not one of us.

M.M.'s kindness was another reason that one loved her – and oh, my Lord, the priest *did* love her! – but this wretched kindness of hers did mean that she filled her house with bores! Like all the lame ducks, the priest did not recognise himself as one. Only the others fell into this pathetic category. He knew that M.M. and Fergus entertained him because he was what is called 'good value'. No point in being falsely modest! There was a certain degree, in this line of thought, where the Jesuit wished to eat and have cake. On the one hand he told himself that the Nolans were woefully unambitious. There were

72

– he knew there were, for he had met them on weekdays – a number of 'interesting' people in Birmingham; some younger members of the English department, for example, at the University were becoming 'known' as novelists, and the Nolans could so easily have invited them. (The young men in question were terribly unpretentious people!) Some of the older families in Edgbaston, too, had their interest, but the Nolans did not appear to know who they were, let alone be on terms with them. While mildly despising them for this, the priest rather enjoyed being the only person in the room, on an average Nolan Sunday, who had 'met anyone'. Julian Ramsay certainly did not count as anyone, though James Petworth Lampitt did. During his novitiate, Linus Quarles had once met Lampitt; he never bothered to tell this fact to Ramsay. When, so amazingly, the Nolans had produced none other than Raphael Hunter out of their hat it was a different story. This was a real catch!

One had often seen Raphael Hunter on television, and, as Father Quarles frequently told some of the more baffled students and novices with whom he was obliged to share the Jesuit house in Birmingham, one was *just* of an age to have known, or at least to have met, some of the people mentioned in Hunter's pages. Some of the things which Hunter had recorded were shocking; but perhaps, Father Quarles considered, more shocking to those of a suburban frame of mind than to those who were used to mixing with sophisticated folk. After all, who are we to say what, in the heart of the Divine Mercy, constitutes the worst of sins? And, though Mr Hunter had attributed to James Petworth Lampitt one of the four sins crying to heaven for vengeance, did we not have evangelical authority for believing that those would be forgiven much who also had loved much?

Father Quarles only regretted that, instead of their all managing to have a decent and civilised discussion with Mr Hunter, it had to be spoilt by Father Bonaventure Reilly or – as the Dominican appeared in Quarles's descriptive soul – 'that red-faced baboon at the end of the table.'

Mr Hunter had asked a perfectly reasonable question: were there not indeed changes afoot in the Eternal City? But he was in the foothills (Father Quarles regarded everyone as a potential convert to his own creed) and should not be dragged up the rockface by this drunken oaf.

73

'Nothing changes much in Rome,' said Father Quarles, still with regard to *On Tiber's Bank*.

'That's not what we read in the papers,' said Mr Hunter.

'Would anyone like some coffee?' asked Fergus.

'Oh, I'm afraid too much has been changing,' said Miss Dare in her rather high-pitched, mincing little voice. 'When I was instructed we were told the Church would never change.'

White hair was piled in a bun on top of a white face on to which a haphazard application of face-powder had been made. Her startled, pinched features prompted the thought that the powder might have reached the cheeks by accident – perhaps by a bag of flour having been upset over her as a practical joke. Miss Dare, who was a fairly recent convert from Anglicanism, seemed to be one of those emotionally constipated people who might conceivably have been made happier by the acquisition of a dog.

'The Church has been changing for every second of its existence,' thundered Father Bon. His tavern loudness, as distasteful to Miss Dare as to Father Quarles, made the Mousey Mrs Mount-Smith feel that the party needed to break up; Joyce and her children were already going, and now Chantal began a pathetically ineffectual attempt to marshal her children into outdoor clothes.

Against the noise Father Quarles said, 'When I was a scholastic in Rome there was this talk of the liturgical movement. The Marce did not change then, and I do not believe that in any material way it will change now. These dialogue Marces are all very well.'

'They've started having them at the chaplaincy,' said M.M. 'I don't like them, I'm afraid. They've even had one in English, I hear.'

'Of course one can be too fastidious,' said Father Quarles. 'There were those who were even upset by Pius XII's reforms to the Easter liturgy. I can remember Evelyn Waugh saying . . .'

'That was just *tinkering*!' It was by now apparent that the huge, sweating, scarlet Bonaventure Reilly was drunk. 'Of course there'll be a regular Mass in the vernacular before long.'

'I don't agree with you there, Jim,' said Fergus quietly.

'And the Council will eventually change the whole Church, root and branch!'

'Of course there's every reason why they might continue with the experiment in a context like the chaplaincy; but, for the everyday parish Marces, they'll never go into the vernacular. Marce in English!'

'It's possible!' Miss Dare was brave enough to pipe up, but they all laughed. They did not mean to be unkind, they thought she was joking, but the over-sensitive lady felt that they were mocking her, all that is except the red-faced friar whom she could not like! She simply was not used to clergymen who were coarse, and a wave of nostalgia possessed her as she thought of nice Mr Ramsay, the uncle of the rather peculiar Mr Ramsay who was there today.

'It's not only possible,' said Bon Reilly, OP, 'it's inevitable! Just open your minds to what's happening, can't you? Are you all completely blind?'

As if to restore a polite calm – and Mousey was now in quick retreat, shoving the frail little arms of Magdalen into her anorak sleeves as if she really did not wish her children to hear any more of this – Hunter quietly asked, 'And Fergus – I know your work has been highly confidential . . .'

Fergus Nolan looked furiously at Hunter, for he could guess what was coming.

'. . . but do you think there is any chance that the Pope will change his mind about the question of contraception? You see – and I'm sure you will forgive me for saying this, as someone who isn't a Catholic – '

'I'm sorry,' said Fergus, 'that's a subject I do not discuss.'

But, before the sentence was past his lips, everyone had begun to talk at once. Hunter's lips twitched with the satisfaction of a terrorist who had just hurled a Molotov cocktail into a petrol tanker.

Mousey had stopped wrestling with Magdalen's stick-like arms and left the anorak to drag behind the child like a train. Father Quarles was saying something but it was drowned by two of the women. Even the inaudible Persy was trying to shout.

Mousey Chantal suddenly turned into a lioness. 'But this isn't taking a human life, or even taking a potential human life,' she said furiously. 'It's simply . . .'

'. . . against Nature,' said Quarles.

'What isn't against Nature? If you have a headache, it's against nature to take an aspirin, but there's nothing sinful about that. And I'm just telling you that we've all had it up to HERE . . .'

'Thomas,' put in Fatty Reilly, OP, 'Thomas . . .'

No one knew who Thomas was except Father Quarles, who noticed with irritation that Dominicans always called him Thomas in their proprietorial way while the rest of the world politely kept its distance by calling him Aquinas. Was it conceivable, the Jesuit quietly asked himself, that Aquinas – a big fat intellectually-conceited Dominican like Bon Reilly – was quite such uncongenial company?

'Look, Thomas would say, you have to distinguish between the essence of a thing and its substance. No, listen – listen, love . . .'

'And DON'T call me love!'

'I'm sure,' said Henry, Chantal's husband, 'there's a distinction between people living in shanty-towns or whatever and people like us who can easily . . .'

'Easily?' Chantal looked capable of violence. 'You stand there – you who have never changed a nappy in your LIFE, never woken up in the night, never helped with the children in any way and talk about EASILY. This makes me SICK.'

Persy Nolan was talking equally animatedly but Chantal Mount-Smith still held the floor.

'Do you actually know what this pill does? Do you even know how the female body works, do you? Your bloody Saint Thomas didn't, for a start! No, I'm sorry, no – but he didn't, he did NOT, Bon, and just admit it. Thomas Aquinas thought, like Aristotle, that the human soul was all contained in the man's seed. He did. He did!'

'Look,' said the Dominican, 'let's get one or two of these arguments sorted out. There's Henry's point – it's a perfectly valid one – about the shanty-towns. There's Chantal's point about the actual biological – '

'I'm asking you to answer me,' said Chantal. 'Did St Thomas Aquinas know the facts of life? Did he? Because if he didn't I hope you're not going to sit there and ask me to accept him as the great authority on . . .'

Chantal, in her fury, had paused to light a cigarette.

The silent Julian Ramsay, who had absolutely nothing to contribute to this debate, noted the contrast between the troubled face of Dr Fergus Nolan and the serene expression of Raphael Hunter.

'Look – if a woman's got three kids already,' furious Chantal, no longer Mousey, was well away, exuding the smoke of Number Six like a fire dragon as she warmed to her theme, 'and she's poor, and she's living in a mud hut – '

'Children are her only consolation in this situation, Chantie! You're not going to tell me she can be translated into a white, suburban two-and-a-half kids way of life; anyway, why should she be? Are you saying that white, suburban mid-twentieth century . . .' This from Persy, who today seemed willing to put forward points of view more reactionary than Torquemada when the authority of the Church was questioned.

'And you're telling me,' pursued the Number Six Fire Dragon, 'that some rich old bachelor – all right, he's the Pope. I'm sorry, Persephone, I'm sorry, Bon, but I – '

'The Pope's celibacy has nothing – '

'Look, love, remember that the Church's job – '

'Oh, DAMN the Church!'

In Fergus's long, private and agonised discussions about the question with his friend Jim Reilly, they had both, like good mediaeval debaters in a *disputacio*, been prepared to argue either side of the question to see if they could understand it better. What had emerged was that this was not just a debate about sex and not just a debate about the Pope. To the two friends it felt as if the human race in the West had reached a turning point.

Jim Reilly, who became increasingly radical in his theology, believed that this was an issue of human freedom and human rights.

'He came that the people of God should have life, more abundant life, Fergus, and that did not mean become slaves to huge families which they could not afford, whatever the pro-life lobby makes of that text. The whole point of Christ coming into the world was that the human race could grow up; Paul says it – we are no longer babies. For Christ's sake – literally, Fergus – we are no longer babies!'

(Fergus noted this tendency of the Dominican to quote the Scriptures, where in the past he would have alluded almost exclusively to the scholastics, and to Aquinas in particular.)

'And Christ the Liberator is alongside women in their struggle for equality; just as he is alongside the people in their struggle against oppression in Central America; in their struggle against materialism and capitalism in the West. We've just got to get away from the idea that Catholics are a load of kids who can be told what to think by the Pope.'

'I agree with nearly all that, Jim, I'm not disputing the fact that we live in a very exciting time and that the mind of the Church has already started to express this; it was bound to express it because the Church is the Holy Spirit speaking through the People of God. The Council has been a miracle – it has restored to the People of God an idea of who they are and what their purpose is in the world. We are alongside the poor and the outcast and the oppressed, and it's no longer possible' – he had smiled as he thought of all the Mount-Smiths and their friends at Ampleforth Abbey – 'to be a Catholic and not be excited by all these developments. This is new life. I grant you all that. But what we are discussing, Jim, is human life itself, the very stuff of human life. Is it something we can just play around with? I have to think about these questions in the lab every day of my working life. It isn't just the old argument about the seed of life – every scientist has known that was crap for centuries. And it's not just the fact that the Popes have condemned contraception in the past. We all know they have condemned almost everything. Paul V condemned Galileo.'

'Leo XIII condemned the use of electric lights,' Reilly had said as he emptied, one late night, the last drops of Jameson's whiskey into his friend's glass.

It was on that half-jokey and half-deadly earnest level that the two friends had so often discussed the question over the last year. Now it was being yelled about over Fergus's lunch-table. No one would ever think of Chantal as a mouse, ever again. Persy had an expression in her face which the enemies of their grandfather must have seen when, as a loyal member of the Republican army, he had fought in the Independence war and fired his shotgun at point-blank range in the face of Black and Tans; Chantal's husband Henry Mount-Smith, thirty-five years old, had the pop-eyed expression of an apoplectic major who had read in his *Daily Telegraph* that they were letting women into the MCC. Anarchy and violent anger had occupied the room; the sort of mad frenzy which Homer describes taking possession of his heroes at the arbitrary whim of the Immortals.

They prayed to St Michael each Sunday after Mass – 'St Michael, Archangel, defend us in our struggle: be our protection against the wickedness and snares of the devil. May God restrain him, we humbly pray: and do thou, O Prince of the Heavenly Host, thrust down to

78

hell Satan and the other wicked spirits who wander through the world for the ruin of souls.'

Mr Hunter bore the archangelic name of Raphael. Fergus reacted to him, however, as if the ruin of souls was his primary business and desire. Why? He just – to use the sort of phrase which his late father-in-law would have used, and which Fergus parodied, in a clipped imitation of upper-class English speech – he just didn't like the cut of Hunter's jib. There was something primitive and instinctual about gentle Fergus's dislike of Hunter; even though scientific Fergus tried to explain his sudden onrush of rage against Hunter by the fact that everyone in that kitchen seemed to be yelling about contraception – everyone except the children and Julian Ramsay, who sat in a foolish, cheerful but semi-somnolent state (Valium, Fergus guessed), saying nothing. This was all Hunter's doing – Persy going red and shouting about natural law, Jim Reilly even redder and sweatier, Chantal Mount-Smith who had become a crazed suffragette . . . And Hunter just sat, smiling, entirely unruffled, and youthful for his forty-something years, while all around him decent folks contorted their faces with anxiety and rage.

Fergus hated him for this. What was this, if it was not the ruin of souls? He loved his friend Jim Reilly's vast sweaty face going at it hammer and tongs against the suave Jesuit, but both men seemed victims of some demon that Hunter had released into the ether – even the sophisticated Father Quarles. Persy, when roused, gabbled so fast that she became incomprehensible; she might have been speaking in tongues. Poor Miss Dare's powdery face lost its slight vestiges of colour, and became corpse-like as the others yelled of semen and ovaries.

Some phrase of Belloc's about the household of faith would have explained Fergus's reaction to this troubled scene. 'Within that household the human spirit has roof and hearth. Outside it, is the night.' Everyone in the kitchen save two belonged to the household. The silent Julian (M.M. said afterwards he was worried about a dying grandmother) claimed to be an unbeliever, but at least he was C of E and knew roughly speaking what was meant by the Mass and so forth. Hunter, by contrast, was a complete outsider; he reacted to the Catholic faith as if it were something completely alien – as if it were Hinduism or Mormonism, seeming, in his superiority to it all, to

79

disregard not merely his own imaginative failure to take in the Faith, but also the fact that (true or false) that Faith had shaped Europe – its habits of learning, its systems of administration, its notions of justice, as well as so many abbeys, churches and universities.

Hunter might have sprung up without tradition, without a past. If Fergus and his friends were of the Household, then Hunter was decidedly of the Night. In his presence, Fergus felt like the good creatures of the River Bank confronted by a weasel or by the other alarming beings who inhabited the wild woods. The fact that he thought in such childish terms (it was nearly forty years since he had read *The Wind in the Willows*) told Fergus that he had ceased to be rational about Hunter. Nevertheless, as the man sat there in his fashionable clothes, with his 'hair-do' and with his smooth, impassive, rather sexless face, which looked as if it had had no experiences at all, Fergus felt instinctively that Hunter was up to no good, that he was wandering the world for the ruin of souls.

Why should a cosmopolitan atheist media star – this was how Fergus now saw Hunter – choose to spend his Sundays driving up the motorway to Birmingham for lunch with 'people like them' unless he felt he could get something out of the Nolans? Fergus knew the obvious answer. Everyone eventually fell in love with M.M., and this had been the cross he had borne since he married her. He had to share her with her lame ducks. But what she gave to Father Quarles and to 'poor Julian' was no more sexual than what she gave to Miss Dare and the scores of others she brought home from the Urra-tree (as Miss Dare pronounced that place). Margaret Mary had never strayed, nor, Fergus opined, could she – any more than he could. He had never, since marrying her, felt the slightest desire to commit adultery; it would have been imaginatively and physically impossible.

The thought of Hunter committing adultery with Margaret Mary was therefore, in the cranium of Fergus Nolan, unthinkable. It occurred to him that Hunter had some ulterior motive for his visits (it was the third time he had been to lunch and it looked dangerously as if it was going to turn into a habit; Fergus did not know if he could bear Hunter becoming one of the regulars). Fergus thought that Hunter was in some obscure way an emissary of Virgil D. Everett and so of Lixabrite. Fergus was convinced that Hunter's job for Lixabrite was to soften up the Nolans; in some intrusive way to ensure that,

80

when the day came for the Pontifical Commission to make up its mind on the matter, it would collectively say – Go ahead! Let Lixabrite produce contraceptive pills with papal approval and they'll soon be selling them all over Africa and South America! Probably every single member of the Pontifical Commission was being oiled up to by someone like Hunter at this time. And Hunter's slick, English, godless manner, his air of condescension to Fergus, summoned up all manner of atavistic responses in the Irish doctor. It was the condescension of an arts man to a mere scientist; of the privately educated to the grammar school. Above all, it was the condescension of the Englishman to the Irishman and Fergus felt this even more strongly than he felt distaste for Hunter's presumption in flirting with M.M. Viewed in this light, Hunter's flirtatiousness seemed no more than the ascendancy landlord coming to exercise his *droit du seigneur*.

Hunter's smoothy manner was therefore deeply counter-productive in 43, Wiseman Road, Edgbaston. If he had been sent by Lixabrite it was the most foolish move they ever made, for Fergus was feeling by the time the party broke up that, as a gesture of hatred for Hunter and all his ways, he, Fergus Nolan, would never countenance the Pill. Yes – if Montini himself went down on his knees and begged that there should be some relaxation of the Church's teaching, Fergus would now wish to say, No! Hunter had hardened Fergus's heart and determined *that he should do the right deed for the wrong reason.*

'Surely you don't have to go already . . . afraid we must seem very dull dogs to you . . . so kind of you to come . . .' These were the sycophantic and absurd social formulae on the lips of M.M. when Hunter eventually rose to depart.

'Oh, Birmingham's become *very easy* since they built the motorway.' Accessibility to London was, apparently, the only thing to be sought in a place. Poor Birmingham, once difficult, had become easy, just as the Gentiles once 'afar off' before the Incarnation had now 'come nigh' to the Redeemer. Smiling loftily, Hunter placed a valedictory hand on Julian Ramsay's shoulder; was this Hunter's absolution for Mr Ramsay's extraordinary behaviour when they had last met in New York? Neither man, however, met the other's gaze. Evidently, they had known one another before. Fergus did not regard this fact as remarkable – they both worked in the 'media'. Hunter smiled at his

81

company, but he did not bother to take leave of each in turn. Only to Father Quarles, SJ, did he make a small bow.

'I'll ask Mr Everett about that – it is absolutely fascinating if true,' he said.

(The Jesuit had told Hunter of the whereabouts of a cache of letters, very much up Mr Everett's street, between Canon Gray and Raffalovitch; as a result of this tip-off the great financier bought the letters before they reached the sale rooms.)

Fergus watched while his wife was enfolded in the arms of Mr Hunter.

'It was a terrific meal.'

'Oh it was nothing.'

'Fergus . . .' Turning his back on the wife with no further ceremony, Hunter took his host by the elbow as they went out into the wide, encaustically tiled hall.

('Room for a pram there and no mistake!' Jim Reilly had quipped when they first bought the house. 'You could have three prams lined up there and there'd still be room to walk around them.' Well, that had been their purpose in buying such a large house.)

'We shall be in touch,' said Hunter and then with an air of impishness, almost the coquette, he added, 'Had I known that it would stir up such a hornets' nest I'd have kept off that subject.'

'Most Catholics blow hot and cold about the subject at the moment.' The sheepishness of his own grin was something which made Fergus blush; he felt he was having to apologise to this metropolitan sophisticate for the 'primitive' thought processes of 500 million people throughout the world.

Fergus had never told Hunter that he sat on the Pontifical Commission; it was one of those cases where 'he knows that I know that he knows'. No open acknowledgement had ever been made – except in confidence to Jim Reilly – that this was what Fergus had been doing for the last five years. When Fergus once suggested to M.M. that Hunter was 'fishing' for information about the Pontifical Commission she had reacted so angrily that he almost feared she was insulted – that is, insulted by the idea that Hunter did not come to see her, but to milk her husband for information. She had hotly denied ever telling Hunter anything about Fergus's work; but Fergus knew that she must have let things slip – for example about his reasons for being in New York on the first occasion of their meeting. Their rows, Fergus's and M.M.'s, had been so rare. It was disturbing to quarrel about this. He could not help wondering what she had artlessly given out during those walks which she allowed herself to have in New York, when Hunter had insisted on taking her to 'sights' which Fergus had never seen, the Frick, the Morgan Library . . .

'We never seem to get a chance to talk,' said Hunter. 'Maybe on one of your London visits, we could get together for lunch or a drink.'

This was the most overt, the most blatant exchange on the forbidden subject which had ever passed between the two men. They quite obviously had nothing in common; why, then, should Hunter wish to buy Fergus lunch? What (apart from information nosed out of the guileless M.M.) could have led Hunter to suppose that Fergus *did* make regular visits to London? Only his work for the Pontifical Commission made him do so. He had never liked London, and he had never much made a habit of going there; it had been, simply, a venue for shows and concerts which he or M.M. had wished to 'catch', otherwise he had steered clear of the place, having no wish to master its geography or to absorb its heathenism. 'Your London visits'; did the phrase suggest a belief that everyone who had the misfortune to live in the provinces must, in order to survive, make London visits? Or did it, as Fergus thought, display in a quite calculated and deliberate manner, a knowledge of those regular contacts which had been established with the Cardinal and with those international conventions of different members of the Commission which sometimes, for convenience, met in London?

'You must be very busy,' said Fergus. Though he had no English blood in his veins, Fergus Nolan knew how to speak English as it is spoken in England. This sentence, translated into any other language in the world, except perhaps Mandarin Chinese, would mean that he did not wish to have lunch with Hunter; that, far from ever wishing to have lunch with him, it would not have disturbed Fergus Nolan if Mr Hunter had fallen from the top of a skyscraper.

They stood by the front door together, Hunter's careful *coiffure* framed by the rusty survival of seven-week-old lilac blossom. The deciduous trees in the gardens up and down the road were heavy with leaf. In Fergus's eyes, everything about this well-planted, nondescript suburban road – where children of dentists and businessmen played

83

safely; where their grannies walked to coffee mornings and whist drives; where some polished cars and others attended Protestant conventicles on Sundays – everything about it was innocent. He knew that this was theological nonsense, and that decent, well-heeled Birmingham Quakers and Unitarians were as much tainted with original sin as were the prostitutes in Balsall Heath; there was, however, something guileless about Wiseman Road. It had so obviously been built by people wishing to lead comfortable, unshowy lives. The slight chill in the air gave the sense that the Serpent had slithered into Eden.

'You know your way to the motorway by now,' said Fergus Nolan.

'Oh, well, I shall find it – no doubt I'll be guided to it by St Christopher!' This parody of superstition came from *de haut en bas*, and made Fergus, as he watched the Jag scrunch away, even angrier. Moreover, he longed for all the others to go, leaving M.M. and him alone together. There were still enough hours of daylight to allow them a trip to the Botanical Gardens or – if they were about to close – to take the car and have a walk on the Lickey Hills. Sometimes those Sunday lunches were socially delicious affairs which naturally spilled over into tea; on other occasions they simply became boring. In such moods of discontent he feared that the Lame Ducks would take everything; that their demandingness would remove M.M. from him forever, leaving him bereft; for still, after twelve years, he loved her, yearned for her as a lover.

Returning to the large unruly room he found that his sister Persy and Bon O'Reilly, OP, were doing the washing-up – a domestic snapshot which stayed in the brain, making subsequent developments in the friar's life less surprising than they would otherwise have been to his pious friend. Neither Persy nor Bon showed the slightest sign of wanting to leave, but at least they had stopped yelling about birth control. Linus Quarles, SJ, who had settled in a comfy chair by the fireplace at the Arts End, showed no cognisance that washing-up was in progress at the Selden End. He was half way through an anecdote, which Fergus had heard several times before, about Monsignor Ronnie Knox at the Old Palace in Oxford. At least, now, Julian Ramsay could perform some useful function, because he was sitting beside the priest providing a notional audience. It allowed others without rudeness to drift away, or at least to ignore the Jesuit. Henry and Chantal had decided that the evening would be intolerably noisy if the children did not get some sort of an airing, and were shoving the last little arms into anorak sleeves. Miss Dare normally left first to attend Benediction at the Urra-tree. (Her fondness for this service caused the Nolans quiet amusement; M.M. said that, poor thing, she probably missed the Anglican hymns; while Bon said that the theology behind Benediction was downright unsound.)

On this occasion, Miss Dare lingered. She too seemed pleased that the dreadful particularity and physicality to which the contraception quarrel had descended should have been replaced by the harmless theme of Monsignor Knox; but, halfway through his limerick, Father Quarles looked up at Fergus as he returned to the room and said – 'What a *charming* man Raphael Hunter is! A real charmer. Of course we all read the Lampitt book when it first came out and I see his *Sunday Times* reviews which I always think are completely *brilliant*. So well-turned. I see signs there, you know.'

'Of Mr Hunter becoming a Catholic?' asked M.M., with bright credulity.

'Oh, certainly.' No one contradicted this surprising view, so the priest continued, 'You know, they do say that old Lampitt became a Catholic in secret on his death-bed.'

'Jimbo Lampitt – you mean James Petworth Lampitt?' Julian Ramsay was roused from his stupor.

'Julian's rather an expert,' said M.M. politely.

Fergus Nolan's mind drifted away while the melancholic actor, stirred again into tedious liveliness, expressed his doubt concerning the claims of the priest: Lampitt, it would seem, far from becoming a Catholic on his death-bed, did not even have a death-bed – was found dead, upside-down in a dustbin; not content to leave it at that, Julian Ramsay was prosing about the Unitarian ancestors of the writer; the old Norwich brewer, who was a Radical; his advantageous marriage to Lady Selina Isleworth in 17–something. How strange it was, Fergus reflected, that insubstantial *thought*, mere cerebral activity, can be so all-consuming to human beings! He seldom, if ever, dared to divulge to non-professionals the nature of his concerns about hormones, knowing that, even if he could make his company understand, he could not make it attend him. The difference, no doubt, between arts and sciences – the arts, represented here by the prolix Mr Ramsay, quite confident that his tale would be not just comprehensible, but fascinating to his audience.

'You must remember the libel trial,' he was saying, not really *to* anyone, but to the air. 'A writer called Albion Pugh claimed that . . .'

'Now, there's a name!' said Linus Quarles, SJ. 'A pretty peculiar Catholic, that one – I've always suspected, reading between the lines of his books, that he was one of those faithful northern families who never apostasised; not aristocrats, you understand. There are families like that all over Lancashire and Yorkshire who have kept the faith since penal times. Salt of the earth.'

Like many ultra-snobs, Linus Quarles, SJ liked to express from time to time a completely unconvincing admiration for the lower-orders, just as some homosexuals feel moved, in certain company, to make rather wild gestures in the direction of praising women's breasts or legs.

'I don't think Albion Pugh is a Roman Catholic,' said Julian Ramsay. 'Or North Country. He's pure Cockney'.

Everyone laughed at this temerarious attempt by Ramsay to contradict the Jesuit; he would be saying next that Mario Lanza or the Kennedys were not Catholic!

'Yes, yes,' said the Jesuit to clinch his argument. 'Albion Pugh wrote *Memphian Mystery*, a wonderful story all about the Pharaohs; Agatha Christie, you could say, with a real metaphysical twist.'

'You could ask Persy. She actually knows him,' said Julian, 'as do I. He really isn't a . . .'

But his words fell on completely deaf ears. 'Albion Pugh', the *nom de plume* of Rice Robey, had certainly been a figure in Persephone Nolan's life, if not in any conventional sense her lover. He was not, however, a Roman Catholic, or, as he would probably have called it (for he employed his own idiolect for most things), a Western Papalist ('Pipe-List').

Only two in that room really believed that a perception of the supernatural, or an understanding of metaphysics, were vouchsafed to those who were not members of the Roman Catholic Church. One was Julian Ramsay and the other was Miss Dare. All the others believed instinctively that the human race was sunk in a moral fog which Catholicism alone could lift.

'Do you remember,' Miss Dare surprised everyone by asking, 'old

86

Mrs Lampitt at Timplingham?' And, having established this claim to a special stake in Lampittry, she said quietly, 'I don't think you remember me, do you, Julian?'

'Oh, but I do, Miss Dare, I do!' Was he telling the truth? No one could tell, but all could see that his manner became more actorly as he made this profession. 'I didn't want to embarrass you by reminding you of your Protestant past!'

'Julian's uncle is a vicar in Norfolk,' said Miss Dare, turning a little pink. 'I used very much to laik the services at his church, but I left the district when Julian was quate a little boy.'

'We still speak of you with affection, Miss Dare.'

'And your uncle – Mr Ramsay – he's still . . .'

'Still going strong – still maintaining the old Sarum Rite in the middle of Norfolk.'

Miss Dare looked so pleased at this news that a very faint tinge glowed through the floury texture of her cheeks. She pressed both hands together, an attitude expressive of prayerful thanks.

Fergus Nolan sighed. At the Selden End, Jim Reilly was burbling to Persy; they had reached the stage of washing-up where all but the greasier pans had been washed, dried, stacked. Chantal and Henry were quite definitely going now. But everyone was still hovering, still maddeningly there, and Fergus, as he looked at them and did not quite hear, let alone listen to, what any of them was saying, felt a disconsolate sense of wasted time; they had simply gobbled his day, these people, taken his time with their jabber, and their eating and their feelings!

'I think we had better all have a cup of tea!' announced M.M., who was quite unaware of her husband's irritation, and did not want the company to disperse. More than that, she perhaps positively needed company, needed an hour or two, after the departure of Raphael Hunter, in which she was cocooned in society rather than being exposed to the company of Fergus alone.

'We are terrible people!' exclaimed Father Quarles, crossing his legs and settling deeper into his armchair. 'We stay and stay! I'm sure we are keeping you.'

But Henry and Chantal and the children were leaving – they too must make tracks for Cheltenham (where Henry worked in GCHQ) and they had the school run in the morning – everything about the lunch as always marvellous – mmwah, mmwah! – fancy meeting Raphael Hunter, isn't he sweet – don't forget to ring Cecilia on Thursday about Papa's birthday . . .' Jabber, jabber out into the hall, echoing jabber as the kettle boiled.

It was Persy, assisted by Bon Reilly, OP, who took charge of the tea-making at the Selden End.

'Do you never help your wife with anything?' Bon asked Fergus. The childishness of the banter irritated Fergus at that moment. Providing tea for – his eye made a hasty calculation – seven people whom he had not asked to stay for tea was not what he would call helping his wife; and no, in any case, he did not in that sense 'help' his wife; he saw it as no part of his function in life's scheme.

The subject of the Sarum Rite, which sparked a degree of interest in the Jesuit and had led to a troika of talk – Ramsay, Quarles and Dare – at the Arts End, carried no weight with the washers-up. Persy and Bon had neither of them crossed the threshold of an Anglican church in their entire lives, even to look at the architecture.

Fergus had been to one of their funerals once (a colleague in the department) and thought how bleak it was; how uncompromising, with its absence of any second chances, its refusal to pray for the dead. Being aesthetically blind he had not noticed the architecture (of Edgbaston Old Church). Persy and Bon were thrashing out Liberation Theology.

'Christ's work is by definition subversive,' said Bon, 'there's no getting round that because that is His nature, and it's bound to be the nature of His Church.'

'But you can't say there isn't something new in the idea of the social gospel, Bon.' This from Persy, who had surprised Fergus by an apparent return to the Faith since they went to America. She went not merely to Mass but to Holy Communion, something Fergus had not known her do since her first term at Cambridge, eight years before.

' "I make all things new." The Gospel always seems new to every generation. It was new when it told people not to worship Caesar, new and subversive. It was new when it told another generation to punish heresy. It must have seemed very new in the Middle Ages when it condemned usury, but it's always been new; it's always undermined the established order, what the Fourth Gospel calls the *kosmos*.

88

That's why the real radicalism in the nineteenth century isn't found in Marx alone, but in the Papal encyclicals. *Rerum Novarum* now . . .'

'You'll be wanting a drop of this with your tay, Father.' Fergus parodied and exaggerated his own very slight Irish intonation when he poured whiskey for his Irish friends. He never did so when speaking to his English friends, least of all to his Mount-Smith in-laws. He hated the Englishman's idea of the stage-Irishman; he hated 'Irish jokes' which were a barely covert way (not the only way either) of asserting the English superiority to his race (and on what was this strange sense of superiority based?!). But when confident that he was in purely Irish company he liked to be a parody-Irishman, which was different from the stage-Irishman of the English jokes.

'You see in some ways – thanks, Fergus,' the friar accepted the brimming tumbler, 'in some ways – and I don't know when you last read it – *Rerum Novarum* is as radical as anything the new theologians have come up with. It condemns capitalism root and branch. It asserts the rights of the working man, it warns against the consequences of materialism in Socialism as well as in Capitalism, and when you see what happened in Stalin's Russia, you can . . .'

'There are ways and ways of getting involved in political action, though,' said Persy. Perhaps the few sips of whiskey, perhaps the very word *political* spoken among Irish friends, was enough to ensure that they would all speak at once.

Bon Reilly asked her where Ireland would have been if the Church had been afraid of getting its hands dirty with politics, and, lest she gave him a wrong answer, he supplied her with the right one, 'I'll tell you where Ireland would have been – still under the English boot, that's where, depopulated and licking the boots of the English, like the bloody Welsh.' And Fergus was saying that this wasn't making all things new, this was the besetting sin of the Irish, this rehearsal of old grievances, old battles, old issues. Not listening to either, Persy, her voice for once audible and several octaves higher and several decibels louder since she had gulped her whiskey, was chasing a different hare and saying that de Valera, Collins, MacBride and all the other heroes – and should she not know, she whose own great-uncle, their nan's brother, had fought alongside Collins and strung up Ascendancy farmers' wives with his own bare hands? – their whole

Creed was rooted in Christ alone; it was untainted by the atheism of Marx.

Our Lady of Fatima's condemnation of Bolshevism had been dragged into the argument before they were recharging their tumblers.

While at the Selden End the whiskey coursed through Celtic veins, the effects of alcohol wore off at the Arts End, and, with the arrival of, and consumption of, tea, Miss Dare, Father Quarles, Mr Ramsay and M.M. became momentarily more sober. Memory and desire haunted both groups; but, while the Selden group grew hotter and more passionate, the Arts group were visited, collectively and severally, by that poignant atmosphere of melancholy which so many in England feel towards the close of a Sunday – an atmosphere which some would explain in terms of apprehension, a dread of the approach of a working week, and others would associate with the fear of death, the closing-in of the dark, the increased likelihood, at that hour, that the past, the individual and the collective past, will come to haunt our consciousness. Had they all been characters in an Albion Pugh novel, the reader could at this juncture have been made aware of all their secret thoughts, their aspirations and prayers emanating soundlessly from them and forming their own potent *mélange*, contributing to what in the present more prosaic narrative has been called, a little feebly, 'atmosphere'. Pugh would have wished to emphasise the unquestionable fact that everyone present except Persy, was in some sense 'in love with' Margaret Mary Nolan. Fergus was conscious of it, but he had long ago realised that he would become insane were he to allow his mind to dwell on the fact that children, animals, men and women, all had this tendency to fall for M.M., to be bewitched by her.

Deliberately shielding himself from the generalised human tendency to worship Margaret Mary, Fergus managed to overlook – actually did not notice – the fact that his best friend Jim Reilly was in love with his wife. Had he fully observed how completely the friar was in love with his wife, the friendship, which meant so much to both men, would have been brought to an end.

As he drank more whiskey, Bonaventure Reilly, OP, talked more and more fervently about politics in an effort to distract himself from thinking about M.M. He could see her at the far end of the room, sharing a sofa with that smoothy Jesuit! One of the things which drove Bon Reilly wild with lust was the surprising contrast between M.M.'s elfin head, and her substantial tennis-player's legs. The facial features were so small, so delicate, that he could imagine kissing the eye-lashes and the tiny boy's-lips so gently that she would hardly know that he had done more than breathe at her. The legs by contrast were sturdy, and beneath his capacious cream habit the large Irishman felt, with a terrible, throbbing erection, what it would be like if those legs of hers were to be wrapped around his legs. This uncontrollable lust was so strong that Father Bonaventure thought that he might pass out. He was frightened that he might suffer from some sort of seizure, a stroke or a heart attack; and, as his innumerable confessions made plain, he could do nothing, nothing whatsoever, to undo such feelings! Masturbation only made things worse. He was absolutely the victim of particularised lust.

Bon Reilly had become addicted to the torture of being erotically obsessed with M.M. Nolan. Its pain fascinated him. He had never had such a specifically directed erotic temptation before in his life, but it had now grown on him, during the last three or four years, so that it had become an obsession. Up to this point – when he acknowledged to himself his absolute servitude to lusting after his best friend's wife – lust had merely been a periodic 'problem', solved by shaky attempts to rise above it, or – when he failed – a frequent resort to the confessional. Before the M.M. obsession, 'it' was just a miscellaneous series of images, a dirty-postcard collection in the mind. He had never actually seen any of the things about which he fantasised – for example the pubic hair of female redheads. His confessor's advice – that self-abuse was the Almighty's way of keeping us humble – 'worked' for Bon until he had unburdened himself of the M.M. obsession. So many things besides lust were at work here – his feelings of friendship for Fergus, his buried feelings of student rivalry for the lad! He wondered, Reilly, whether it had not been a mistake, even in the sacred confines of the confessional, to mention his M.M. obsession; for confessing it seemed to increase the desire he felt. He knew that he should have applied to be sent away from Birmingham. His provincial could easily have arranged for him to go back to London, or go to Blackfriars in Cambridge or in Oxford. Or he could have gone to a parish for a while, to work it all out of his system by getting involved in the real griefs, bereavements and worries of parishioners. Instead, when the prospect of a move was mooted, he had pretended that it was vital that he should remain in the philosophy department of Birmingham University; that no one but he could give the students a clear grounding in mediaeval philosophy and that if he went the whole department would fall a prey to logical positivism. So, he continued to visit the house in Wiseman Road, and to torture himself, and to feast his eyes and heart on M.M., who barely sensed more than a whiff of his feelings.

To M.M., to Fergus, to everyone who saw them together, to everyone except Bon Reilly himself, it was becoming obvious that Persy nursed feelings for him which were comparable to his feelings for M.M. With the telepathy cruelly granted by the Goddess of Love to all who fall under her spell, Persy was granted (as no one else except his confessor and Jehovah knew) exactly what Father Bonaventure felt for Margaret Mary. Persy instinctively knew all his lusts; this knowledge released in her a terrible capacity to hope; a capacity to believe – in spite of the fact that he had taken life vows of chastity and obedience to his Order, that he might one day marry her. If he had been without sexual feeling, her own hopes would never have been aroused; the fact that he was so obviously enlivened and charged up by the presence of a woman, enabled another woman to fall for him completely. The telepathic knowledge of love told Persy that he was prevented from loving her by devotion not to St Dominic but to M.M. Nolan. She could not tolerate this knowledge, nor would she ever have risked humiliation by mentioning it; so she thrust it down, deep into her heart where it bred a wild fury. She was now, particularly in her cups, incapable of saying anything to Bon Reilly which was not hypercharged with murderous anger. Her love for the friar included a love of his argumentative mind, so that these furious verbal exchanges provided her with their own curious satisfaction; but her love was intensely physical, and the pong given off by this large intellectual athlete, a smell which was not in the least charming to the Nolans' less fastidious guests, excited in the young woman thoughts of the great bear-like body which his vast sweaty habit concealed. Even the yellowing cheesy socks which the friar wore with black sandals dissolved Miss Nolan into ecstasies. Her lust was increased by the certainty that he was totally inexperienced in the ways of physical love. Now that she approached the age of thirty, her desire to be overwhelmed by Bon Reilly's body mingled with a gut-wrenching, soul-breaking, heart-dissolving passion to bear a child again in her womb.

'But come on, Persy, we all know that Fatima was just being *used* by the Fascists. I'm not saying the kids did not see Our Lady. I'm saying at the time, in the context of history – '

'You'd explain away the Assumption, you'd explain away everything,' now she was totally scarlet, 'you'd explain away the resurrection of our Blessed Lord himself.'

'I wouldn't explain them away – what's *away* doing in that sentence I'd like to know! – but everything has a social context. The whole of the Catholic faith is grounded in the idea that Nature is redeemed by Grace; and that means the Incarnation; and that means that theology starts when you've had the courage to master the actual *sitz im leben* in which the Gospel first grows.'

'Do you have to teach me all the time, condescend to me – do you?'

These were the words which hotly flew between them, but Eros knew how empty, on this occasion, they were; and that Persy wanted more than all things to nuzzle in the friar's huge chest, and to banish from it all love for Margaret Mary. Wisdom taught her that if she could only make him perform the sexual act with her, he would forget his silly 'crush' on Margaret Mary, and go on making love to her until they had a whole squalling family of Reillies!

Fergus, for whom any German word smacked of the heresies of Luther, verbally wished his friend would not talk of *sitz im leben*, but speechlessly gazed down to the Arts End – an Adoration Scene such as painters might have depicted. Presumably, since Miss Dare had forgone the pleasures of Benediction at the Urra-tree in favour of tea with M.M., thought Fergus bitterly, she loves my wife more than she loves the Blessed Sacrament Itself. That Julian Ramsay was staring like a besotted spaniel at M.M. was no surprise; Fergus was not threatened by the devotion, merely threatened by the heavy knowledge that the more he adored M.M. the more Mr Ramsay would wish to come and stay with them, rather than doing what they all wanted him to do – break off this affair with Persy and *get lost*.

As for Father Linus Quarles, SJ! Well, he too loved M.M., and loved within her the blood of the Mount-Smiths.

'. . . and I remember your darling old Uncle Bill,' he was saying, 'when he was up at the House at exactly the same time that I was at Campion Hall doing Mods. He had tremendous difficulty getting up in the mornings, so of course he overslept for Marce. Now Ronnie was such a gentle priest . . .'

They all knew (except Miss Dare) the limerick which Ronnie Knox composed to nudge the conscience of Bill Mount-Smith in the matter of Eucharistic attendance. Its recitation played its part in the strange epiphany or unconversion which took place in Miss Dare's soul as the afternoon turned into evening.

Besides, our narrative makes no claim to omniscience, certainly not to the divine omniscience with which the Pugh novels made such play. (When asked in the *Paris Review* interview in 1968 why he had been unable to write novels in his maturity, Pugh had replied that only a young man could be sufficiently arrogant to write at that pitch – 'And by arrogant I *mean*, to arrogate to myself' – moyself – 'the All-seeing Eye of the Offspring of Kronos'.)

Therefore, the thoughts of those present in the kitchen of 43, Wiseman Road are unseen to us. Pugh in his youth would self-confidently have laid them bare, seeing the loves and hopes of all present ascending like invisible balloons to hover above the heads of the individuals there. A desire for historical accuracy, however, makes us wish to insert one small footnote into the narrative, and to assure readers that, on one point at least, the 'telepathy' of Fergus Nolan played him false. He was completely wrong to imagine that Miss Dare was sitting engrossed in Margaret Mary's spell.

Something quite different had occurred in the breast of this highly religious English spinster of sixty-eight years old. For some weeks past, she had been asking herself why she had joined the Roman Catholic Church. The reasons for doing so at the time – three years previously – had all been perfectly coherent. She could still recite the *arguments* but emotionally speaking they had gone dead in her. (The conversion had happened as a result of reading a volume by the same Monsignor R. A. Knox whose limericks and detective-stories so obsessed Father Quarles – *The Creed in Slow Motion*). Like Bon Reilly, Miss Dare had no sexual experience at all, but she imagined that what had happened to her was a little like falling unsuitably in love – perhaps during a seaside holiday – and then, in retrospect, not being able to recapture in one's imagination what had made one do it. Just as the memory that one had really woken up in that stranger's bed must puzzle the mind of the impulsive lover, so Miss Dare told herself that she had, truly, gone through the form of being received into the Catholic Church, but what it felt like to *want* to do it – that sense now eluded her!

This chance meeting with Julian Ramsay, the nephew of an Anglican priest to whom she was once devoted, excited memory and desire to a painful degree in Miss Dare's breast. As he spoke boringly of the Lampitts, Miss Dare remembered the Norfolk village near to which she had once lived, and where old Mrs Lampitt had lived in the 'big house' – Timplingham Place – and where Mr Roy Ramsay, Julian's uncle, was still apparently the rector. Still there, after all those years! Miss Dare thought of Mr Ramsay, arrayed in the full, manly vestments of the Sarum Rite, looking, as he stood in the airy aisles of that marvellous fifteenth-century priory, like a figure in a mediaeval book of hours, and reciting, in his melodious tones, the words of *The Book of Common Prayer*:

> Simon Peter answered him, Lord, to whom shall we go? Thou hast the words of eternal life . . .

In one of those doodles which many believers make with familiar, scriptural words, Miss Dare applied her own private meaning to a particular Gospel phrase; and she allowed her brain to believe that 'the words of eternal life' were quite specifically the English words chosen by Coverdale and Cranmer and the other compilers and revisers of the English Prayer Book, as recited in the voice of the Reverend Roy Ramsay. These were, in her inner mind, the words of eternal life, the words of salvation.

> Lighten our darkness, we beseech Thee, O Lord . . . O God, who knowest that we have no power of ourselves to help ourselves . . . teach us who survive, in this and other like daily spectacles of mortality to see how frail and uncertain our own condition is . . . who has safely brought us to the beginning of this day . . . we beseech Thee with thy favour to behold our

most gracious sovereign lady Queen Elizabeth . . . Lord have
mercy upon us and incline our hearts to keep this law . . .

The words, like some highly specialised form of *glossolalia*, made no
particular sense but played a full diapason inside her head and filled
her with spiritual homesickness and yearning. The tea party at Wiseman Road was Miss Dare's last. She missed, but did not miss, Benediction. She never went back to the Urra-tree. Like an addict returning
to a favoured narcotic, or (depending on your own religious
predilections) like a prodigal returning to the bosom of the Father,
she immediately and inwardly resumed the practice of Anglicanism.
She was too late for an Evensong that day, but the next morning found
her, weeping with joy, at the Early Service in St Philip's Cathedral.

And we sat, the two of us, on a garden bench near the back door, lit
only by the few electric lights, behind and above us, still bright in
the house. Beyond a thick beech hedge the carriage lamps and globular
paper lanterns of neighbours winked and glowed. Margaret Mary and
I were alone together. At last. The darkness and the fact that we were
chainsmoking Marlboro somehow deepened the bond. Our tendrils of
tobacco-smoke entwined with one another and lingered on the warm
air blending with the sweetness of tobacco plants, night-scented stock
and summer jasmine.
   Father Quarles, SJ, had at last gone. His lingering, his preparedness
to accept supper from the Nolans and to continue to sit, even when
Fergus, rather pettishly, had gone to do some work in his study –
fuelled my own competitive desire to outstay him. The others had
now been gone for hours. Miss Dare was a faded memory. The roister-
ing friar was one of those who liked to round off a day's drinking by
visiting the pub and Persy had surprised me by saying she'd like to
join him. (How blind I was – I thought of them simply as two
individuals who had begun to bore me with a theological obsession.
It did not occur to me that their wish to spend more time together
could be explained by mutual attraction.)
   Now I had what I wanted, more, at that hour, than anything. I was
sitting in the dark, smoking cigarettes with M.M. and feeling very
close to her; not touching her, but almost more aware of her physical
presence than if she were actually wrapped around my neck: aware of

her scent and of the faint down on her bare arms and of the movement of her chest as she breathed.

We talked in a disconnected ramble, punctuated, always, by her laugh. She was always laughing. At the time I thought it must have been my wit which kept her so amused; and her excessive politeness encouraged me in my vanity.

'*You used to keep us all in fits with stories about Sargent Lampitt.*'

This was M.M. language for, '*What a bore you were!*'

Perhaps I was, for some of that time in the dark, talking of Sargie. For a few years, until it became impossible, I had done my best for Sargie in London, not being his 'minder' exactly, but working as his amanuensis and keeping up, in a desultory way, with Sargie's help, with my Lampitt book. There were 'funny stories' galore about Sargie. Had I really, at thirty-five, already turned into the bore who makes anecdote a substitute for conversation?

No doubt I did prose on about my own life, as we sat there in the dark; my perennial doubts about wishing to act for the rest of my life in a second-rate radio drama series; the possibility of other work; the expense of living in London.

'You could always live here.'

'I couldn't possibly.'

'Of course you could. You have to come up to Birmingham most weeks in any case to record "The Mulberrys". Why not live here? There are worse places to live, you know, and it's much cheaper than London.'

A rush of feelings, not all of them pleasant, was occasioned by this suggestion. 'Living with' the woman whom I idolised, seeing her each day – what could be better? But she could not have made such a proposal if she had felt even the smallest attraction for me. She always spoke to me, punctiliously, as if the reason for my presence in her house was that I was Persy's boyfriend. The word 'fiancé' was even used although I never recollect proposing marriage to Persy and I can imagine the flea in my ear I should have received if I had tried that one on.

Margaret Mary's invitation that I should stay in her house, at least on those nights of the week when I needed to be in Brum to broadcast, could only be construed therefore as the most crushing blow to my hopes – fantasies – that we might become lovers. The insane and unrealistic optimism of love, however, gives plausibility to the most laughable hopes. Together with my wounded disappointment, I irrationally persuaded myself to half-believe that Margaret Mary was suggesting an arrangement which could make it easier for us to become lovers. Of course, it is impossible that such an idea so much as crossed her mind. I do not believe that there was ever a moment when she cared for me, except as a rather dopey friend of her sister-in-law. The friendliness with which she had treated me from the first should have warned me off; she behaved as a woman might do with a brother or with a trusted male homosexual, happy to hug me, hold my hand, kiss me if she chose to do so, without the smallest *frisson* of desire.

I think, as we sat there in the dark, we did draw up plans for a trial period in which I might stay for two or three nights in a week in exchange for a rent which I knew would never be paid.

'I shall be glad of the company,' she confided.

'Poor Margaret Mary. You can't be lonely.'

There was a very long silence in the dark. She couldn't be crying? What about? As well as blinding me with egotism, love makes me incredibly stupid. The fact that she might be unhappy at first caused a leap of joy in my heart. I really supposed that if she were 'unhappy' with Fergus, she might become 'happy' again by falling in love with me. To put a check on this absurd idea, I expressed what I thought was the more realistic (in fact crassly unimaginative) notion that she couldn't be lonely since she had so many relations, and so many friends met at the Oratory.

A sniff – then a resort to Kleenex, before lighting up a cigarette once more – told me that she was indeed weepy.

'Oh, Margaret Mary.'

She allowed me to put an arm around her, and she rested her head against my chest, and we sat there for what was probably twenty minutes in silence.

'Have you ever wanted children?' she asked me.

A bull's-eye: how had she known? Again, I was so encased in selfishness that I at first thought she was revealing an extraordinary telepathic awareness of my own preoccupations. There was no reason to suppose that she and Fergus had even guessed that Persy and I (though a pair) had ever been lovers in the full sense. Quite regardless of religion, in those days affianced couples were not expected to copulate on anything like the scale which became fashionable later in the century. Some readers might find this hard to believe, but it is true. It would, I am sure, have shocked M.M. and Fergus to have known that Persy and I were, or had been, lovers. The fact of the abortion would have been to them simply incredible.

So, I did not suppose that M.M. was telepathically guessing anything about my recent emotional history when she asked if I had ever wanted children. I told her, at some length, about losing my own parents when I was a child, about the illness of my grandmother, the seeming imminence of her demise, the atavistic yearning in such circumstances to perpetuate one's species. My self-absorption was so total that it did not occur to me, as I spun this narrative to the fine hair and elfin skull which reposed upon my chest, that M.M. had asked the question about children because of something on her own mind. Having aired my own views on the subject I said, for politeness, 'How about you?'

'What do you think?'

'I never know what to think, Margaret Mary. Not about the wishes of other people.'

'Want a baby so much I'm almost dying with it.'

This was said abruptly, not in her normal voice. After a silence I said, 'Oh, my dear. Oh, poor, poor Margaret Mary.'

She let me squeeze her hand – let me lift her long fingers and press them to my mouth.

'It seems so – so cruel. Particularly now Fergus spends all his time on this Commission.'

'What's that – what Commission?'

'It's advising the Pope. It's meant to be a secret, but everyone at lunch seemed to know about it.' Her laugh returned, and I realised for the first time how mirthless it was.

'Isn't that a contradiction in terms – advising the Pope? Isn't he the one who gives advice to the rest of us?' This was the sort of point-scoring which I endeavoured with Persy. It dismayed me that I could hear myself saying such things to the Beloved, but RCism, I am afraid, brought this out of me.

'I wish you were a Catholic,' she said simply. 'It's so hard to understand us if you're not. Fergus is off to Italy tomorrow. You won't tell anyone, will you, Julian? Promise?'

'Who should I tell?'

'You see, neither of us can get this silly idea out of our heads.'

'What idea is that?'

'That – well, that the reason we haven't had a baby – that it's a sort of punishment for Fergus's work.'

'You can't really believe that?'

But I was always saying this aloud or inside my head, for all the time that I was such close friends with the Nolans – 'you can't really' – and blow me, they did.

'I know it sounds ridiculous. But so many of the things which Fergus has been doing in his work, in all innocence, have led to the evolution of this wretched pill.'

'Is it wretched?'

She stroked my hand.

'Don't let's have a repetition of the conversation at lunch,' and, again, the metallic laugh. 'I shouldn't be telling you any of this. Fergus is such a good person.'

'Of course.'

This conversation was changing my perception of them both. One's view of the husbands or lovers of women with whom one is in love is never likely to be generous. Having supposed that Fergus (like most scientists) was a bit of a bore I now began to suspect him of being a crackpot as well.

'Fergus feels – and I agree – that if he can persuade the Holy Father to take a firm line on birth control, we might have a bit more luck.'

'You mean, if Fergus tells the Pope to condemn the Pill, God will make you pregnant.'

'It sounds silly if you say it like that. It's so hard if you aren't a Catholic.'

'In some ways.'

I squeezed, and slowly massaged, her shoulder. At that moment I was considering the implications of her belief. To gratify her personal need to have a child, God's representative on earth might counten-ance a population-explosion which would cause plague, murrain, famine and war. I wanted to say to that beloved skull on my chest, 'Empty yourself of this trash; unload your beliefs; just stop thinking nonsense; stop thinking at all; and turn to me – love me, for I love you with a slavish devotion which no one could guess; and if you did, I could give you a baby! I should love to do so. Oh, my darling M.M.'

But in silence I held her and allowed her to say, 'You promise, don't you, Julian, not to tell anyone.'

'Of course I shan't tell.'

'He has a audience; a personal audience.'

Not being *au fait* with papalist terminology I was slow to grasp the significance of this.

'You mean he's going to Rome to see . . .'

'He's going to Castelgandolfo actually.'

'Oh.'

'You won't say, will you? Promise?'

'Let's have another cigarette. Of course I won't say.'

'I've run out. I'll get some more.'

Was this an excuse to arise from my embrace? When she came back with a fresh packet and two more glasses of red wine, she had decided to abandon intimacies.

'Isn't it odd that you nearly met my brothers at Les Mouettes all those years ago?'

'I might even have met you if you'd come with them.'

Silvery laugh in the darkness.

'The awful thing is, they decided at the last minute, they just couldn't face going. Mummy thought of the first lie that came into her head and sent a telegram to announce her own death. She never really knew Mme de Normandin, you see; but Papa – poor Papa. He had known the Normandins for ever; and it meant they could never really see one another again. They had been such good friends. Once Mme de Normandin had been told that Papa was a widower.' More joyless laughter.

'Isn't lying a sin?'

There was too much aggression in my voice as I asked the question.

'Oh, Julian, the whole point of being a Catholic is that we are all sinners and we go on committing sins right up to the hour of our death.'

With a twinge of homesickness for Norfolk I realised that this was probably the reason why my uncle and aunt, who managed to get through life without sinning very much, so heartily disliked the largest of the Christian denominations.

'Besides,' she said, speaking of the casually false declaration by the Mount-Smiths that their mother was dead – a declaration made simply in order to get out of a summer holiday, 'it was only a white lie.'

FIVE
(Spring 1968)

What do you mean by a mystery?
By a mystery I mean a truth which is above reason, but revealed by
God.

Like any addict of detective stories, I had often read of the death rattle. Never having attended a death-bed, I had no idea what it sounded like. I was sitting with my grandmother in the Norwich hospital, and we were alone together. Since her mild stroke, a week or so before, we had taken it in turns to keep vigil – we four, Aunt Deirdre, Uncle Roy, Felicity and I. For years now, Granny had been, if not exactly comatose, then lost in a semi-somnolent condition, with her eyes half-closed. Now, at eighty-seven, there could not be much doubt that death was near. She was slipping inexorably away, and no one wished to yank her back into a life for which she had always displayed ambivalent feelings.

How she had survived in this world at all since the death of her kind friend Mrs Webb was, if not miraculous, certainly mysterious. It had been Mrs Webb who, during the War, had queued in shops with my grandmother's ration-books ('You couldn't expect Thora to queue, not with *her* feet') just as, during the peacetime years, it had been Mrs Webb who had done most of Granny's shopping and cooking. Mrs Webb, likewise, had been the one who searched for Granny's spectacles and changed her library books. (A fondness for Ethel M. Dell and Elinor Glyn had given place gradually to Mazo de la Roche,

Barbara Cartland and Catherine Cookson). When Mrs Webb died, Granny came to live with her sole surviving child, my Uncle Roy. It then became Aunt Deirdre's task to 'look after' Granny. There was not much looking after to do – once she had entered her ninth decade, Granny did almost nothing except loll in a chair with a copy of the *Daily Mail* resting on her lap. (My aunt, who often denounced this newspaper as 'frightful twaddle' and 'not quite the thing', was often, I noticed, to be found in the kitchen, before throwing it away at the end of each day, with her nose buried deep in the horoscopes and the gossip column.)

And now – at last – the end! The death rattle – was that it? A dreadful gurgling from the back of the throat and a stertorous roar. I ran from the room – 'Help! Can someone help?' (Private treatment was completely beyond Granny's means, but in view of her frail condition they had placed her in a small room on her own near the ward sister's desk.) A staff nurse came at once when I raised the alarm.

I was approaching my mid-thirties and, like many Westerners of my generation, I had never seen a corpse, and never before watched a fellow-human being die. And, now that this woman whom I loved so much, almost the last link with my childhood and my parents, was about to die, I felt a spiritual dread of her departure but also an intense physical fear of being in the same room as a dead body. I wished, fervently, that my cousin Felicity was with me. I was afraid of my own panic. How could I fear something inanimate, something as lifeless as a pig hanging upside down in a butcher's shop? Yet I retain my horror of dead bodies; they are to me the ultimately terrifying thing. (How anyone dares to work with them, either as a nurse or as an undertaker, is beyond anything I could possibly understand.)

The staff nurse who came into the room had very pronounced breasts and her plump legs, swathed in black tights beneath the blue uniform, worked a powerful effect on me. (The increased randiness of human beings in wretched circumstances, in cities under siege, in prison or in concentration camps, is widely attested. I've noticed, in a minor way, in my own life that the body, as if to console one for some extreme of misery, can simply *take over* from one's unhappy mood, and perform its own strange sexual tricks, offering its limited range of little ecstasies, while the brain remains detached. This is particularly the case when one is suffering from unrequited love. The fact that things were going badly with Persy, and that I was miserably aware that I had no chance with Margaret Mary – in fact, would no more think of having sex with M.M. than a devout Catholic would think of 'dating' a Mother Superior – only left my body freer to pursue its own randy life. Looking back, I should say that this was the most promiscuous period of my life; not that this fact has much to do with the present story.)

So – the nurse; the black tights, the eye-contact and the smile and the everlasting question, even in the presence of my dying grand-mother – would this young woman be interested?

'Now, Mrs Ramsay!' The nurse spoke to Granny as if she were in full consciousness and vigour. 'What do you want us to do, eh? Straighten your pillows for you, is it?'

This brisk, plump young woman, straightening pillows (and, did I imagine it, or could I detect full nipples, the size of broad beans, shaping the outline of her uniform?), was so inconsistently alive, was so gymnastically *there*, while Granny was not really 'there' at all. The nurse, with one podgy white hand, took Granny's pulse and with another stroked her forehead. (Fat little hands do not look beautiful but they are much sexier to the eye, as well as to the touch, than beautiful elegant fingers like those of M.M.) In a brisker tone, the nurse spoke – her briskness explained by the fact that she was address-ing me rather than my grandmother.

'Probably just choked on a bit of her saliva. That can happen, though it shouldn't when patients are propped up nicely.'

'Then she's not . . . she's not . . .'

Either the nurse did not understand my unfinished question, or she had made it her professional business in the case of each patient to regard death as unthinkable until it actually happened. Perhaps one can only be a proficient nurse if, imaginatively speaking, one blots out one's empirical knowledge of a patient's mortality and concen-trates only on symptoms – a fever, the need for a bedpan, an uncomfortable pillow – never the unalterable fact that in the end no amount of plumping pillows, nor pulse-taking, nor brow-stroking, nor injecting, nor dosing will stop the patient turning into one of those *things*, one of those waxy, moist, white inanimate things which are not merely in themselves grotesque but which mock life, parading as they do the fact that every being comes at length to this – all artistic and commercial enterprise, all wit, all laughter, all grief, all joy, all desire, turns to this, this putrescence, this cruel stillness.

'The drip's probably made it that bit difficult for her to swallow,' said the nurse brightly.

A plastic tube came from one of Granny's nostrils; another plastic tube was attached to an arm. From beneath the sheets emanated another arrangement of tubing, rank in smell.

'We'll deal with all that in a minute,' said kindly, matter-of-fact, oozing-with-sex nurse.

While she was gone – and her black-stockinged presence had brought a whiff of soap into the room to confront the other odours, and a whiff of youth, vitally and painfully at variance with the human decrepitude on the bed – my grandmother opened her eyes. The assemblage of tired, decayed limbs which, a moment earlier, had seemed but a snore away from metamorphosis into a corpse, became once again the woman I had loved so much, all my life. The eyes retained the air of amusement which had always been one of her most marked characteristics; however querulous she was, she always *liked a joke*, and much of what passed before her eyes seemed to have amused her. Did she mock me now? No, for mingled with that amusement in her eyes there was a deep tenderness. She could see my panic and my agony. The dying have more cause to pity us than we to pity them. They have no grief ahead of them.

My grief for my parents, when they were killed in the air raid during the War, had been so intense and so imperfectly worked *through* (as the therapists would now say), so self-absorbed and so solipsistic, and so long-lasting that I seldom allowed myself to speculate on the effect which those deaths must have had on her. The air raid which deprived me of Mummy and Daddy took from Granny her first-born son, David. To me, her David would always be simply Daddy. I was not such an egotist, in youth, as to be unaware that she grieved for David; she often spoke of how she valued the letters of condolence which had come to her at the time of the funeral, and she treasured the allusions made to Daddy in an annual Christmas card from Mr Pilbright. But, such knowledge on my part was surface-deep. I did not allow myself imaginatively to recognise that my parents' death, so much the most important event in my own life, had been of immense significance to others. I could remember my Uncle Roy's face, and his voice, choked with tears, as he read the burial service for my parents, but only now, as Granny lay dying, did it occur to me to speculate on the effect of those deaths on Uncle Roy. Perhaps many of Granny's 'lazy old ways' – which Aunt Deirdre found so exasperating – were her way of dealing with grief? Her strange, take-it-or-leave-it approach to life (she distrusted medicine, for example, and likewise to my knowledge she never went near a dentist) implied an impatience with patching up the body before the longed-for end. Aunt Deirdre used to complain that her mother-in-law was so lazy she could not be bothered to attend a surgery. But what was the point – Granny's attitude implied – of stopping a tooth or correcting some minor bodily ailment, when she would soon be *off*? This had always been her attitude, in the almost three decades since my parents had been killed. It must, this 'lazy old view', have sprung from a sense that, since her son was dead, there was 'nothing left remarkable beneath the visiting moon'.

So completely did she dictate the terms of her own life that no one, in my recollection, ever questioned that Granny was too delicate, too muddled, too put upon, to live as the rest of us. Mrs Webb had often said it: 'You couldn't expect Thora to look after the boy, not with this Blitz.' The natural inference to be drawn was that the Luftwaffe had chosen to rain down torrents of explosives on London, to expend millions of Reichsmarks, to kill tens of thousands of people, with the sole mischievous purpose of inconveniencing Granny. (I can remember, even before my parents died, sitting in an air raid shelter in Fulham with Mummy, Granny and Mrs Webb. As enemy bombardment reached its loudest in the middle of the night, and buildings were collapsing in flames for miles around us, Mrs Webb opined, 'All this thumping will bring on one of Thora's heads.')

In these trying circumstances, you could hardly have expected Granny to undertake my upbringing when I had been orphaned.

No one seemed to question the justice or the logic of this. Perhaps, in peacetime, I could have returned to London and been brought up by Mrs Webb. But by then I was installed as a child of Timplingham Rectory, a witness to my uncle's friendship with Sargie Lampitt, an heir to my uncle's inexhaustible preoccupation with the Lampitts and all their tribe. When the German surrender was signed it might have been supposed that I should have spent at least a part of my school holidays with Granny, but this never happened. As things transpired, the Luftwaffe had no sooner stopped making my grandmother's life a misery than along came Sir Stafford Cripps, Mr Attlee, Vernon Lampitt ('bless him', my uncle would wish to add, when mentioning his name) causing all those highly inconvenient shortages.

Perhaps, buried within me, there is some resentment at this state of things, an anger with the old lady which a well-trained therapist would winkle out. I am not aware of being angry with Granny, though; I have always accepted, as a given fact, that I should live with Uncle Roy and Aunt Deirdre. I never expected Granny to take me into her tiny house in Fulham, nor in retrospect do I think she would have been well-equipped to look after me. Later, Granny came to live with us all at Timplingham even though – again, one of those obvious facts which never occurred to me at the time – this involved considerable sacrifice on the part of Aunt Deirdre, who never liked her mother-in-law.

And now it was all coming to an end; the woman who gave birth to my father was dying, recumbent in a hospital ward, with tubes sticking out of every orifice, attended by a nurse she did not know. And although the black-stockinged beauty had 'plumped' Granny's pillow and asked the semi-comatose body if it was feeling more 'comfy' I knew now that Granny was dying – I realised it completely for the first time. And I thought of all our past together – my early childhood holidays, for example, when she can have been barely past the mid-fifties (much younger than I am now as I write these words!) but when she seemed to my eyes so infinitely old. And as I sat in the ward and took her wrinkled old hand – the one which did not have a drip attached to it – I wanted to say this last thing to her; I wanted to say that *for the first time, I understood*; that she and I, alone together in this world (with the possible and mysterious exception of Uncle Roy), had been carrying this burden together of grieving for my parents; and we had never talked about it; and I had never realised that she was carrying it too; and now she was about to lay this burden down. Words like this I wanted to say, though I knew that it would be hard to say them without making them sound like a speech or without crying.

Another gurgle – this time, it would seem, not the death rattle –

and she opened her eyes. The smile she gave to me was radiant. I felt she had never looked so pleased to see me, nor loved me so much.

'David,' she murmured.

It was quite distinct; there was no mistaking it; she used, not my name, but Daddy's. She continued to focus on me with the rapt expression of pure love. Of course, she had never looked on me like this in her entire life; nor had I ever seen such an expression on her face when she looked at Uncle Roy. Why could I not allow that smile, and the deluded joy which it betokened, to remain on my grandmother's face? I certainly felt a stab of disappointment. In one selfish moment I wanted her to love me, and not her dead son!

'Granny!' I said, and squeezed her hand.

And I watched all the joy drain from her face like colour, like life itself. She had opened her eyes and thought she was in heaven. My childish need to be loved had reminded her that she was not.

She did not open her eyes again that day. It was some time that morning that I summoned Black-Stockings to tell her that in my opinion we had reached the end. The more the nurse told me that there was nothing to worry about, the more insistent I became that Granny was on the point of death. A ward sister was again called. She said there was no noticeable deterioration in Mrs Ramsay's condition, but that if I felt strongly enough I should summon the other members of the family.

Timplingham is not far from Norwich. Within half an hour of my telephone call, the cast for a deathbed scene had been assembled in the tiny hospital room – the four of us, sitting or standing around the bed – Felicity, her parents, me. I was so preoccupied by the imminent death, so certain that it would happen within an hour or so, that I did not pay much attention to the others or their demeanours. It was only to be expected that Granny's surviving son should display signs of agitation. When half an hour had passed, and my grandmother had done nothing except snore, however, even I was conscious of a particular restlessness in my uncle which could not be explained by the fact that he was sitting beside his mother's deathbed. He kept consulting the pocket-watch which was suspended from the lapel of his violent green tweed jacket. I could not believe he was so heartless as to look at his watch out of impatience for his mother's death and I could therefore only conclude that the watch itself (a present from old Mrs Lampitt; she had meant it for her godson and nephew Orlando Lampitt, who had then so amazed everyone by going on the stage) gave him some pleasure, for I could not but notice how his soft cheeks were suffused with colour and his eyes were sparkling with excitement.

'I'm *afraid*,' he said at last, lingering out the vowels of this word, 'that I am going to have to go.'

His wife and daughter looked completely unsurprised by this announcement. To whom was he making his excuses, the tone of which would have been more suitable for leaving a sherry party than slipping away from this hushed and important scene? Parish business could surely wait? I was genuinely puzzled – a sure sign that Granny's death was muddling my wits – as to what in the world could seem more important to Uncle Roy than his own mother's last hours.

Then he said – 'It's what *old* Mrs Lampitt, bless her, would have called a "council of war", and Pat calls a "pow-wow"!'

Ah. Lampitts called. All was explained. Aunt Deirdre's face, brick red with gardening in too much sun, gave nothing away. Nail-brush fingers from which all soil had not (in her haste to get to the hospital) been removed were folded on a tartan lap. It was certainly no time of the year to be sitting indoors – with onions, leeks and beans to plant out in the kitchen garden; bedding plants to be put out in the herbaceous border from the seed-trays in the greenhouse; and hours of daily weeding after a very wet spring. Over the years she had become crossly accustomed to her husband placing the Lampitts first in everything, and she had lately come to reserve her explosions of impatience for only the more extreme manifestations of my uncle's Lampitt-mania. (For example, she would not allow him, when speaking to me, to refer to 'Uncle Sargie' – 'He's not Julian's uncle,' she would erupt.)

'Go, Pa,' Felicity's large moon face had the authority of an abbess. It was she who was in control of this situation while I panicked. 'You need only be gone for a few hours. Nothing is going to happen today.'

'We can all go,' said Aunt Deirdre. 'Only, Fliss and I will need the car to get back to Timplingham. I want to be back by two because I'm trying out a new boy for the rough.'

This was less adventurous than it sounded, and merely referred to the recruitment of a village lad called Ron, who had dug over the trenches for the onions and scythed the long grass around the rhodo-

110

dendrons, and who might if he was lucky be taken on regularly to
assist in the large Rectory garden. My aunt was anxious to borrow,
and have a go with, his strimmer.

'This wretched wind,' said my aunt, 'has absolutely wrecked the
rhodos this year.'

I began to remonstrate. It seemed outrageous that we should all be
abandoning Granny at this moment, and for such a reason. Eventually,
however, I yielded to Felicity's argument. Once one reflected upon it
rationally, there was no reason to suppose that Granny had reached
that moment so repeatedly anticipated in the Hail Mary, the 'hour of
her death'. Felicity said it would do me good to get away from the
hospital for a while. (Granny did not die for months after this; Fliss,
as so often, was right. By that stage I had begun to enter such a very
strange state of mind that I can remember very little of Granny's
death; and her funeral has been blotted from memory.)

So it was that I found myself at the wheel of my Anglia, driving
down the familiar road that led to Mallington. Once beyond the
ring-road, with the sprawl of Norwich behind us, landscape and sky
reasserted themselves. Huge fields rolled beyond hedgerows heavy
with may and cow parsley. Uncle Roy, his pipe ablaze, leaned forward
in his seat and explained the nature of the Lampitt family crisis.

Sargie Lampitt had been asked to leave yet another nursing home
– this time an establishment in St John's Wood – and there seemed
genuine difficulty in getting him into another.

'Old Mrs Lampitt, bless her! She told me they had had just the
same trouble with Sargie and prep-schools! He went through six
before he won his scholarship to Winchester, where, as you know, he
did so brilliantly . . .'

The prep-school trouble had happened at the turn of the century.
Though not quite as old as Granny, Sargie Lampitt was obviously
entering the final furlong; his (long-estranged) wife Cecily had done
her best to persuade nursing homes to take him in; but now she
herself being past the age of eighty and far from well had appealed to
Sargie's family to come to her aid. Hence a family 'council of war' at
Mallington Hall. To judge from what Uncle Roy told me, Cecily had
suggested the idea that Sargie might be taken in by his cousins Lord
and Lady Lampitt at Mallington Hall itself. An absence of space
was not a problem. Mallington probably had more than twenty-five

bedrooms. Whether Vernon Lampitt (Ernie as he preferred to be known in the Party) would have much time to look after his cousin was questionable, since in spite of advancing years he appeared to play more and more part in public life, addressing rallies, cheering-on 'demos' and even, quite recently (as I'd read in the paper) getting arrested after an altercation with a policeman outside the American Embassy in Grosvenor Square. Even had Vernon not been so much occupied, Mallington would have been no place for a man in Sargie's condition, who was obviously drinking heavily and in need of psychi-atric care as well as more general nursing.

It was not clear why the Lampitts needed Uncle Roy to discuss Sargie's future. True, he had, for twenty years or so, been Sargie's best and closest friend, but the two never spoke to one another now. (The row was all of Sargie's making as far as I could see.) Perhaps they assumed that any clergyman, even one as eccentric and as apparently indifferent to pastoral concerns as Uncle Roy, could automatically dispense information about such matters as district nurses, old people's homes and geriatric hospitals.

The Sargie-crisis appeared to have the effect, as we drove along, of taking my uncle's mind off the illness of his mother; indeed he did not allude to Granny in any way for the rest of the day, preferring to discourse, as the Anglia rolled northwards towards the coast, of his favourite theme. Just as in other religions, the holy names of Prophet or Deity can not be uttered without some qualifying epithet – Blessed Be He – so Uncle Roy peppered his Lampitt talk with the familiar epithets of piety – 'dear old', 'bless her', 'darling', qualifying the names even of the obscurest members of the sainted tribe.

These days, actual meetings with any Lampitts were of rare occur-rence for Uncle Roy. Like the Confraternity of the Blessed Sacrament in the head of Father Delmar, they were now all in Barking. Safe inside our heads, other people are easier to handle. Far from condemning my uncle for his apparently unfilial desertion of his mother's bedside, I quickly came to rejoice in it myself. I had learnt from him very early on to fill up my head with rival attractions to the sideshows physi-cally on offer. As he spoke, and as I drove, I saw the face of Margaret Mary Nolan, and wondered if there was anything more heart-breaking in the world. Let us all keep our saving illusions.

'It was only a matter of time before a crisis such as this would blow

up,' said Uncle Roy. 'Dear old Sargie always was *extraordinarily* difficult.' He harrumphed with mirth. So often, he had driven along
empty Norfolk roads beneath a vast white sky, as we did today, only
with Sargie instead of myself for company, that it was hardly surprising
that the car journey should have stimulated a recitation of some of
the oldest chestnuts in the repertoire. Anecdote, that deadliest
of conversational forms, had become my uncle's almost sole means of
communicating. The familiar old tale of the drive to Cromer – Sargie's
insistence that they stop to check the tyre pressure at innumerable
garages – the exasperation of garage men from Norwich to Fakenham
and beyond – was slowly and lovingly repeated. Then he spoke of
Sargie's much younger sister Sybil Starling. Apparently the nursing
home had been fairly tolerant of Sargie's drinking habits, even when
a paper bag containing hidden empty gin bottles had fallen from the
top of a wardrobe on to a cleaner's head. What necessitated Sargie's
departure had been a row between Lady Starling and the matron of
the home.

'Darling Sibs – always the complete doormat. I know, if you repeat
what she actually said, the words sound harsh, but someone had to
say them, and *as usual* the lot fell on little Sibsie.'

'The comparison between the nursing home and Dachau was unfortunate.'

'The point is, Julian, was it just and . . .'

'I did visit Sargie there – admittedly months ago. A very comfortable room, charming staff and rather a nice view of the garden . . .'

'And it obviously was a remark that was justified.'

'Anyway, Sibs has got Sargie into this mess but shows no signs of
getting him out.'

My instinct to contradict everything Uncle Roy said was strength-
ened on this occasion by a recollection of squabbles I'd had with
Sybil Starling myself. (She had, after all, been my mother-in-law.)
The same mournfulness came into my uncle's eyes that used to be
visible when, during my teens, I made galumphing denunciations of
religion.

He hastily settled into a numbingly tedious recollection of Lady
Starling's War work, when, as the young Sibs Lampitt, she and her
mother had joined the Women's Royal Voluntary Service.

While the wondrous tale unfolded, I sank into my own Lampittreflections. Some years before all this Sargie and Vernon Lampitt had surprised me into agreeing to write at least one and possibly two books about the Lampitts. One was to be a general history of the family – from its origins in a Norfolk brewery in the eighteenth century, its rise through judicious marriages and the accumulation of wealth to a position in the county; and its genesis of a number of scientists, artists, and leftish politicians who were not without interest. (Having no training as an historian, this book was entirely beyond my scope, but it was years before I recognised this and handed over the project with complete relief to my friend Professor Wimbish.)

The other book, which you, my dear William Bloom, agreed to publish, and urged me to write, was the True History of Jimbo, an attempt to set the record straight after the publication of Hunter's scurrilous Volume One. It was Sargie, Jimbo's sole heir, who had sold his brother's papers to the Ann-Louise Everett Library, thereby placing them in the hands of the man he most wished to spite, Raphael Hunter. The prevailing view at the time of the sale, certainly one to which I still adhered, was that it would have been much better for all the Lampitt Papers to be kept together in one place – in the muniment room at Mallington Hall. This room, to which Professor Wimbish had introduced me, contained a vast archive of the family – the voluminous political diaries of Vernon's father and grandfather for example; the hundreds of caches of eighteenth- and nineteenth-century letters; the records of Joe Lampitt's friendship with Doctor Johnson's friends the Thrales, and the purchase by Joe of the Thrale brewery in Streatham when Henry Thrale died; all this as well as hundreds of deed-books, rent-books and wills which to a trained historian provided a richly abundant story of a family and the house into which they had married. (There is also a huge amount of Isleworth material at Mallington, but that is a different story.) In such a collection, the papers of James Petworth Lampitt (the best known, but by no means the only man of letters in the family) would have been at home, far more obviously at home than in the air-conditioned library where I had already spent a week or two working, in New York. Sargie had always maintained that he had deliberately hoodwinked the Americans, and that Virgil D. Everett, happy for some obscure reasons to throw away his money on rubbish, had bought what amounted to no more than a collection of swanky autographs.

114

'Anyone who was really interested in old Jimbo,' Sargie had said, 'would want to read letters *by* him, not letters *to* him, even if they were written by Henry James.'

This was only partially true, of course. Already, by reading James's letters to Lampitt, I had discovered the interesting fact that for a fortnight in 1899 (when he had just left school) Jimbo had been James's amanuensis at Lamb's House, Rye, and brought forth on the Remington, to the slow dictation of the Master, those crucially important chapters of *The Ambassadors* in which Strether enunciates his creed – '*Live all you can, it's a mistake not to!*'

How much this was advice taken to heart by Jimbo himself, this was much harder to decide since Hunter's book, which so totally failed to penetrate the mystery of Jimbo's character. Whether such a penetration can ever be achieved in the case of anyone, or if it can be achieved, whether it can ever be truthful – these are highly questionable things. Maybe such illusions are best left to the illusionist, of whom James was perhaps the greatest. Jimbo's own attitude to biography was far removed, on the one hand, from the novelistic preoccupations of the psychologist or the more ploddingly forensic approach of Hunter. Jimbo looked for truth in the sketch or the elegantly crafted caricature rather than in the full-length portrait in oils.

Perhaps it would have been better to tell his own story in his own way, and to represent him, in a well-turned, stylish, two hundred pages, as an Edwardian fop, a nineties stylist, born slightly out of time, and surviving bizarrely, to see the Second World War and Attlee's Britain. To speak of his 'surviving' implies longevity, but Jimbo was not particularly old when he fell from the balcony – he was in his mid-seventies. No evidence had ever been advanced for Albion Pugh's outlandish claim that Raphael Hunter had murdered the old gentleman, even though Cecily Lampitt had been prepared to appear as a defence witness at the libel trial. She had implied then that she was privy to some sort of evidence, but she could not endure the pain of making it public. Later, I gathered that she had lodged all *her* 'Lampitt Papers' at Mallington in the muniment room. The time was surely approaching when these secrets would be disclosed, if not to the world in general, at any rate to me.

Though I had written not one word of my Jimbo book, I had given a great deal of thought to the matter of his relationship with Cecily. The two had become friends at the time of Cecily's marriage to Sargie, and they had continued to be friends after Sargie and Cecily parted company.

There is so much we do not know, and so much we do not *need* to know about one another in life, but which comes to light after we are dead. I cannot remember now when I discovered the 'truth' about Cecily's marriage to Sargie and how it ended. Sargie, at the time, was a very promising young don at Oxford. The story conveyed to me, first by Uncle Roy, and then by other members of the Lampitt family, was that Sargie had fallen into an emotional decline, suffered a nervous collapse, gone off his head, and that after this experience he had been obliged to retire from academic life and live with his mother at Timplingham Place. Cecily and he had parted, she remaining behind in London. All true, as far as I can gather. But only in Cecily's papers, which Vernon allowed me to read when she was dead, did I discover about the sad little case in the Oxford magistrate's court. A complaint had been made against Sargie for an alleged misdemeanour one afternoon at a cinema in the town. The 'victim', or accomplice, in the misdemeanour was a fourteen-year-old kitchen boy from one of the colleges. What exactly had taken place in the darkness of the cinema when the lights went down it is hard to say. It would seem to have been little more than a fumble. Perhaps a man with more guile than Sargie would have been able to hush the matter up, but he had blustered, pulled rank, and hired one of the grandest KCs in London to represent him at the magistrate's hearing. What might have been passed over as an extraordinary (and perhaps drunken) aberration in the life of a brilliant young man was taken up by the newspapers. Sargie was fined two hundred pounds and given a sus- pended prison sentence. He had resigned his fellowship at New Col- lege at once, and since then his marriage had effectively been at an end.

Did Uncle Roy know any of this? I could never have brought myself to discuss it with him; and my suspicion is that he knew nothing. How often, when in his cups, Sargie had fallen into comparably silly adventures, none of us was ever likely to know. Having known him quite well during my own boyhood, I had never picked up the slightest hint of pederasty in his character (and any of us educated at English

boarding-schools are quite good at nosing this sort of thing out!).
Before Cecily, and Sargie, died, one had assumed that Jimbo was
regarded (perhaps falsely) as having homosexual leanings. Hard to
say how helpful such classifications are when dealing with actual
relationships between people. Cecily and Jimbo are a case in point.
For as long as I could remember, Sargie used to complain that his
wife and his brother were 'as thick as thieves'; the alliance certainly
fuelled his incurable persecution mania. Cecily in turn had plenty of
reasons to be violently antipathetic towards Hunter – not least
because, in the first instance, Sargie had been so much on Hunter's
side, offering him full access to the Lampitt Papers. At the libel trial,
however, Hunter's counsel had put up a powerful case for other
motives being at work. Cecily, it was implied, had been frustratedly
in love with Jimbo and unable to control her vitriolic jealousy when
she saw the old man fawning on youth.

Jimbo was – what? – nearly twenty years older than Cecily. My
own hunch now is that their friendship of more than thirty years
went through many phases. Some of the early letters which he wrote
to her and which I was to read in the muniment room at Mallington
were quite simply love letters. Hunter, who had never seen these
letters and did not know of their existence, contented his readers by
reminding them that Cecily had a 'gamine' charm and that when she
followed the fashion in the twenties for cutting her hair in an Eton
crop, her 'boyish athleticism' was 'all the more alluring'.

I would not wish to deny that Jimbo's obsession with Shakespeare's
Sonnets, and his not very good book on the subject, were jumbled
up in his mind with his feelings for Cecily; and that he identified her
with the youth 'too dear for my possessing' rather than with the Dark
Lady. (When my turn came to be obsessed with the Sonnets, I felt a
particular empathy with him – but that lies ahead – out of the scope
of this volume.) Cecily and Jimbo were many things to one another.
She had begun as the Boy to whom Shakespeare wrote his most
impassioned lines.

Truth about human relations is not fixed like Newtonian physics,
but fluid. The mercurial quality of human characters, and of their
interactions, can more easily be captured by works of literature which
do not proclaim themselves to be 'true'. Novels and plays tell us, in
their darting and haphazard manner, more than the scientifically

117

researched biographies with acknowledgements to all the big American libraries. There is no one truth about a pair of human beings who have known one another for more than thirty years. Lives are lived first, chronicled afterwards, and the attempt to write it down distorts and changes the nature of the reality even if the writer is trying to tell the truth, or has a sufficiently developed moral sense to know what a complicated thing this would be if it were attempted. Cecily was, and was not, the bitter woman who allowed herself to be irritated by Jimbo's young friends. She was, and was not, the beautiful Boy of the Sonnets. She was a life-companion. At different times, she and Jimbo had both been buffeted by the overpowering egotism of Jimbo's younger brother Sargie. They were both refugees from Sargie, and that was how they met. As Sargie became a recluse, living at Timplingham with only his mother, and then Uncle Roy for company, Cecily and Jimbo were together in London. Jimbo was a man who really did know Everyone – a much wider circle of Everyones than had ever crossed the path of a minor snob such as Father Quarles, SJ.

Jimbo had known Everyone when Everyone contributed to the Yellow Book and dined at the Café Royal. (In the old broadcasts, which I played again and again while rehearsing my One Man Show, Jimbo pronounced these two words Café Royal not as most Englishmen do, but in Edwardian French – *Rrrwah-yall.*) He continued to Know Everyone when Everyone clustered around the Sitwells or flocked to the drawing-rooms of Sybil Colefax and Nancy Cunard. Indeed, by the time he gets his brief mentions in the diaries of Chips Channon and Harold Nicolson, you would hardly know that Jimbo had been a Man of Letters at all, rather than simply being a figure in society. The generation who devoured the novels of Evelyn Waugh and the poetry of Auden and MacNeice left the works of Lampitt largely unread, though he continued to be an accomplished and widely admired reviewer to the end. On the day when he fell to his death, he left behind a chimney-piece in Hinde Street, laden with tokens that he still knew Everyone. Yet how many of the Everyones who met him at publishers' parties, dining societies or dinner parties, had read *Lagoon Loungings* or savoured, as I in boyhood had done, the sheer stylishness of his *Prince Albert* or his *Tennyson?*

No wonder Cecily, who also liked going to all the parties, should have spent so much time in Jimbo's company. They were far better

118

suited to one another than Cecily had been to her actual husband. Cecily's motive for appearing as a defence witness at the Hunter libel trial was, like much human behaviour, impenetrable; the experience can only have been painful and humiliating. She had obviously wanted, however, the world to believe that she and Jimbo were lovers. Nothing else could have explained her preparedness to volunteer as the only defence witness, and to proclaim so self-confidently that Jimbo had no interest in his own sex.

I can't make up my mind on the matter. Instinct tells me that, if they had actually been to bed together in the early stages, they would not have remained such firm friends for thirty years; but this assertion probably tells you more about my attitude to sex than it does about Cecily and Jimbo. I think the friendship was sustained in its initial stages by flirtation, by frustration, by anticipation, by promise – aren't all these words for the same thing, as far as sexual relations are concerned? While she was the Shakespearean boy, *anything* could have happened. Later, when they became 'thick as thieves', they had, I suspect, passed the stage where sexual intimacy could have been attempted without cringing embarrassment on both sides. But – who knows?

Writers and artists and actors are lucky enough to make money out of an activity in which most human beings indulge – which is the creation of worlds inside their heads. We are all hearing voices – when we wake and dream, but only the artist makes hearing voices his way of life. The extent to which literature is self-projection is in most cases hard to exaggerate, but it can be a pointless exercise to disentangle (as I have just fleetingly done by my Cecily/Shakespeare's Sonnets identification in the Jimbo *œuvre*) the unlikely shapes and patterns of an individual's fantasy and think that by so doing one can reconstruct the biographical 'truth' which inspired a work of art. (Jimbo, in his various writings on Shakespeare, frequently subscribes to this error, postulating that *King Lear* was written after the playwright's own father lost his wits, and that *Timon of Athens* reflected Shakespeare's money worries.) It was, for instance, a long time before I hit on the idea that *James Petworth Lampitt: The Hidden Years* was Hunter's way of writing about various aspects of his own character with which he found it difficult to come to terms; projecting various snobbish and homosexual tendencies of his own, and which he probably wished to conceal even from himself, on to the defenceless figure of 'Petworth' as he would insist on calling Jimbo. It was equally long before I realised that any act of writing can be viewed in some lights as an exercise in autobiography; and that the same can be said of the act of *reading*. We need to become selfless and highly motivated intellectually to attempt a 'pure' reading of a book, a reading which does not make the activity an exercise whereby we suck out from a text those elements most gratifying to our ego – which is why as a child, having enjoyed some particular story, we wish to *be*, and in some senses actually become, the figures in the story we have most admired. The habit which began with our 'being' Alice or Mole or Emil and the Detectives is (often without our realising it) carried on into the mature years, the success of many *soi-disant* serious books owing quite as much to this phenomenon as the trashier end of the bookshop. It is indeed fairly obvious that we partially 'become' the sleuth or the special agent while we read a thriller. It is less obvious that comparable acts of make-believe are at work when we read a treatise on the spiritual life or a book of philosophy or astronomy. The image of ourselves reading the book, ourselves-as-intellectuals, can be just as strong as the fantasy that we are men or women of action. All reading is therefore equally 'escapist' unless we purify ourselves from time to time by a recognition of the fact.

It was, I suppose, extraordinarily appropriate that I should end up 'being' Jimbo on stage, since, from the moment when I first read him, I had found myself aping his attitudes and stylistic quirks. When, in later years, I discovered that he had been unable to advance beyond his first Edwardian literary mannerisms, and, for all his high intelligence, that he had been unable to come to terms with modernism, I found him all the more sympathetic. But, if I had wanted to be Jimbo, Hunter had had the more perverse desire for Jimbo to *be him* and it was this, surely, which had informed Hunter's cardboard portrayal of the Edwardian Literary Scene with its own coarse vibrancy.

The journey from Norwich to Mallington Hall took about three-quarters of an hour. Uncle Roy had time to rehearse an admirable number of Lampitt anecdotes before the road followed the familiar, mile-long wall of brick and flint. Then, the gate-house and, once we were past that and had swung into the long drive, we were able to see, beyond rolling parkland and the clumps of ilex, the substantial eighteenth-century mansion which housed the people's friend, Ernie Lampitt . . .

Squeezing past the old perambulator in the stone-flagged back passage (still laden with its electioneering pamphlets and posters from the 1906 election and their desire that we should VOTE LAMPITT FOR A FAIRER WORLD), we discovered that the council of war – as befitted such very unpretentious folk as 'Ernie and Pat' – was being held in the kitchen. Pat was in her usual rig, a pair of hideous brown 'slacks' made from artificial fibre (I always suspected that she ordered them by post) and a white cable-knitted nylon jumper which covered her vigorous torso. Pat must have been sixty-odd, Vernon somewhat older. Snowy-haired now, he sat at the end of the huge pine table. No introductions were required to the others who sat round the table: their daughter Kirsty, still unmarried and now 'filling out', Ursula Lampitt their academic cousin (Principal of Rawlinson) and Cecily, who had shrunk several inches (osteoporosis) in the few years since I'd last seen her, and seemed several centuries older – Rider Haggard's *She* just before her final dissolution, a figure of dusty feebleness, but still talking animatedly about the old worries and obsessions. In fact, when we entered, and greeted the others, Cecily still went on talking, and it was only when we sat down that we caught her mid-sentence.

'. . . I know that will seem far-fetched to some of you, but I really' – *reely* – 'do think it.'

'No,' – Vernon was self-appointed Chairman of the proceedings – 'have yer say, Cecily, have yer say.'

'Well, if Mr Everett really is a clever man, and on some level, he must be – I mean you don't make a lot of money without being clever, do you?'

Pat made her formulaic wish that in that case she wished she was clever. It was always hard to know whether she expected her protestations of poverty to be believed.

'I mean, Mr Everett – if he looks at all those papers he bought – he must know by now that Mr Hunter has – well, not to put too fine a point on it, hoodwinked him!' Cecily's tiny vole's face, now plentifully supplied with wisps of hair which increased one's sense that she was one of the dressed animals from a Beatrix Potter watercolour, lit up with amusement at the thought of such villainy. 'I mean, we all know that Mr Everett paid Sargie a fortune for that archive, and he only did so because Mr Hunter says he found out about Jimbo's private dealings, shall we say,' – at this point Cecily's satirical smile was matched by a sympathetic giggling fit from the Mistress of Rawlinson, Dame Ursula – 'by research. But suppose Mr Hunter just made it all up. Suppose Mr Everett has been through those papers, what then? And he sees that it isn't true what Mr Hunter wrote, that Jimbo wasn't, you know, quite that way inclined – horrid phrase but you *know.*'

'Well then, Virgil'll at last do what we've all been wanting for years; he'll give Mr Hunter his come-uppance,' – this from Pat, *con brio.*

The 'council of war' was summoned, it would seem, with a dual purpose. On the one hand, they were trying to decide what to do about poor Sargie, and on the other, while they were about it, they were attempting to see if there could not be one last act of literary revenge against Hunter for what they believed to be a travesty of the truth – *James Petworth Lampitt: The Hidden Years*. I had been so *distrait* in the hospital that I did not realise that I as well as Uncle Roy was asked to the 'council of war'. From me they wanted to know the truth of a rumour – that Hunter was on the verge of completing Jimbo's life in a second volume. Since they now withheld from Hunter any permission to quote from Jimbo's work – published or unpublished; since they, who had known Jimbo, all refused to speak to Hunter; and since, in particular, Cecily kept her huge number of Jimbo's letters (well over 2,000) from Hunter's eyes (he did not even know of their existence) it seemed to me less than reasonable to complain that Hunter made things up. After all, since he was not allowed to consult the true source material he would have little alternative but to lie. I was much more partisan, however, at that time, and did not see things as I see them now. Also, I still retained a hope that I might finish my own book, so that the news that Hunter was about to launch a second large Lampitt volume could not please me.

'Mr Ramsay,' Dame Ursula leaned forward, folding the arms of her thick cardie and beaming at me as if I were a shy undergraduate whom she was about to submit to examination *viva voce*, 'when you have been working in the Everett Archive, have you come across any of this' – giggle, giggle – 'what shall we call it – salacious material?'

'Filth more like,' said Pat.

'Julie knows what yer mean, Ursula.'

'It's a strange library to work in,' I said. 'You are brought your manuscript material – and I don't exaggerate – one leaf at a time. The catalogue, compiled by some research student at Hunter's recommendation, would not pass muster in a proper research library, and it is impossible to cross-reference from it. For instance, let us suppose, for the sake of argument, that I wish to find all the references to Henry James . . .' I watched their faces glaze over as I became a research-bore and told them about my 'discovery' that Jimbo had actually worked with James on *The Ambassadors*. 'Now what I can't do,' I concluded, 'is to rummage. I can't say, May I look through every box of papers to see if I can find all your other Henry James references? I can only ask the librarian to bring – one page at a time – the known, catalogued letters which James wrote to Jimbo. So you see how painstakingly slow the work is, and how difficult it would be for any visitor to find out whether Hunter was pulling the wool over our eyes.'

'Yes,' said Cecily in her little mincing insistent voice, 'Mr Everett doesn't have to get permission to look at his own things? He's the owner of them, Mr Everett, and he can go in and rummage as much as he likes; and what happens if he does do that? What happens if someone says, "Mr Everett, you've been made a fool of, you've been had by Mr Hunter", what then?'

It was a good question. Cecily never got much closer to knowing the truth, for she died a few days after this conversation – she collapsed by the flower-stall at the bottom of Kensington Church Street and died instantly. Uncle Roy went up to town to take the funeral at St Mary Abbots – a church he had always much liked. Sargie – the other great subject of debate that day at Mallington – was too ill to attend the obsequies of his wife.

'You both know Sarge,' said Pat, who, like Lady Starling, enjoyed reducing Sargent Lampitt's name to this unsparing monosyllable. She spoke, as I have observed before in these chronicles, in a curious Cockney twang, not because she could conceivably have been old enough to speak in that 'aristocratic Cockney' which, we read, was the accent of some sections of the upper class until the First World War, nor because she had been born of modest stock within the sound of Bow Bells. (She was *née* Dawnay.) I'd always assumed that Pat's voice had developed over the years, in some bizarre way to match or blend in with her husband's egalitarian views. 'Oid've thought yew both knew Sarge better than any uv us.'

'It's an indictment uv the system uv course,' said Vernon, who had got his pipe alight. 'Here you've got a chap in need uv help – no doubts on that score.'

'Sargie needs a jolly good kick up the BTM,' said Cecily with childish savagery. This made Dame Ursula burst into such a giggling fit that I thought we might all have to stop speaking until she had finished – and how, with such a peal of semi-hysteria, could she be stopped? Would we be compelled to hold the Principal of Rawlinson, this academic equivalent of the laughing policeman, under the cold tap until she quietened down?

'Do you know,' Cecily continued to say through Ursula's wholly mirthless yelps, 'when that nurse opened the top drawer of the wardrobe to get out the pillows he said he wanted, three bottles fell out – empty I may say – and she could have been hurt, the nurse, those bottles could have hit her on the head.'

'And it's old people like this the system's failing. By golly if Nye were alive today! I mean – our old people don't just need shoring up physically. They've got very specific needs and if this were a Socialist country we'd address each of those needs.' It was never long, in any paragraph spoken by Lord Lampitt, before he began counting out lists with the dottle-damp mouthpiece of his pipe on to his orange old fingers. 'They need help psychiatrically, uz I say; they need help funancially – the pensions are a long way frum keeping up with inflation let alone beating it which is what they should be doin', help with – '

'I thought Sargie was staying in a private hospital,' I butted in.

'Um afraid 'e's bin forgettin' some of 'is Socialist principles.' Lord and Lady Lampitt spoke at once for, while Vernon was saying this, Pat was saying, 'Oi think any hospital that tikes in Sargie is *asking* for it.' *Arse King.*

'But' – giggle – 'it is rather a problem, as it were,' – like all the Lampitts Ursula said *problim* – 'since none of us would be willing to have' – giggle – 'Sargie to live with, as it were, us.'

I wonder if any of them saw, as I who knew him so well could see, the emotions passing over my Uncle Roy's face. It was obvious that he could not possibly ask Aunt Deirdre to bring Sargie to live with them at the Rectory; equally obvious, if Sargie's condition had deteriorated thus far, that this would not be the right solution even if it were an option. Yet Uncle Roy's face was that of the child who knew there was no chance of persuading his mother to allow him to keep a pet rat but who could not conceal his longing, nor an unrealistic faith that – somehow – it might one day be possible . . . The Great Estrangement between the two friends had been going on for as long as I had been grown-up; the origins of the estrangement were hard to reconstruct – Hunter had certainly muddied the water, and the cause of the final row – Sargie's unpardonably vandalistic decision to demolish Timplingham Place – was clear enough in the memory. The further you draw away from events, though, the harder it seems to say that they happened for any specific set of reasons. There are times to draw together and times to separate, in friendships as in marriages; it is not always easy to see why such times are reached, but that they are reached cannot be denied. From the expression of loving expectancy which played across my uncle's soft, gentle face, it seemed as if there was a chance that this estrangement might, *might* . . . But the brightness faded from Uncle Roy's eyes. He knew that if half the reports were true, Sargie was too far gone for any hope to be realistic which promised a possible revival in their friendship. Into the sadness and desolation of Uncle Roy's features there returned a defiant expression which brought back the old days. He wore it when he was about to tell his wife that he would be spending the next few days driving Sargie up to town, or taking him to Cromer. I knew that the present expression of defiance would never presage any such suggestion – that it was created by involuntary longings and Quixotic dreams. Sancho Panza was dreaming that he might set out with his knight of the sorrowful countenance on another series of fantastical adventures. The fact that they were all now too old, or that Granny lay dying, or that parish business, or his obligations to Aunt Deirdre, would make such a thing utterly impossible, could not stop the dream from forming itself in my uncle's brain, and I am sure I do not invent this, I am sure that I saw it pass. Old and mad as Sargie apparently was, why should the two of them accept defeat? Where there was life there was hope! Might not Sargie force my uncle to sit through a few more humiliating scenes in restaurants or hotels, and make him the witness to a few more pointless and inebriated altercations with lift-boys, head waiters, taxi-drivers and barmen before they went back to the Savile Club for a snifter and a duet of shared belief that the world was full, crammed, with awkward *buggers* (on Sargie's lips), *so-and-so's* (on Uncle Roy's), conspiring to make Sargie's life impossible? Uncle Roy, I suspect, was the only person who had ever loved Sargie on his own demanding terms (except perhaps for the sainted and long-since dead old Mrs Lampitt – bless her – Sargie's mother, regarded by the rest of the family as responsible for spoiling Sargie, though what he had been before, and what she had spoilt, no one was old enough to recollect). As his anecdotes all made plain, Uncle Roy did positively enjoy it when Sargie was 'acting up'. With what loving affection my uncle would recall behaviour which was by no normal standards acceptable. True, having wiped away tears of mirth and repeated, 'I really think for two pins that waiter would have struck Sargie', he would add, 'but an *extraordinarily* intelligent man, Sargie. Possibly the finest brain of his generation, but all gone to waste you see, through being . . .' And here my uncle would shrug and tap the side of his temple with a well-manicured fingertip.

It now seemed as if medical opinion was veering towards my uncle's oft-expressed viewpoint. As we had guessed, the Lampitts were under the impression that any priest – and my uncle was the only priest they knew – would know all about finding a 'place' in a local lunatic asylum. In spite of their impeccably Socialist credentials, they were in danger of showing some of the desire for preferential treatment which might have been expected from middle-class vulgarians hoping to get their offspring into a good private school.

'We thought you'd know, Roy, well, that it ud be up yer street, so to say.'

'Oi mean it'd be sow much easier to 'ave Sarge in the area where iz people could go over and see 'im.'

If they wanted practical counsel about the geriatric and psychiatric establishments in the county they had clearly consulted the wrong man. It was years, really, since Uncle Roy had been any great shakes pastorally. Indeed, he made very little secret of the fact that the human race did not really interest him – that is, the large proportion who could not claim the privilege of kinship with the Lampitts or, as he would put it, who were not of the Blood Royal. (Like so much language, this phrase had started life as a joke but the inverted commas had long since dropped off it, with the result that strangers who were hearing one of my uncle's narratives for the first time wore a puzzled expression as, in the course of his unstoppable anecdotes, he would appear to be asserting that Vernon, a great economic brain, dear old Vivian-bless-him in Mombasa, Dame Ursula of Oxford or the lost Orlando, who went on the stage in 1928, had some family connection with Sandringham or Balmoral.

Realising that they had drawn a blank and that we were not going to find some easy saps who would, in effect, take the Sargie problem off their hands, the Lampitts would have been glad if they could have asked us at once to leave; had it not been for my desire to mention the Nolans in their company. There was no possible reason why Fergus Nolan, a professor of obstetric medicine at Birmingham, should know any more than Pat did about geriatric nursing in Norfolk. But, with that obsessive need which one has, when in love, to mention the beloved's name in the most inapposite circumstances, I found myself bleating out that I would ask the Nolans and that, while her husband was a clever scientist, it was really Margaret Mary who might have the answer – since she volunteered once a year to help the sick on the Lourdes train.

The women continued to talk of the Lampitt Papers, but Vernon had turned to the state of the world. It would be invidious to suggest that one of these topics was more important than the other. While Pat and Cecily urged me to fly back to New York at the earliest possible opportunity to establish whether Hunter had indeed been hoodwinking Virgil D., Vernon, by contrast, was wallowing in the fact that the Americans were losing the war in Vietnam, that young people everywhere were in revolt, that the students in Paris were gouging out the very cobblestones from the streets and hurling them at policemen. Bliss was it in that dawn to be alive; to be an elderly peer of leftish persuasion reading about it all in the newspapers was very heaven.

'And yer see, Julie, and um sure you've found this,' – did he think because I knew a few Catholics that I had actually 'gone over'? – 'the Pope's with us, oh yes, by golly. 'E's a good social democrat, this Pope – whatsis name, Mantovani.'

127

'Montini,' said Uncle Roy.

'That's why the Fascists hated 'im so much – you see 'is old dad ran an anti-Fascist newspaper in Brescia all through the thirties. They are very much on our side, the Mantovanis, and in my view 'e's goin' ter show 'imself a real radical. A mean, 'e's goin' ter drop all this nonsense about birth control, you mark me words.'

'Oi don't agree with you there,' said his wife. 'They'd never change that. Any political party would ban birth control if they could get away with it. We'd do it ourselves if we could get it past the National Executive – it's the best way of guaranteeing that the next generation of supporters is four times as great as the last.'

There are those who follow the movement of human ideas the way others follow the sports results. Not being one of these, I had failed to catch up on the alliance which had been forged between the more go-ahead sections of the Nolans' Church and the more idealistic section of Vernon's party. I suppose, as the would-be historian of the tribe, I had assumed, in a simple-minded way, that the Lampitts, from purely dissenting stock, could have no truck with priestcraft and mumbo-jumbo. I had always admired – given his devotion to the Blood Royal – the dogged persistence with which Uncle Roy remained loyal to an admittedly distinctive persistence in the 'bells and smells' end of Anglicanism. (Aunt Deirdre, never slow to point out the more humiliating aspects of her husband's friendship with Sargie, crossly, but incontrovertibly, would say that 'None of that family has ever darkened the door of a church. My father used to say "The Lampitts are the sort who chopped off the King's head".')

Vernon's republican credentials were impeccable. If openly charged with responsibility for decapitating Charles Stuart The Man of Blood (as he liked to call the Royal Martyr) he would have taken it as a compliment.

His endorsement of the new Pope and his ideas came as a slight surprise, though he had given indications in the past that he saw the Pilgrimage of Grace as a populist uprising, anti-capitalist in spirit. Evidently, some of the Liberation Theology, so much propagated and admired by Bon Reilly, OP, and now by Persy, had found its way into some of the newspapers over which Vernon's protuberant eyes had played. (I'm sure Vernon never, strictly speaking, read anything *through*, except perhaps his own pamphlets and articles.) So – some rum alliances were being formed in the world at that juncture, what Albion Pugh could have called 'conjunctions of polarities and con-sanguinities of opposites'. At prep-school, the cricket master would yell at Darnley and me for making daisy chains on the outer perimeter of the playing fields rather than concentrating on the conflict being enacted at the wicket. This incorrigible tendency was still with me. I knew, when in Birmingham, that Jim Reilly and Fergus and Persy were 'thrashing out issues' of the utmost importance to humanity; all I could think of as they spoke – and think is the wrong word, used here merely for the sake of shorthand – was the loveliness of M.M. And, here at Mallington, mention of the Pope's social policies only sent me off into such reverie, and the thought of her rather fine boyish hair pressed against her skull beneath a lace mantilla as she emerged into the Hagley Road from Marce; and the brain began to devise a feverish excuse why I might telephone her that evening. And I thought of her bright, blue-green eyes and her very thin arms, and I found myself superimposing on M.M.'s face memories of Mummy: Mummy kissing me in the bath; Mummy reading aloud to me from *Alice* as we sat in the air raid shelter with Granny and Mrs Webb; Mummy waving goodbye to me on Platform One at Paddington.

'The Pope has picked up many of the Anglican ideas at long last!' said Uncle Roy, who had lit his pipe, and showed no sign of wishing to cut short his precious Lampitt-time, deathbed or no deathbed, Granny or no Granny. 'As you say, Vernon, he's very distinctly a man of the Left; many of his ideas seem as if they might have been borrowed from William Temple and Maurice Reckitts. And you see, Percy Dearmer anticipated *all* their liturgical movement.'

Here he had moved well outside the area in which all those present might conceivably be interested. Embarrassment at his insensitivity awakened the truculent adolescent need to contradict everything my uncle said.

'I'm sure they'll have Mass in English soon, just like us,' said Uncle Roy.

'My Catholic friends say that's most unlikely,' I snapped.

After Cecily's death, I felt it had been an 'important' visit to Mallington, particularly when I had at last read her correspondence with Jimbo. The letters which he wrote to her – playful, fantastical,

129

full of jokes and gossip, brought him alive as no printed word of Jimbo himself had done. There is no whole truth about a human life, but here was *a* truth, so much at variance with the Hunter version – one which was so much funnier and lighter and more innocent, that I did feel a sense of mission: hence my extravagant decision, later that summer, to revisit the United States and see whether the archive in New York would yield any new secrets. I had no sense then that Hunter was about to finish his book – nor that by the time it was published Virgil D. Everett would be dead, and the Ann-Louise Everett Library would have been dispersed. The Lampitt Papers, so called, purchased by Virgil D. from Sargie, were all divided up; private collectors bought most of the nineties material; the Henry James stuff went to Boston; Magdalene College, Cambridge, bought the Benson letters, such as they are. In none of the sale catalogues was any of the 'material' thus dispersed regarded as very interesting, except for the Gray and Raffalovitch stuff – which has no bearing on this particular story. Those who believed that Virgil D. had been 'sold a pup' by Sargie might thus have been justified in their opinion. From my point of view the interesting thing was the light all this shed on Hunter, his methods of scholarly approach and the position which he had occupied in the Virgil D. Everett world.

As the Anglia swept down the enormous drive, the mirror at eye-level showed Mallington at its most splendid, and – behind ilex clumps at the end of the Long Walk – the Isleworth Obelisk, built before the Lampitts came on the scene. (Walpole, when Prime Minister, had been driven over from Houghton and had complained to his son of Lord Isleworth's obsession with planting, and his relentless wish that neighbours should survey each tedious sapling.) On this very patch of the drive, arriving at the house with Darnley some months before his marriage, I had narrowly avoided a motor-collision with the Leader of the Labour Party. I thought, though, not of the great men who had come and gone at Mallington, but of Darnley, of whom I was so fond, and who had – for no special reason – drifted apart from me over the years. Uncle Roy, sitting beside me in the passenger seat, had a sad expression on his face. No doubt he too was hearing the voices of old friends.

SIX
(Summer 1968)

What is Satisfaction?
Satisfaction is doing the penance given us by the priest.

KNOCK! KNOCK!

The terrible knocking on the door caused paroxysms of spiritual terror to pass through the student Raskolnikov. If only he had not been forced, through circumstances, to murder that second old lady! Still, in his dreams, he found himself washing his hands, trying to rid himself of the blood-stains. And now . . .

Knock, knock!

It would be the police. It would be Porfiry Petrovich, who knew perfectly well that Raskolnikov had murdered the old ladies and who was simply playing a game of cat and mouse.

Gingerly, and wet with perspiration, the sallow, unshaven student opened the door of his room and came downstairs.

From a neighbour's open window, the sticky night air bore the voice of Mick Jagger: 'I can't GET no –

Satis – FACK – shun . . .'

His room was above a taxidermist's shop and, even in the shared hallway, there were a number of stuffed animals – heaps of bones – various animal-parts, including three separate zebra feet which might or might not be usable as lamp-stands and a giraffe's head and neck, which reached to the dirty ceiling.

Through the grille of the glazed front door, he – I – the person who had been Raskolnikov and was now winding down, and turning into another *tabula rasa* – could see a visitor.

The state of mind in which we are absorbed in a book can be likened to that induced by narcotics. One comes down from a trip by degrees. The scruff who opened the door was me; but upstairs on the sweaty divan lay *Crime and Punishment*, into which I would dive again when the distraction of the visitor was passed.

'Is Christopher at home?'

'I'm afraid he's away.'

'Is anyone else . . .?'

An unpleasant leer had possessed the face of my visitor.

He was an Englishman of perhaps forty-five years of age, every inch the NCO. He spoke with the unmistakable voice of Sarf London. In fact, for a moment, my head still dizzy with *Crime and Punishment*, I supposed that he actually was one of the foul-mouthed sergeant-majors who had persecuted me during my period of National Service.

'I'm alone in the house,' I said, feeling a fool to allow such a confession to blurt from me.

'Are you now?' A curl of the Enoch Powell moustache.

His short hair was brylcreemed to the top of his head. He wore a short-sleeved white shirt, from which firm brown arms extended; track-suit bottoms added to the impression that he might be an army gym instructor.

'Mr Everett was expecting a visitor,' he said meaningfully. 'Perhaps you could tell Christopher.'

'But I told you, he's gone away.'

'And you aren't' – again an unpleasant leer – 'standing in for him?'

I slammed the door in the man's face and bolted it, running upstairs in the dark and lying for some half hour afterwards.

The sinister sergeant-major had frightened me; but, alone in New York at the height of a very hot summer, I was easily frightened. The place steamed. It was no wonder that those lodgers who were able cleared out of their rooms above the taxidermist's shop in E. 14th Street and left town. Whenever I returned to my second-floor apartment, a malodorous hutch ten foot by eight, I faced a choice of being broiled, or listening to the ancient air-conditioner whirr and roar. It was louder than Aunt Deirdre's Atco lawn-mower and made sleep impossible.

I could not cook in such a place, and I could not afford to move out to an hotel. Evenings, therefore, were either spent sweltering alone above the shop or hovering on high stools in bars and diners with a book balanced beside my plate of fries. I read a lot of Dostoevsky that way – perhaps not a bad way to do it. Absorbing that writer in extended concentrated gulps, without the interruption of embodied human discourse, sent me, quite often, back to the little room in a strange state of mind. In such a condition, as I swatted flies or turned on the thunderous air-conditioner as an accompaniment to my thoughts, I easily became a Dostoevskian 'underground man', identifying readily with all the central figures of the novels as I lost myself in them.

It is possible to become enamoured of solitude however painful it is. My reading increased my terror of the New York streets at night, and after the visit of the sergeant-major it was hard to convince myself that he would not return and force me out of the building. I remembered Christopher's account of a girl – Melanie – being dragged out of her room and forced to . . .

Mr Everett? *Mr Everett?* Had the sinister sergeant-major really named Mr Everett? It was perhaps a common enough surname – but there seemed too much of coincidence here. Could he have been referring to my Mr Everett, to Virgil D. Everett, Jnr?

It was an unhappy time for me, but not an unfruitful one. *Joys impregnate: sorrows bring forth.* I was beginning to make progress with the Lampitt book. My mind was awake, though dead to the world. I had become a hermit, never buying a newspaper and seldom hearing a radio. Sometimes, in the corner of my nearest diner, the TV screen would flash up an image – of aeroplanes over an Asian forest, or a senator addressing a crowd. The great upheavals in the world since spring – the new French revolution, the assassinations in Memphis and San Diego, the manifestations of the counter-culture in student demonstrations and happenings and love-ins – made small imaginative impact on me.

This was the beginning of the – beginning! What am I saying? The beginning was in the womb. Correction. This was the first time that dissociative symptoms in my mind began to trouble me. Lying on my bed, shaking with fear, I could not remember whether the sergeant-major had named Mr Everett or whether this was something which I

133

had made up. Was Mr Everett trying to murder me – or was I trying to murder Mr Everett? Had I been responsible for the death of Ann-Louise Everett herself? I was no longer quite sure that I knew the difference between being Raskolnikov and being Julian Ramsay. Sometimes, I would give myself some entertainment by going to a diner one block up the street and 'being' a different person. I was no longer Julian, but Jason Grainger, the character whom I depicted in 'The Mulberrys'. It was hilarious to see the expressions of surprise on their faces – waiters, and bartenders – when confronted by Jason at his snootiest. He made a very amusing companion, Jason. With Wilmie not answering her telephone, and with all my acquaintances almost certainly out of town – people such as Pigtail or Christopher – it was not surprising that there was no one with whom I could spend my evenings. Thank God for the busload from Barking whom I had brought along between my ears.

No wonder, too, that my visits to the Library began to take on a distinctly desperate air. My dusty, smelly, cramped lodgings stank of poverty. The Everett Foundation provided consolations where it did not seem outlandish to remember Scriptural images of the parched hungry soul, yearning for the water-brooks. To step from the baking street, one entered at once a world where Mr Everett could control the very seasons. The perpetual feel of an English spring was present in the cool air of the atrium, with its huge plane tree swooping towards the glassy air; its cascades of cool water tumbling down beside the glass elevators in which the hundreds of Mr Everett's employees ascended and descended like the angels of God. On the top floor of this strange kingdom, and reached by a private elevator, was the penthouse occupied by Mr Everett himself. Some way down, on the twentieth floor, was the Ann-Louise Everett Library and it was not surprising that the two staff there, Dorset and Mr Leegrober, should have loomed large, for a while, in consciousness. For over a fortnight (a long time if you are lonely) Dorset and Mr Leegrober were the only persons with whom I conversed.

Mr Leegrober was what in England would have been called the Library clerk. A wizened, pale man with paper-thin skin and enormous ears, he wore pale blue sleeveless shirts and some rather handsome trews of (I think) the Maclean Dress Tartan. His slowness used to infuriate me. I wanted to *go through* the Lampitt Papers, to rummage.

134

It was Mr Leegrober who (acting under orders, of course) made this impossible.

I began to feel that I should never get a freer access to explore the 'stacks' and that my second visit to New York had been a dreadful waste of time and money. I cursed myself for having come. At home, the doctors said that Granny might live for months, possibly years more; they were, in the event, wrong. The affair with Persy, if such an unsatisfactory arrangement could still be called an affair, had reached the stage where it was actually more painful to leave it alone than to be with her. In my loneliness I certainly missed Persy – not for purely sensual reasons. In spite of our painfully obvious incompatibility Persy Nolan and I had grown to like one another; and I liked her family; I missed M.M. and the whole household at Wiseman Road. I even rather missed Father Quarles. It seemed crazy to be sitting, three thousand miles from anyone I loved, and twenty storeys up in E. 63rd St, reading letters which had originally been written to Sargie's brother!

> My dear Lampitt,
> I am touched almost to dissolving by your heroism, your self-denial, your, dare I say it, your adventurousness in making the cumbersome and, at this far from incalescent season of the year, arctic railroad journey to Rye in order to refresh, entertain, enliven, your poor old friend. And I am yet further touched by your parting gift, a gift whose thoughtfulness could not fail to delight my heart as, no doubt, it will, when I have read it, resurrect in my mind those memories of the last century which you, in our dear conversations, appear so patiently eager to provoke and, once provoked, to attend.
> You will know that an old Yankee such as I must always have an exaggerated sense of reverence for anything which, for want of a kinder word, smacks of rank, blood, dynasty and all the arcane, but to us enviable, trappings of old Europe; so that, my dear Lampitt, your sketches – I refer of course not so much to what you have written as to what you have so delightfully told your old friend – of English and Germanic royalties have always been a source of delight. And you will recollect what

135

I told you of the dearest Duchess of Albany, when she met your old friend at Mentmore, last summer . . .

There were untold boxes of letters like this, preserved because they came from famous people, but containing, strictly speaking, no biographical information whatsoever beyond the fact, which I knew all too well by now, that Jimbo had dined here, lunched there, and stayed with this or that titled or notable contemporary. Having finished the letter, which was signed 'ever your most devoted, dearest Lampitt, Henry James', I replaced it in its cellophane container and took it back to Mr Leegrober's desk.

The Ann-Louise Everett Collection was not the sort of scholarly library where any scholar could wander in at random to do research. Only by considerable string-pulling with Sargie himself had I been granted permission to do research there at all, and, during that particular week, I was the only researcher in the Library.

'Is Mr Leegrober not here today . . .?' I asked, for Dorset, rather than my wizened old helper, was the one who took back my document.

'What else can I get you?'

She wore a T-shirt and no bra; a shortish blue and white skirt. Her body was that of a healthy tennis-player and swimmer, and it had not even occurred to me, until that moment, that I had any chance in that particular direction.

One thing, as they say, led to another. A stroll, during the lunch hour, to a nearby deli, a brief exchange of autobiographies – we'd both been married, both been divorced, both felt hot, and a little lonely. The rest was somehow inevitable. There was no one else in the library that afternoon. Dorset was an extremely willing participant, and the fact that, thirty years later, I did not immediately remember her face when I met her after the 'One Man Show' should not be taken to indicate that, once her name and number had been recovered from my creaking mental filing-system, I did not recollect that the pleasure of that afternoon had been extreme and, I hope, mutual. (She was one of those lovers who like making a lot of noise which, in a library, surrounded by notices which read SILENCE, greatly added to the excitement.)

Mr Leegrober, it appeared, was away for a week in Cape Cod, leaving me, and the library, in Dorset's hands. Whether it was actually and immediately in a post-coital situation, or whether it was because of the new nature of our relationship, I do not recall; but it was Dorset who allowed me to break the rules and to *rummage* in the Lampitt Papers.

'I shouldn't be letting you do this, honey.'

'This – or *this?*'

And – on a large writing-desk in the middle of the spacious reading-room – the strange rituals of love were repeated. Pass thirty years, and I could meet Dorset again and not even remember who she was. When memory had reproached me by recalling her identity only a few snapshots of our intimacy remained – that table; and the gratifying fact that she was so wonderfully ready for what took place between us. People talk about others as 'good' or 'bad' in bed (or, in our case, on the table). I have come to the conclusion that this phrase is largely meaningless, an extension of playground cruelty. Just sometimes, though, sex rises above the ordinary level of pleasure and becomes the sort of thing which so many modern writers believe (wrongly, I think) that it is easy to describe or chronicle. It would be facile to set down for the reader the snapshots which remain in my head of Dorset – extent of mutual excitement, number of times, and so forth; as easy as scrawling on a lavatory wall. Less easy to convey the strange cheeringness of it all, and its ephemeral quality. Sex in my experience, what moderns would perhaps wish to classify as 'good sex', is the most perfect example of what Blake called 'the joy as it flies'; heavyweights and erotic mystics like D. H. Lawrence and his admirers perhaps made the mistake of – in the Blakean phraseology – binding to themselves a joy and thereby destroying 'the winged life'.

Not surprising, therefore, that I can remember only fleeting moments on the table with Dorset; but that the rest of the scene is preserved in my mind with cinematic clarity.

'Mr Leegrober is just going to kill me if . . .'

'He won't. He won't know. No one need know.'

In this, the second sortie into the stacks, I must have made a strange spectacle, clad as I was only in socks and drawers, and taking down one cardboard box file after another with greedy grabbing gestures.

In the first few boxes, I read each page carefully. Quickly, however, my long suspicion was confirmed. This huge assemblage of what

Hunter called 'material' contained almost nothing of the slightest biographical interest. The seven surviving postcards from Sybil Colefax, imploring Jimbo's presence at soirées or dinner-dances, would have had their charm to the autograph-collector; likewise, the jolly exchange of mutual compliments which seems to have taken place when either Jimbo or Arnold Bennett wrote a book, and sent each other a copy. The only box which did contain fascinating information was the large bundle of letters from Albion Pugh. How fast and how well I recognised the large, babyish hand of his letters to his mentor. Had anyone been choosing to write a biography of Albion Pugh, they would have found these jejune outpourings (mostly penned when Pughie was between twenty and thirty) of the utmost interest; but, they told us nothing about Lampitt himself beyond the fact that he had clearly been a sympathetic listener to Pugh's literary aspirations and dreams, and been generous enough to reply, not only with letters but also, fairly often, with dollops of cash. Cash too, I was surprised to see, had been sent to the young Day Muckley during some marital crisis before the War; indeed, as I pulled down box after box, it was striking to me how many young writers Lampitt had helped financially, and even more striking, perhaps, how many of them had written thank you letters.

Hunter's first volume, *James Petworth Lampitt: The Hidden Years*, had been sold on the strength of his close, and unique, acquaintance-ship with the Lampitt Papers. Felicity, my cousin who had helped to get these papers into a rough and ready order preparatory to sale, had always maintained that there was not much there, by way of biographical stuff; certainly nothing to justify Hunter's implied suggestion that Lampitt had led a life of unbridled homosexual promiscuity. Even the Diaries, on which so much of Hunter's work was supposedly based, could never justify the innuendoes and hints which Hunter made. (From some passages of *The Hidden Years*, though nothing is spelt out in four- or even in six-letter words, the reader could be forgiven for believing that Jimbo possessed an irresistible erotic magnetism which even the chastest of celibates or the most rampant of heterosexualists could not resist. The hints about Cardinal Manning rival the rumours about Lloyd George for sheer audacious improbability.)

I was therefore determined, during my few precious hours of rummaging, to discover those diaries; and this was not, as it transpired, at all difficult. Although Sargie had been paid – and this in the mid-fifties – something in the region of ten thousand pounds for the papers by Mr Everett (and you could buy a substantial house in England at this date for £4,000), I can remember Felicity telling me that the actual papers were not so very extensive. Most of what Everett bought, and which filled the trunks and boxes (eventually stacked up in the offices of Denniston and Denniston – family solicitors), was pure rubbish – yellowing copies of the *New Statesman and Nation*, old insurance certificates, scrap-books containing notices of Jimbo's books and other scrap-books of Jimbo's own journalism. If Mr Everett wanted to pay big money for a few old magazine cuttings, that, concluded Sargie, was his affair.

He disregarded – it was the cause of a tremendous rumpus in the family at the time – the fact that Hunter had already got in on the act, made himself the custodian of Jimbo's sacred flame, and actually grabbed for himself a position of authority in the Everett Empire. Had the Lampitt Papers been kept in a more conventional academic institution, either in the United States or in Britain, other scholars would have had much freer access to them, and would have been able to challenge, indeed to refute, most of Hunter's wilder assertions. As it was, by persuading Mr Everett to buy the papers in the first place, Hunter had effectively silenced the opposition, and since his literary reputation, and his subsequent success as a media bore and a televisionary, had been built on his expertise in Lampitt-lore, it was not surprising that he should wish the secret of the Lampitt Papers to be kept: their secret being the Sphinx-like enigma that there was no secret.

'What is it, hun? Read it out if it's funny.'

Dorset was sitting on a chair at the other side of the library, her lovely, honey-coloured athletic limbs still unclothed.

'I've found the box with all the Diaries in them!'

'Boy! Bet they could tell a tale or two.'

'Yes – but not quite of the kind we've been led to believe.'

'Excuse me?'

'*15th May 1911. Rather colder than of late. I think that the turtle soup last evening at Lady Elcho's cannot have agreed with me, for I was bilious in the night. Clayhanger. 16th May 1911. Bilious attack cleared up.*

Lunched with Lascelles Abercrombie who told amusing anecdote about Swinburne which I had not heard before . . .'

'Don't we get to hear what it is?'

'Don't we hell. That's just it. *17th May 1911. Lunched with Wells. Vulgarian. Dined with the Literary Society. Sate beside Arthur Benson, who is always so full of charming old reminiscences of days of yore. He told me a story about his brother Hugh – the Romanist priest – and the mountebank Baron Corvo . . .'*

'It's all like that?'

'As far as I could see.'

I flicked here and there. A tiny little Diary, no more than an engagement diary, from 1899, was of interest in so far as it recorded a visit, when Jimbo was just eighteen, to Wilde after his release from imprisonment and decision to live in exile; but Jimbo was not a great diarist and he had not thought to record a single aphorism which fell from Wilde's lips. Flicking ahead to the later years – the years of *entre deux guerres* – there was absolutely nothing to shed light on any of Jimbo's friendships, loves, thoughts about the world, or even – a subject which was not without fascination for me – his thoughts about the rest of the Lampitt family.

'I'm going to take you to have something to eat and I'm going to show you a proper American sandwich,' announced Dorset.

It seemed like a good idea. After the sandwich (a largely flavourless pitta into which someone had ladled coleslaw), we walked about arm in arm; and we went to a bar. Dorset didn't suggest coming back to my place – something of a relief, since I guessed she would have been shocked by its squalor. Having it half in mind that she might ask me back to hers, I inquired where she lived.

'I live in Brooklyn,' she said and looked at the bottom of her beer-glass, as if examining tea-leaves for some insight into the future.

'Listen, Julian, if what you're saying's right, and I'm sure you wouldn't lie – you're a very warm sincere person – then Mr Everett hasn't gotten what he thinks in there. The Lampitt Papers – they're not papers at all.'

'That's what it looks like.'

'So – it's like someone sold him a fake picture by Dali.'

'Yes.'

'And that was the Lampitt family themselves who did this. That was real sneaky.'

'In a sense it was the Lampitts. But you could say that the man really responsible was Raphael Hunter. It is in his interest, you see, to make the world believe that the Lampitt Papers are much more interesting than they really are. And locking them up in the Ann-Louise Everett Archive is a good way of making sure that no one gets to read them.'

She looked at me as though I'd uttered blasphemy.

'Oh, no! Raphael would never do anything mean,' she declared with a smile. 'He's so sweet and gentle.' She sighed and was silent for a moment; Hunter's sweetness had evidently taken her heart for speech. 'He'd be real interested to know what you've found out about those papers. Sure he would.'

'I wouldn't be quite so sure myself.'

'You know what I gonna do?'

'No?'

Hopes that she was going to drop this subject, ask me home, give me a night of passion, were beginning to dwindle.

'I'm gonna tell Mr Everett myself. Yes, sir. He can read those Diaries for himself and see what he's bought.'

Did she do this? If I had only recognised her thirty years later, after the 'One Man Show', that is what I should have asked her. Had she done so, was it not possible that she opened the Pandora's box which led to Mr Everett's death? What if he had denounced Hunter, and threatened to expose the learned volumes of biography as the shame they really were?

'You're not a Catholic, are you?'

This was a pretty abrupt change of subject, brought about by my ordering another round. It made me even less hopeful that I'd be spending the night *chez* Dorset. It seemed to be my year for Catholic girls.

'Why, are you, Dorset?'

'Was,' she smirked. 'Not very likely to be now. Can you imagine what the Pope is doing, Julian?'

'What – right now? Saying the Rosary? Taking a friend to *Song of Bernadette* followed by a Chinese meal?'

'I mean with this encyclical. I mean, for Christ's *sakes*, Julian.'

While I buried my nose in my Bourbon glass, she gave me a brief *résumé* of the *Humanae Vitae* encyclical, as it had been *précised* on a recent news bulletin. I had not heard about it.

'Hey. Hey,' I said. 'Stop giving me a hard time about it. I didn't write the bloody thing.'

'Can't he see the world's too full of people already?'

'Perhaps not.'

A dreadful chill had passed over me. I was remembering my conversation with Margaret Mary of two years earlier. Doubtless, the Pope would never have changed his mind about the birth control matter. Fergus Nolan probably had nothing to do with it. And I was not even a believer. But there was that superstitious contract, to which M.M. had made me privy. If Fergus took the old-fashioned line, and the Pope took the old-fashioned line, the Almighty would give a baby to Fergus and M.M. If she became pregnant, I knew that I would have lost her for ever; the nature of my love for her would change; the unrealistic fantasy of it would be broken.

'Listen, Julian – when I said I was divorced, that was true. What I forgot to mention was that since then I've gotten married again,' said Dorset abruptly.

'Oh.'

'What happened – it was real nice but . . .'

'A lot of things are like that. Real nice but.'

'Don't be sore, Julian.'

'I'm not. Honestly, I'm not.'

She laughed and imitated the way in which I pronounced the word *honestly*.

'What does your husband do – and won't he be wondering where you are?'

'He's visiting his mother who lives in Miami, and he's a very wonderful guy and I' – she swigged the last of that fizzy beer – 'I feel like a complete bastard.'

'Is it the first time something like that's happened?'

'Uh-huh.'

'I feel honoured.'

'Still friends?'

'Of course.'

We remained on this footing for the remainder of the week, during which I was surprised to receive a written invitation to stay with Mr Everett on the following weekend. That is, I was asked to stay not in his New York apartment but at Greenlawns, Yorkshire, Connecticut, one of his places in the country. No need to worry about transport arrangements since he needed an extra car brought up to Yorkshire, and he had deputed Dorset to drive a spare Chevrolet from the parking lot under the Everett Foundation in E. 63rd St.

As the day approached – a Friday – we both had plenty of time to reflect upon this journey together. I looked forward to getting to know Dorset a little better. We could not discuss what had happened in the Library, since the day after Mr Leegrober returned from Cape Cod – amazingly, just as pale as when he went away and no less wizened. I was not going to press my suit where it was not wanted, but I should have liked the chance to clear the air – to do something with Dorset which was companionable but non-sexual. A three-hour drive to stay with the boss might have been an ideal way of making friends.

Maybe I underestimated the extent to which our romp in the Library had made her feel like a 'complete bastard'. That old perennial, the unknowability of other people's marriages, which I experienced so painfully in Wiseman Road with the Nolans, came into play here. Did Dorset fear that a drive with me would tempt her to further disloyalties – verbal or physical? Or did she, by contrast, so much regret what had taken place between us that she could not tolerate the idea of spending three hours alone in a car with me? Or – another possibility – was her husband meant to have been of the party and did she feel she could not face this?

Whatever the truth, she waited until the Friday morning to leave me in the lurch. I turned up at the Library as usual, and Leegrober brought me, together with one leaf of the juvenile Albion Pugh – it was a letter to Lampitt describing his joy at reading what had evidently been recommended by Jimbo himself, William Morris's *Earthly Paradise* – another letter which concluded *Best, Dorset*.

A sore throat, a high fever, a fear that it might all turn to influenza were adduced as excuses for her withdrawal from the party. I got the picture. Our afternoon and evening together in the Library had been the sort of crazy thing which married women sometimes have to do. There was no point in trying to speculate what marital tension (or lack of it) had led her to the sexual rampage in the Reading Room;

the hot weather, or a simple question of hormones, such as Fergus Nolan would have understood, could have explained the way in which she had behaved. In the subsequent days when we had met in the Library she had handled the situation with consummate tact; but a long drive in a hot car, and a weekend at Greenlawns were different kettles of fish. In retrospect I salute Dorset's delicacy in withdrawing from a situation which would either have been embarrassing to us both, or led to an emotional entanglement which both of us would have come to regret. At the time, I was left, despite her copious written instructions, in a state of panic. I had never driven on American roads before; the prospect of having to go to the parking-lot, take the Chev. and drive to Yorkshire, Connecticut, filled me with foreboding.

Dorset's directive was, however, punctiliously detailed. I followed its instructions to the letter that Friday morning. Already, at 9 a.m. the cockroaches on my bedroom floor must have baked, for there was an eery stillness and a strange odour which even overpowered that of my unaccomplished laundry as I locked my door and headed downstairs past the still-closed door of the taxidermist. I took the bus up Madison Avenue and alighted at E. 63rd Street.

A man in a pale grey peaked cap and matching frock coat with epaulettes was expecting me at the door of the main entrance. He telephoned for another man, this time in a black peaked cap, who escorted me to the garage beneath ground level. There was awaiting me the Chev. with the keys in the ignition. The car itself was several times larger than the apartment which I had left behind in 14th Street – or so it felt. It took a while to realise how generously I could spread myself in its ridiculous proportions. Hal (he of the black peaked cap) had been detailed to make sure that I knew my way out of town. The details were repeated to me several times over and I listened. I hated the idea of missing my turning and being marooned in a rich man's car in some adventurously poverty-stricken part of the city. The very words 'Spanish Harlem' were enough to bring me out in a gooseflesh of terror.

In time, I was cruising along the fairway having left Manhattan behind me. The sky above the open roof of the car was blue. Suburbs grew boskier, then gave way to open country; larch, birch and oak, heavily in leaf, splashed refreshing washes of green on either side of me. Dorset's written notes even informed me (quite accurately) when I should start to feel hungry. An hour and a half down the road, I was told, there was a roadhouse where I could eat a burger and fries. Obedient to her whim, and to the pangs of my own stomach, I pulled off the road at exactly the point decreed.

It was a small roadhouse, not much more than a wooden hut set back from the side of the highway, with a large parking-lot where patrons were evidently expected to consume their meals. Wooden tables with benches had been placed there for the purpose. I settled myself at one such table with my flavourless bun – a quarter-pounder – and the fries which were crisp but also flavourless. I never mastered the fact that, by contrast with the cuisines of Europe, flavour was not something which you got out of American food; it was something which you squirted on to it from ketchup bottles and mustard jars. I swilled down the bun and the mince with some Coca-Cola, thinking that it was actually what my aunt – in those days of rationing when one wasted nothing and even the nastiest bits of an animal found their way into the kitchen mincer – would have called a rissole. Aunt Deirdre, in quite a different mode, eschewed flavour when food was in question, so in my strange way I felt perfectly at home – though suffering mentally from the knowledge that all the food set before me would lead to trouble the next morning. Presumably, in their own homes, Americans eat as much in the way of roughage as we do; and in the period slightly later than my narrative, in the 1970s, I know that the craze for health food, bran and high-fibre diets swept the northern Americas as it did Europe. In my very limited experience, however, of their public eating places on my three visits to the United States – those two for research and my more recent return to New York for the theatrical 'One Man Show' – the menus might as well have been headed RECIPES FOR CONSTIPATION. (I so well remember the inquisitions each morning at Seaforth Grange, when Mrs Binker would quiz us about the success or otherwise of our matutinal motions; only complete idiots would ever own up to a failure, since the remedy proffered by Mrs Binker if she ever managed to extract a confession from us produced extremes far worse than the slight lethargy induced by a lazy bowel action. Timpson, the head boy, later an evangelical bishop, had once owned up that he had not 'been'. The extravagant overdose administered by Mrs Binker, had

145

led to appalling noises and smells from Timpson for several days. Since religious psychology is of perennial interest, I have often wondered whether Timpson's early manifestation of a tendency to be constipated might bear any relation to his adoption of the more determinist varieties of Protestantism, it being a noticeable fact that Luther, for example, was a martyr to the condition which Mrs Binker, with her lethally efficacious syrup of figs bottle, was so vigilant to keep at bay in her young charges at Seaforth Grange. Bowel movements tend to be a pre-pubescent – and then again, much later, a senile – obsession. Intrusive as the regime was at the public-school to which I went, aged thirteen, after I left the Binkers' care, I never remember anyone expressing the slightest interest in whether or not I'd crapped; and even Mr Treadmill, my charismatic, hypochondriac English master – he who first introduced me to the works of James Petworth Lampitt, an old boy of the school – never made obvious or overt reference to this particular activity, obsessed though he was by the digestive process in general, and its pitifully frequent malfunction in his own particular case.

Thoughts of Treadmill flitted in and out of consciousness; though thought would be the wrong word for my state of mind when consuming the quarter-pounder if it suggests to the reader any logical or linear process of ratiocination. It is, however, one of the examples of that extraordinary phenomenon, very common in my experience, whereby somebody one has not seen for months, or even for years, comes to mind a few minutes before one hears their voice again on the telephone, receives a letter from them or even meets them again in person. It is one of the many tiny areas of experience which would appear to undermine rationalism, for, while it would be mad to draw any conclusions from the phenomenon, it would be perverse to deny that it happens, and it is impossible to see how it could be explained in a purely materialistic or Darwinian scheme.

While having such a random mental magic-lantern show in which stray impressions, opinions and memories flashed up on some interior screen, very much like the old slide lectures we used to have at school in lieu of entertainment (some of the pictures upside down; some mirror fashion because the slide had been put in back to front, and many only approximating to a clear focus), I munched on my dry food, regretting the snobbery which had made me eschew any of the brightly coloured sauces, and half noticing my fellow-wayfarers at the roadhouse. A high proportion of them were truck drivers or travelling salesmen who seemed as fittingly in place as the cars in the parking-lot which surrounded us. Here and there, however, a character stood out among the crowd. The precise, smooth, shaven figure at the table next to my own, for instance, seemed painfully at variance with his surroundings. In the absence of a table-cloth, he had laid two paper napkins before him and he was eating his chips delicately with the help of a plastic fork. He took extremely small mouthfuls and if there was the smallest danger of some salt or a fragment of chips falling from his lips he dabbed them with short frantic gestures with a third paper napkin held perpetually in his left hand. I found it hard to guess his age – though assumed he was well past sixty; his stretched, perfectly-smooth skin seemed more female than male. A face-lift? And whose face? There was, distinctly, something familiar about it. He noticed me staring, and allowed a watery smile to play over those much-dabbed lips. I looked away, embarrassed by his eye-contact; he returned to his paperback which I then noticed, to my considerable surprise, was *Prince Albert* by James Petworth Lampitt, the very book which had prompted in Henry James so emptily effusive a 'thank you' and in myself, reading the book in the school sanatorium half a century after the Master, an addiction to Jimbo's books. For a short moment I indulged the fantasy that the old party at the next table was the emanation of Jimbo himself, for that, as I realised, was whom he so strikingly resembled. Then the old man, and his book, were jerked out of my consciousness by the group of young people congregated at the far end of the picnic-tables. I took it that they were travelling in the couple of dormobiles parked in the lot. Such travellers were a familiar sight at that date; the eye had grown used, in England, to the feebler imitations of the real thing in the United States.

It was (*mutatis mutandis*) as if we had returned to the Middle Ages when troubadours, beggars, friars, religious crackpots, pilgrims, wandered the highways of Europe. This particular band of pilgrims – fifteen or so in number – seemed so much like the others whom I saw daily sitting in Washington Square in New York City that I had hardly given them a glance. Both sexes wore their hair long, the men favouring beards and everyone tending to be draped in beads. Some-

one was strumming and slapping a guitar and intoning, in a strangu-
lated voice, 'SADDIS – FACK – SHUN'. It did not sound as if he
had achieved satisfaction. In fact, from his screwed-up features it was
almost as if he had been eating too many burgers, and clogging the
bowels; but his companions swayed along sympathetically to his words,
and repeated – 'Satisfaction'.

Having 'dropped out' of the stultifying conformity of suburban
middle America, they had lost no time in acquiring a uniform and a
set of conventions, and even a language which – so it seemed to
someone who was at home in neither world – was just as rigid as the
world they had left. That was why I hardly noticed this gang – they
blended into the roadhouse as flavourlessly as the hamburgers. It was
therefore all the more a surprise when one of their number – the
only one who was neither young, nor bearded, nor long-haired, nor
American – arose and waved to me.

It was Treadmill. A letter, some years before, had told me the news
that he had left the school and, as a result of some domestic upheaval,
emigrated to the United States. He had got a job in a Liberal Arts
college somewhere in upstate New York, and it had been half in my
mind, in the intervals of research, that I should try to re-establish
contact.

'My dear Julian.'

Yeeair.

The Treadmill voice and mannerisms seemed all the more comically
pronounced when heard in an American setting. When from time to
time I had seen him in London, and even done some broadcasting
work with him (though never quite daring to address him by his first
name, Val), I had come to think how crude our schoolboy imitations
of him had been. Among his American students, however, it seemed
as if Treadmill was hamming up the crudest Treadmill imitation of
them all – or so I initially decided, perhaps unfairly. In their company,
he seemed radiantly happy. The dreadful gloom which, together with
a powerful odour of TCP, had almost perpetually surrounded him in
the foggy Midland town where I was educated, seemed here to have
lifted. His skin – in England an unhealthy pale yellow – had turned
nut brown, and his moustache pure white.

'We're making our way -- yeair – as I expect you can guess – to
Amherst.'

148

'Why?'

'You know,' one of the girls at Treadmill's side explained helpfully, 'like Senator McCarthy's giving a speech.'

She was a spectacularly beautiful person, whose perfectly straight, very long yellow hair fell to a tight, blue-jeaned waist. Her upper figure amply shaped the cheesecloth blouse. Lilith, or Eve before the Fall, she seemed entirely lacking in guile. The serious innocence of her features, and their fanaticism, challenged one's cynical old European assumptions. I did not necessarily find it in my heart to admire this new order of being, even then; but this did not obviate the problem of politeness in such a gale of purity, and the perennial English question, always in mind when conversing with strangers, whether it is more ill-mannered to admit total ignorance of (therefore indifference to) a subject of burning concern to one's interlocutor, or to attempt some form of bluff. My state of knowledge, as far as American politics was concerned, was a perfect case of a little learning being a dangerous thing. I was on the verge of stating that I believed Senator McCarthy was dead (or anyway removed from the scene) and that it amazed me that someone as obviously on the side of love, peace and joy as herself should have taken the trouble to travel in very hot weather to hear the famous denunciations of unAmerican behaviour in black film stars or pinkish university professors. She would never have believed me if I had come out with this opinion, believing it to be a joke in incredibly poor taste, since she was obviously one of those who looked to the *other*, the new Senator McCarthy, as to a Saviour.

Like everyone else, I had been shocked by the assassinations – Dr King's in the spring, and now, more recently, that of Bobbie Kennedy, but as for knowing the names of American politicians, or where they stood in the spectrum of political ideas, I was as ignorant as the average American would be if questioned as to the causes of Vernon Lampitt's exclusion from Harold Wilson's Labour Cabinet of 1964. The enormous following of Senator Eugene McCarthy among the young, his popularity, as a poet and a friend of Robert Lowell, with intellectuals, his straightforward moral objections to Vietnam, the growing tide of popular support for him among students, had all been in the newspapers, but this was precisely the sort of news – when I got round to buying a paper – which I always skipped, turning for

149

preference to the murder stories and divorces on page three and to the obituaries.

'Lowell said to me, as it happens, in a letter written only two weeks ago, yeair,' said Treadmill, 'that quite possibly we have not had such a man in American politics since the days of Jefferson.'

'So you've known Val in England?' asked another of the young women – not quite in the Lilith league, but still of a heart-stopping Caravaggioesque beauty – a head of boyish curls, and the muscular brown shoulders and arms emerging from the singlet, suggesting the young Bacchus or David about to slay Goliath.

I explained to her that 'Val' had taught me at school. In such a context, to have referred to him as Mr Treadmill would have been stuffy to say the least, but it was vaguely shocking to find that this man, who could so terrify classrooms of adolescent English boys, had a very different approach when teaching a different age group, and a different sex, in a different country.

'His classes are just – the best.' This from Lilith rather than Bacchus.

'So they were in my school.'

Treadmill's Shredded Wheat moustache stretched across his upper lip to accommodate the proud grin.

'My pupils in England were more diligent – here they are very much more articulate. And, I might add,' – the next two words, which were 'more beautiful', were not exactly spoken, so much as thrown away in that distinctive nasal grunt of his. (It was fifteen or twenty years before such compliments could have landed Treadmill in disciplinary trouble with the college authorities, if not with the police, and no one appeared to object to them on this occasion.)

'Val's teaching modern poetry in this semester?' said another of the hippies on whose lips (a common American idiosyncrasy of pronunciation) every single utterance sounded interrogative. 'Like Pound? Like Wallace Stevens? And, you know, like, I'm doing this course on Fantasy? Like Tolkien? Like Lewis? And, you know, like Val really knew these guys? He even met Albion Pugh?'

'An old friend of Julian's here.'

This fact was not something I regarded, at that time, as much worth writing home about. Its effect on Treadmill's pupils, however, was extraordinary. It was not unlike telling a party of young people

150

at a pop concert that one was on nodding terms with Jimi Hendrix, or mentioning, at the Nolans' lunch table, that one took regular summer vacations with Mother Teresa of Calcutta. The revived popularity of Albion Pugh's novels (first published during the Second World War) among the Flower People of the late 1960s was one of the many strange reversals which that decade brought about.

'But, Julian – you know my address; I don't know yours.'

'Let me write it on a piece of paper.'

From all that group of wandering scholars, it was surprisingly difficult to rustle up one pencil and one piece of paper. When this had been accomplished however and I had written down my address, Treadmill said, 'But you must be near St Mark's Place.'

'I think I am. I live in this strange tenement above a taxidermist's shop. You must come and look me up if you are ever in New York in the next two or three weeks.'

'You've met Wystan of course?'

'Do you mean Auden? No.'

I felt sheepish to admit that – with my few acquaintances out of town – I had met almost no one in the whole of America, this trip, apart from Dorset and Mr Leegrober. Painfully, I lacked Treadmill's ability to pick people up, to collect them as if they were cigarette cards. I preferred loneliness to the possibility of seeming – if only in my own eyes – pushy.

'I shall give you a call,' said Treadmill, evidently meaning that he would communicate by telephone. How interesting that this great purist – who would punish us as boys so severely if we wrote or spoke ungrammatically, and who had once set a boy lines for using the expression 'OK' – was now so cheerfully adopting Americanisms into his speech.

'Do – please. There are things I'd like to discuss with you – things about which you could advise me.'

Treadmill nodded sagely and pressed his lips together, causing the moustache to become momentarily horizontal, an habitual gesture of old, suggestive of thought and care.

Treadmill's parting question as I made to go – 'Are you just motoring round, or do you have an end in sight?' – elicited from me the name of Virgil D. Everett. If my credit had shot up with Treadmill's young friends because I had met Albion Pugh it shot down again, sharpish, when my destination was made known.

'He's really, like sinister?' said Mr Interrogative.

'Yeah, sinister,' said Bacchus, who also spoke as if everything was a question – they all did it. 'You know, like, he killed his wife?'

'It is news to me he was ever married.'

'And now,' said Lilith with a passionate intensity, 'he is helping to murder little children in Vietnam, to murder trees with napalm, to murder birds and . . .' The next two words – rare fauna – I heard as *Ref Honour*. Momentarily thinking that this was yet another American politician of whom I had not heard, I panicked and, like a coward, I said, 'You know, I've hardly ever met Mr Everett.'

'I hardly ever met Adolf Hitler,' said Lilith contemptuously. She spat the words out, and one had the alarming impression that in spite of her generalised commitment to Peace, she would be prepared to make an exception in the case of Virgil D. – perhaps in the case, also, of Mr Everett's house-guests – and wring a few necks with her large, clean, capable hands.

(Strangely enough, if one had to be murdered, I can think of worse ways to go.)

'I would not *wanna* meet Hitler,' she further elaborated.

It would have been useless to debate this question – throw it open, as Treadmill would have said at our school debating societies, to the floor of the house. I am afraid that I belong to the school of thought that I should be interested to meet anyone, just the once, even the worst monster in history (if Hitler fits that description) if only to see what they were like. (Is this actually a moral question, rather than one of taste? As a child, I pined to be taken to the circus because I wanted the excitement of the high wire act, the smell of horse dung, the pathos of the performing dogs. One did not necessarily have to approve of training animals to dance, in order to wish to see it, if only once.) I do not consider *meeting* someone suggests that one endorses all their political views. Nor did I really consider that old Mr Everett (whatever sins he had committed) was really in the Nazi league of malignity. But it was immediately obvious that there would be no point in trying out such ideas on the present company.

'It is true,' said Treadmill, 'that Virgil D. Everett – a close friend of Mayor Daley, incidentally, of Chicago – has made major contributions to Democratic Party funds. I am speaking generally. The contributions have come chiefly from Lixabrite. It's no secret that he violently – and I use the adverb advisedly – opposes everything which Senator McCarthy stands for, not least his religion. Nor is it a secret that he passionately dislikes Humphrey.'

I was just sufficiently clued-up not to ask, 'Humphrey who?' That was the level of my knowledge.

I knew these matters were of profound importance to the future of the United States – hence, to the future of the world. It was frivolous of me to be so ignorant. Sad to say, I was not as enthusiastic about politicians as I had once been. The political territory where I should once have felt at home seemed to have been hijacked by prigs. It did not force me to lurch in any other direction – left or right – but merely to become bored by the whole process. One did not need to have heard of their new hero to know that people like Senator McCarthy get absolutely nowhere in late-twentieth-century politics.

Vernon Lampitt, the only politician whom I met regularly, shared the beliefs of these young people about Mr Everett. I would have conceded that if one were to investigate his place in the general scheme it would turn out to stink. Safer to see him merely as an old buffer who happened to own the Lampitt Papers.

Treadmill waved as I pulled out of the parking lot in the Chev. His light-wristed motions suggested that he was conducting music, in time to the guitarist's rendition of 'Strawberry Fair'. I looked about for the old man whom I had seen at the roadhouse – the one with an oddly familiar face – but he was not to be seen.

The car left behind suburb and lowland. Larch woods and pines and birch climbed mountainous country on either side of the fairway. It could not be long now before Château Everett came into view. Dorset's message suggested that Greenlawns would be difficult to miss.

'Drive right on through Yorkshire and Greenlawns is on your right stuck right on the side of the hill.'

Yorkshire is a small town, first settled, I believe, in the seventeenth century. The old pilgrims' roads can still be traced under the coniferous floor of the forests round about, but they have left no architectural trace. It's a pretty, prosperous little place now where people from New York have second homes. There's a white clapboard Presbyterian

153

church with a steeple and a clock tower. There is a tiny parade of stores selling hardware and groceries. The houses are well set back from mown lawns. Station-wagons wait in double garages, ready to transport their regular cargo between Yorkshire and New York – the grocery cartons, the dogs, the baby buggies, the kids by first and second marriages, the fishing-rods, the guns.

It flashed by in an instant, Yorkshire, more an impression than a place. And then – there it was, Greenlawns, just as Dorset had said, stuck right on to the side of a hill.

The mad King Ludwig of Bavaria would not have been entirely ashamed of its pinnacles, battlements, turrets, and variety of architectural styles. Parsifal's funeral could have been conducted before its old portcullis. As the Chevrolet scrunched the gravel of the drive, I felt that there was something sinister about the place, while trying to dismiss from my mind all the rumours about my host which had been coming my way: Vernon's view that he was an agent of the hard right in American politics – an idea corroborated by Treadmill's students; Christopher's suggestion that there was something erotically threatening about the man and his entourage – his extraordinary story of the hooker being kidnapped and made to 'perform' with the butler in front of Virgil D.'s lecherous gaze. Perhaps, rather than being a Wagnerian fantasy, these towers and gates were inspired by Dracula's Transylvania?

To park a car in front of such a pile would have seemed like a desecration of the wide empty drive, the terraces beneath, the urns bright with geraniums, the flights of stone steps. So, I slowed down, and drove through the stable arch at the side of the house. In a yard at the back there were several cars parked, but no one was about.

I left the car and felt shy about walking round to the front of the house. The front porch would have made the west front of Rouen cathedral seem unassuming. It somehow wasn't the sort of front door you could stroll up to and ring the bell. Besides, the bell, if rung, might well have been a great booming thing like those of Notre Dame de Paris in the film. Charles Laughton as Quasimodo, gibbering and ugly, would probably have appeared swinging on the end of the bell pull. So, I found an open door at the side of the house and I walked down a few corridors which would have dwarfed the cloisters at Bec and found myself in a large stone hall. When I say large, I suppose it would have been fair to say that you could put Timplingham Parish Church in it and rattle it like a die. Gothic columns swooped to a vaulted ceiling where the bosses were emblazoned with heraldic devices. Huge chairs, thrones such as Charlemagne might have lolled in, were placed at each corner of the hall, and in the middle was an octagonal table the size of a skating-rink. The suits of armour stood at the bottom of the stairs. The walls were heavy with spears, targes, halberds and every variety of mediaeval or bogus mediaeval weaponry.

Into such castles in Arthurian legend, knights came with a single task of heroism to perform. Sent forth by the Lampitts to clear Jimbo's name, I had penetrated the Everett Archive, and set eyes upon the Lampitt Papers. Was it now my duty to complete the Quest, and to tell Mr Everett that Hunter was a liar; that his apparently 'researched' book was nothing more than a plodding work of fiction with footnotes; that the only evidence which he ever adduced for Jimbo's sex life was his own mysteriously codified and numbered system of references, since no scholar had ever done what I had done? Surely I had to tell Mr Everett, didn't I? And yet, how was I to explain to him that I had defied all the rules of the Ann-Louise Everett Library and penetrated the inner sanctum? I did not need to confess that I had done so clad only in underpants and socks, but there was some need to concoct an explanation, one which would not land Dorset in trouble.

These thoughts occupied me while I was shown to my bedroom which, if not equal in size to the hall downstairs, was several times larger than any room in which I had ever slept. A large four-poster dominated one end of the room. At the other end, a chintz sofa, a grate. The allusion to the English country house merely served to point up the difference between a place like Greenlawns and – say – Mallington Hall. Everything here was so clean and – my eye began to take in the bedroom walls, hung with Salvador Dalis – so expensive. The difference was further emphasised by the entry of a black maid who placed on the ottoman before the fireplace what was evidently supposed to be an English tea-tray – a very welcome silver pot, silver jug and Worcester cup and saucer. A plate of cheese, crackers, and strawberries.

'Just put the tray down,' said the butler who had escorted me to these quarters. He spoke with unnecessary fierceness to the woman, who made a very speedy retreat.

'And now – you'll be wanting me to unpack,' announced the man, adding, as if by further way of punishment, the word 'sir'.

I have already made allusion to the process of dissociation which was, in me, the first indication that I was losing my wits; aware of these symptoms, and frightened by them, I had begun to distrust the impressions of other people which at first formed themselves in my head. Sometimes these impressions were reliable; but, if I was observing them in the 'wrong' frame of mind, I could very likely find that I had turned them into characters from 'The Mulberrys', or from my own past. The familiarity of the butler's face and mannerisms immediately put me on my guard. Merely because he was 'a bit like' one of the sergeant-majors with whom I'd done Basic Training was likely, in my present frame of mind, to send me off into an inner reverie, in which I could not distinguish between things said by the RSM inside my head and the butler who was threatening to unpack my suitcase.

'I can easily do my own unpacking,' I said to this vaguely terrifying domestic.

'As you wish, sir.' His English voice was a surprise. Was he? Yes he was, he was! He really was – surely? – the mysterious visitor to the taxidermist's shop in E. 14th Street? The man who had asked for Christopher and who, with a sinister leer, had inquired whether I was 'standing in' for Christopher?

'Only – it's a very small suitcase. I'll have this unpacked for you in a jiffy,' he said with quiet pleasure. This time, the pause between the end of the sentence and the enunciation of the word 'sir' was so long as to be satirical. Could he have been both my nocturnal visitor and my old sergeant-major? Not impossible.

With a contemptuous flick of both thumbs, he revealed the shaming contents of my small suitcase – some dirty socks and underpants which I had hoped, while staying at Greenlawns, to get washed; a couple of fraying shirts. A bottle of whisky, half consumed. Notebooks. Crumpled cigarette packets. A British passport.

'Have you lived long in the United States?' I asked him, to distract us both from the unseemly sight of my belongings.

'I'll get someone up to see to these, sir,' he said. 'About ten years, in answer to your question. I was just coming out of the Paras . . .'

So I had got that right.

'This job cropped up – it seemed too good a chance to pass over.'

I wanted, without gross intrusiveness, to know how it had cropped up. He was staring at me now. I could not interpret the steely gaze of those grey eyes. Was he daring me to allude to his visit to my apartments in E. 14th Street? Or was he suffering from a moment of 'double take' similar to my own? Was he trying to place me in his mind?

'Do you get back often?'

'To London, sir?'

'Yes.'

'Mr Everett has always been very generous. And, as you know, sir, he loves London. His favourite city. So, yes. We get back two or three times a year.'

By the time I was alone again, pouring Earl Grey from the superb teapot by the fireside, the butler had summoned the maid to come and 'do something' about my smalls. All the offending garments were spirited away in a plastic bag. An hour later, bathed and pomaded, I descended to the cavernous hall.

This ostentatiously vaulted part of the house – it came to me that evening as I stood there awkwardly with my glass in my hand looking around at my fellow-guests – was an exact replica of the lobby of the House of Lords at Westminster – another Gothic fantasy where I had occasionally lingered in shyness, waiting for Vernon to come and entertain me to the school food on offer in the peers' restaurant. The Greenlawns Gothic Lobby lacked the richness of Pugin's original – there was no gold paint, which is what made its shape initially unfamiliar. The greenish grey stone was quite unadorned, though the walls were hung with some superb old Mortlake tapestries depicting the story of Susannah and the Elders.

'It makes me feel a little as if I've been buried alive,' remarked the man on my left, whom I recognised as the elderly party from the roadhouse; recognised, too, as a face who was familiar but to which I could not put a name.

'Certainly.' I was tongue-tied, and only managed the added word 'sepulchral'.

Ref Honour, had he existed, would certainly have felt at home in that smart gathering of politicians, *hommes d'affaires* and their ladies. I felt hideously out of place. Kind as it had been of Mr Everett to have invited me, I should have been much happier, at that moment, alone on a stool in a diner, drinking a milkshake and reading *The Insulted and the Injured.*

'And they've cast us among the living dead,' he said *sotto voce,* coming slightly closer to my face than I would have wished on a first acquaintance. 'You and I are the only representatives of our,' he cast his eyes down like a shy girl admitting to an unplanned pregnancy, 'our calling.'

He was, I suppose, about seventy years of age. He wore a blue and white jacket and navy blue slacks. It did not look from his taut, pink skin, as if his face had ever needed a razor. Indeed, the short well-cut hair did not in any way diminish one's sense that he could easily have been a woman who had chosen to dress, for some reason, in this severe, but not excessively masculine, outfit. His breath, which I could actually feel on my face he stood so close, smelt of something very sweet and faintly chemical, presumably a pill or gargle taken as a prophylactic against halitosis. I realised within myself the symptoms of an embarrassment which all too frequently comes upon me – the knowledge that I was in the presence of someone who expected me to know who they were.

'I suppose most of them are politicians,' I said, looking at our fellow-guests.

'And their wives,' he hissed, with a smile of malicious triumph, which managed to implicate me in his suggestion that anyone who brought a wife was to be held in derision. Marriage, his smile implied, was foolish enough; but actually to bring your wife to a dinner, this was going too far.

'Do you know the significance of the term "spin doctor"?' he asked. I didn't. It was a couple of decades before I ever heard the compound in England.

All around us they were discussing The Situation: the progress of the war, the likely outcome of the election, the growth of student power.

'But, since Tev, all has changed. Ho is simply not going to give in, even if we send a million boys, two million, five million, and I tell you those kids are not going to stand for it.'

'We never had student riots in my day. I think Governor Reagan has the right idea of how to deal with these things, I do really.'

'You're saying that because a man has to sack his entire staff – and every single one of them fairies – there's nothing "on" him?'

'Newt, that is not reflective in any way upon the Governor's character, and you know it.'

I recognised this conversation – a few feet away from us – was being conducted by the Ahrlichs and a couple of richly-attired bespectacled figures, one of whom had been described by my new friend as a 'spin doctor'.

At this moment – from the direction in the lobby which (its Westminster original) would have led to the Chamber of the House and thrown up a scarlet and golden vista, with a glimpse of the Woolsack – Virgil D. Everett made his stately entrance. When I had first met Virgil D. in Claridge's all those years ago, he had seemed a perfectly amiable old codger who happened to speak rather slowly. Now that I had heard so many disconnected pieces of gossip about him, and so many denunciations of his political standpoint, I began to invest him with qualities which I had not observed before. In spite of his prodigious wealth, was there not something almost seedy about him, tobacco-stained and boozy? His smoothly-shaven upper lip glistened with sweat as did his bald brow and his palm as he clasped my hand. A pair of blue-tinted spectacles added to the impression of 'sinisterness' – the mad scientist who might have human guinea-pigs squealing in some sound-proofed laboratory where he practised fiendish experiments upon them. Yet it would be hard to say precisely what summoned up such a sense of evil as he squeezed my fingers with a large moist paw and murmured, 'I'm pleased . . .' The pause which followed this statement was so long that I thought this was all he was going to say. '. . . that you got here safely, Mr Ramsay.'

'The drive was easy.'

'I wish' . . . Again, a silence full of suspense. What did he wish? That I had delivered the Chevrolet in better condition? That I had brought Dorset? That I had not been illegally fornicating and rummaging in his Library? His absence of speech silenced either me or my new elderly companion, so that the voices around us were heard once more.

'I reckon now it could be anyone's race – Hubert Humphrey, Eugene . . .'

'Do not even say that name!'

159

'Look, you've got to be realistic.'

'You'll be saying next that Richard M. Nixon will become . . .'

'I'm not saying that. I can't see the American people electing Nixon, and for this simple reason . . .'

Perhaps he was prompted by the others; perhaps he had always intended to say, 'I wish you were visiting the United States at a happier period in its history, Mr Ramsay. We've got a nice crowd here, and I hope you have a good time – I believe you know the Ahrlichs, and we've got Karl and Michelle Watts, Jean and Frank Shultzmann – and Ol Pitman is well-known to you already.'

'We've only just this minute met,' said my elderly companion whom I now knew to be Ol Pitman. A 'B' movie actor who had never made any great success until a few years earlier. He usually played unscrupulous con-men or the cold-hearted 'brains' in some criminal gang. His villainy was made apparent to cinema audiences by his English accent. In fact it was a voice which was English only in origin, overlaid by years of exposure to American locutions. Having been a cinematic nobody, he had become famous in a television drama series called 'The Criminals'. Few would have been able to tell you that he was called Ol Pitman, but most regular television viewers, in England as well as in America, would have been able to recognise him as Mr Fettiplace, the member of the gang who could always talk his way into the room with the safe by some implausible claim to an Etonian education or aristocratic acquaintance. It occurs to me now, as I write these words, that Mr Fettiplace was a character not wholly dissimilar to Jason Grainger, the figure impersonated by myself on 'The Mulberrys'.

Holding his cigarette at the level of his ear, occasionally lifting the hand which held it higher so as to smooth the back of his head, Ol Pitman said to me, 'Now, let me get this right; you're doing the whole family or limiting yourself to James Petworth? You know, I suppose, that we all called him Jimbo?'

'Mr er . . .'

In the time it took Virgil D. to say my name, and to inform Ol Pitman that I knew a thing or two about the Lampitts, Ol had said, 'I'll have to watch what I say or I'll find you've put *me* in your book.'

Coral Ahrlich, as kittenish as I had ever known her, had come up to join us, and was heaping praise on Ol's television role as the stylish con-man. She spoke as rapidly as Virgil D. spoke slowly. A musician could have made an interesting arrangement of their voices, Virgil D. as the slow old bass, thump, thump, thumping along, while Coral's voice shot through a great diapason of notes rising to the high octaves and then plunging down into a sort of mockery of self.

'I' (top C), 'just lurvv' (really low on the keyboard), 'all those crazy little shows with really good character actors – Julian, you don't have those so much in England.' There was nothing so very remarkable about Coral's opinions, but the vehemence of her expression guaranteed attention; she shook and worried her words like a dog with a bone. ' "The Munsters", "Bilko", it's great. "Dick Van Dyke".'

Having been happy to be spoken of in the same breath as the other shows, Ol Pitman pursed his lips at the mention of Dick Van Dyke.

'So who are you and your husband *for*, if a non-politician may ask such a thing of a senator's wife, Mrs Ahrlich.'

'Newt's not a senator yet,' she said, 'we're hoping.'

One was fairly sure that Ol had made this mistake deliberately, in order to force his interlocutor to admit that her husband still had a long way to go before we needed to kowtow to the likes of her; this was an ample punishment for putting him in the Dick Van Dyke bracket.

It was while he was speaking that I realised why the features were so familiar; yes, I had seen 'The Criminals' and I agreed with Coral – there was (and, to this day, is) a liveliness about such television shows in the United States which is almost invariably absent from English television. But the long features of Ol's face should have announced to me at once 'who he was' even if he had not given me the clue – that afternoon in the parking-lot – of reading Jimbo's *Prince Albert*.

Years before – when I myself had first started acting – one of my aunt's weekly letters on Basildon Bond writing paper had posed the question, 'Your uncle wonders whether you will come across Orlando Lampitt. Rather a black sheep, we gather!!! A cousin of Jimbo's and Sargie's who went on the *stage* in 1928 . . .'

When, later in the evening, I was placed next to Ol Pitman at dinner, and was able to allude, quite casually, to the fact that his early years had been spent in Mombasa (where his father died of phlebitis),

161

he rolled his eyes in a manner which could not conceal admiration as well as flirtatious delight.

'My, you have been doing your detective work.'

I took the credit. It seemed more plausible that I had found out about Orlando Lampitt's family by means of research rather than asking him to believe that I had first learnt of his father's death by phlebitis, rather in the way that other children might learn nursery rhymes, or master the names of plants and animals, or cricketers or, nowadays I suppose, rock musicians. One did not have to sit down and *learn* the names of the Lampitts. In Timplingham Rectory we had them, as Mrs Webb and my grandmother had furiously agreed, 'coming out of our ears'.

I congratulate Virgil D. Everett, in retrospect, in bringing me together with Orlando Lampitt – as I prefer now to think of him. We very much forgot our manners, and neglected the rest of the company.

'Let 'em get on with it. I hate left-wing politicians – for obvious reasons.'

'These are left-wing?'

'They're Democrats, aren't they? Having not the smallest sympathy either with democracy or republicanism I have never felt tempted to vote in an American election. My family, as you know, have been passionately addicted to both heresies since the eighteenth century. Indeed old Joe Lampitt even entertained Benjamin Franklin at Mallington – and for two pins he might have emigrated to the land of the free if he hadn't been making so much money pouring beer and gin down the throats of the very workers he claimed to be redeeming with all his radical twaddle. We might have had a Lampitt State over here or a Lampitt President.'

'So you are not with your cousin Vernon?'

'Politically?'

'What other ways are there with Vernon?'

'Now you're being a little naughty.'

He spun out a strange tale that night, sometimes muttering under his breath about our host, and sometimes not needing to do so, for we were left alone by the politicians and their wives. What he told me was not incompatible – given their very different political viewpoints – with things I had heard from Christopher on my first visit to New York, and what I heard from the hippy followers of

162

Senator McCarthy. Virgil D. Everett, he hinted, had had a double life. On the one hand, there had been the huge law firm, the investments, the virtual ownership of Lixabrite, the political life and influence. On the other, there was his imaginative life. I do not know to this day how much time he managed to spend on his literary collection, but the fact that he chose to make it at all, rather than merely asking an investment manager to buy him Surrealist paintings in a sale-room, suggested a particular area of interest and pursuit. Nor – if Orlando Lampitt was to be believed – was this particular area of interest wholly imaginative or academic. Some such 'double life' as suggested by Christopher was alleged to take place; and the butler, John, was apparently part of it.

'Do you mean you have met John before?' I asked.

Orlando Lampitt's eyebrows shot up his smooth brown forehead, and down again.

'If I asked you if you had visited the Pacemaker's Arms would you know what I meant?' he asked.

'No.'

'It's a pub.'

'It sounds like one.'

'It's near Marble Arch.'

'And?'

'Do you remember the long passage in Proust, I think at the beginning of *Sodome et Gomorrhe*, in which he meditates on the strange fact that there are actually in this world young men who are attracted to older men? Do you remember that passage?'

'I'm ashamed to say, I'm saving up Proust for my old age.'

Rather than make absurd expressions of surprise at this gap in my reading, he just said, 'Treat in store. Truly. Anyway, he did not lie, Mr Proust. By the way, do you know that Jimbo met him once? It was arranged by Harold Nicolson.'

'It's hinted at in one of the reviews, but I can't find any . . .'

'Oh, you must let me tell you about that in a minute. I just wanted to establish that you were aware of the phenomenon.'

'I don't think I was.'

'Oh yes. All the straight world assumes that the homosexual world is peopled by a lot of older people trying to corrupt younger people. Homosexuals from Socrates onward or downward have been accused

163

of it. The truth is much odder, as the trials of Oscar Wilde make clear, that if it makes any sense to talk about corruption, it is very often the young who corrupt the old. Certainly there are boys and men who prefer older men; and sometimes not just older men but . . .' he paused and looked me up and down carefully. Evidently, I was both too old, too young, or too plain to fit in with what he was about to confide, so he added, 'There are some boys who want old men. Can you believe that?'

'I have never thought of it.'

'The Pacemaker's Arms is not a pub where dirty old men go to pick up boys. It's the old men who are lolling on the bar stools there, and the young men who are cruising.'

'Why are you telling me all this?'

'If you had ever been one of the young men you might have met me before now – on one of my visits to London,' he said. 'It's how Virgil met John,' – with a swivel of his eyeballs, rather than a motion of the head, he indicated the butler – 'and it's also how he met one or two other golden boys we could mention.'

The identity of the others had to remain a mystery because at that point, guilty at neglecting her neighbour, one of the political wives turned to me and engaged me in conversation. I think she talked to me about her children's prospects at college, my own marital status, holiday plans – it was waffle, whatever was said.

It is not entirely possible for me to recall the events of that weekend; they won't focus. It is not hard to see why, since it was while I was staying there that the telegram arrived: GRANDMOTHER'S CONDITION CRITICAL COME HOME. RAMSAY. After Granny's death – not immediately after, but pretty soon – I suffered the mental collapse from which it took over a year to recover. Memory is always selective, but it seems to have made a particularly rigorous job of cutting out details from the moment that Granny's death was made known to me. Lots of reasons for that, I guess – her links with my childhood being chief among them.

So, I am afraid that I simply cannot remember the order in which I learnt the tittle-tattle about Virgil D. Everett's secret life, and his patronage when in London of the Pacemaker's Arms. (This was not its real name, of course – it was the nickname given to it for obvious reasons by patrons.) The fact that Virgil D. – then still married to the late Mrs Everett – had engaged a domestic in this London hostelry was not altogether surprising, nor even scandalous. But this could not be said for Orlando's suggestion that the very presence of the Lampitt Papers in the Ann-Louise Everett Collection was attributable to a convergence of erotic sympathies between Mr Everett and the custodian of his archive, Jimbo's biographer.

'You're not saying that Hunter . . . ?' I asked.

Orlando Lampitt placed the tip of his right index finger against his pursed lips; and suddenly a well-groomed old gentleman became Little Miss Muffet.

'You were surely aware that a certain young woman was, as we might say, on the committee?' he asked darkly. 'Even if you did not know of her *penchant* for the older members of the Club?'

A stream of disconnected, and disagreeable, images came into my head – of Hunter arm in arm with our sadistic old headmaster – at the funeral of the Woolworth Magdalene; of Hunter at Claridge's – having negotiated the sale of the Lampitt Papers to Virgil D. – though we did not know this at the time, coming across the dining-room with Mr Everett, and with my wife, Anne. My certainty at the time had been that Anne was having an affair with Hunter – certainly she was in love with him – but was he merely using this convenient emotional fact as a way of getting closer to Sargie, closer to the Papers? I thought of the hold which Hunter had exercised over Sargie himself, and over my cousin Felicity; I remember even my uncle Roy being rather charmed by him – frightened but charmed – when Felicity had brought Hunter to tea at the Rectory – as her 'intended'. Only Treadmill, to give him his due, had been disappointed by Hunter on the very first time I ever met the man at our school literary society. But perhaps Treadmill was alone among these older men in being one hundred per cent heterosexual; in having no wish, in the smallest part of his hidden soul, to visit the Pacemaker's Arms and to see what alluring creatures might be on offer there.

In memory, now, Hunter seems more than ever like the Angel of Death since his appearance at Greenlawns and the arrival of the telegram from England are indistinguishable. I do not know whether they really happened within a few minutes or hours of one another, or whether in fact one happened in the evening and another in the morning. Nor will I ever know how much of Orlando Lampitt's scandalous talk was true. In my experience, journalistic *exposé* as a literary form makes it harder not easier to perceive the truth. By ripping open their subjects, the exposers present no more realistic a picture than would a surgeon who asked us to judge a person by a swollen liver or a blocked windpipe. One bit of butcher's meat looks much like another. The veil and the curtain can tell us more than the striptease. Several of the people staying that weekend at Greenlawns subsequently found themselves hanging up in the window of the *Washington Post* with a hook through their mouths; I didn't recognise the 'likeness'. By association, Virgil D. was implicated in some of that scandal – skulduggery in high places, bugged rooms, drugs, here and there a transvestite prostitute or a hell-fire preacher – perhaps the same character – photographed in a motel room, laundered bank accounts, assumed names, murders. Into this strange world, it was concluded, Virgil D. somehow fitted; Christopher Johnson – either as a young man, or a druggy, or a political enemy, or a friend who got carried away with some game – was deemed guilty of Virgil's murder, and – so it was generally acknowledged – one hell of a lot of people breathed a sigh of relief when Christopher himself died. It was a good season for deaths, the couple of years covered by this volume, and the Angel of Death had not finished his reaping just because I had received a telegram announcing Granny's long-expected, but somehow hideously shocking, demise.

'You know, long ago,' I began to whisper to my new friend, my new *old* friend, Orlando, 'I was once sitting in the steam-room in a Turkish bath in London.'

'Really?'

'I went there for a Turkish bath.'

'Of course.'

'But I found myself sitting next . . .'

I did not finish my sentence. Even as I spoke, the butler opened the dining-room door and announced a late guest. Flushed but self-confident, a preternaturally youthful fifty-one, Hunter's words were, 'Virgil, I'm *sorry*.' There were settings where these words would have been even more appropriate – some of them I had already been running through in my head.

It emerged that, having jetted from London the previous evening, he had spent the day recording an interview with Robert Lowell for British television.

'That man has some very strange views,' said Coral briskly.

'I promised I'd do this film,' sighed Hunter. 'It had been on the cards for some time.'

The self-deprecatory weariness told us all that a self-publicist's work is never done. Having rushed from his television colleagues, he still wore his make-up, a faintly orange foundation cream which gave his face an even more than usually impassive air.

'Julian,' he said, 'how very nice to see you.'

But, even as he spoke, John the butler was muttering in my ear.

'Mr Ramsay – a telegram has arrived for you, sir.'

SEVEN
(Afterwards)

What do you mean by Limbo?
By Limbo I mean a place of rest, where the souls of the just who died
before Christ were detained.

Pope Paul VI: *It is most irregular to find myself here. In the first place, I have been baptised, and this place is for those who have not been admitted to the Church. In the second place, I have not yet died.*

Socrates: *My dear sir, you cannot imagine what pleasure it gives us – all the more so, since you are, as we understand, a famous overseer or governor in Rome.*

Paul: *Yes, but you see, that very word 'overseer' in your language, which has become 'bishop' in ours, is . . .*

Agennetos: *Before your arrival, Socrates was discussing with us the perennially interesting question of the soul, and its immortality.*

Paul: *I have, of course, read the works of Plato, and I know what Socrates thinks about this subject.*

Plato: *My dear! I'm too flattered. What do you think, boys? I think our new visitor is very sweet in a simian sort of a way.*

Paul: *(squirming) And, of course, given the state of knowledge which prevailed in fourth-century Athens, you, sir, and you, ever-dear Socrates, for I think I can say that I love you, having read the works of Plato . . .*

Socrates: *(laughing) You don't want to believe that I actually said any of the things attributed to me by this rascal! Plato is a poet – which is*

168

why he has such acid things to say about all the other poets in his works. All poets hate one another. You even wanted to banish Homer from your Republic, you bitch!

Agennetos: Homer? Isn't she that dear old blind lady who told me those terribly sad stories the other day?

Plato: No, dear, that was Tiresias.

Socrates: Agennetos is a slow learner.

Plato: Socrates means to say, that Agennetos is slow to remember his former states of knowledge.

Socrates: Oh, yes, I remember now. According to you, I'm supposed to think that because we all had a former existence, the act of learning is really an act of remembrance of this former condition of being and knowledge.

Paul: I'm afraid we can't believe that. You see, that's the doctrine of reincarnation. The Hindus believe that, and in your state of ignorance – the fact that only a limited degree of knowledge has been permitted to you, and you are living without the dispensation of divine grace . . . outside the divine revelation . . .

Socrates: Pause! You have already supplied us with quite a number of useful topics with which to occupy ourselves. How long have we got?

All the other young men, who have heard this joke once too often, say in a weary **Chorus:** An Eternity!

Socrates: Well, it is true that I talk so much that some of you believe that I am capable, quite literally, of going on forever; but Brother Paul here is still bound to the world of time, so let us begin by stating the matters on which we agree.

Alcibiades: Such as that Italian boys are really gorgeous, especially Sicilians.

Paul: I have always thought so, but I in my present position could not possibly comment.

Alcibiades: Hoity, toity!

Plato: Do you remember that slave-boy that Adeimantus found in Syracuse – but ah! Here are Adeimantus and Glaucon with grapes and olives and Chian wine. You see, we do ourselves rather proud in Limbo; we can conjure up more or less anything we imagine, and because we are not bound by your invented new superstitions, Paul, we are quite outside your power.

Paul: Superstitions?

169

Plato: *That blend of my books with Jewish folklore which you entitle universalism . . .*

Paul: *You mean Catholicism. It's the same word, but . . .*

Socrates: *This is all a red herring. Paul and I were trying to establish the matters about which we are agreed. We are completely agreed, for example, that a human being's highest good is to be found in the exercise of virtue.*

Paul: *Certainly, Socrates.*

Socrates: *And we are both agreed, too, that the soul is immortal.*

Alcibiades: (in an all-too-audible aside) *Does anyone realise we've been lolling about, listening to Socrates talk about this subject for the last two and a half thousand years and we still haven't got any closer to understanding it!*

Paul: *Of course.*

Socrates: *Which is why human thoughts and actions are of such profound importance.*

Two fleas: (who are present in Alcibiades's abundant chest hair speak in the language of fleas and, therefore, even in limbo, they are unheard) *We too have souls; why should a soul be 'important' merely because it is immortal? We have mortal souls and so, we should contend, do you.*

Socrates: *Now, if a soul is immortal it must have lasted forever. Is that correct?*

Plato, Adeimantus, Agennetos and Glaucon: *Of course, this goes without saying.*

Paul: *No, no, no. A soul comes into being at the moment of conception.*

Agennetos: *Are you saying that there was a time when I did not exist?*

Socrates: *No.*

Paul: *Yes.*

He sat, Julian, and sat and sat and sat and sat, so absorbed in his own moroseness that, from the outside, it was impossible to know whether, or what, he noticed. Perhaps his silence sprang from an inner confusion, an inability to distinguish what was happening before his eyes and what was going on inside his head. Kind visitors came. Some sat quietly with him. Others tried to talk. If the visitors coincided with one another they would talk to one another, ignoring their truculent and silent friend.

His cousin, Felicity Ramsay, brought a paperback selection of Platonic dialogues, but she was given little in the way of dialogue herself, until the arrival of Margaret Mary Nolan. He hardly seemed to know M.M. Felicity had felt she had to talk to the woman, though they had little enough in common. On another occasion, Felicity tried to get Julian to talk about the Plato which she had brought him. Surprisingly, he did seem to have read it. Many passages were scored with a crayon, and some pages had dots on them which he was later able to explain were drawings of the souls of fleas. At this stage of treatment, however, Julian had nothing to say, although he said – again, afterwards, weeks afterwards – that he had been helped by Felicity's visits, their constancy. He had even enjoyed some of the conversations which she had had across his slumped silent form. What he tried to explain afterwards was the fact that he could not concentrate during the worst phase of his depression. It was not that he failed to recognise his friends; rather, priests, doctors, voices on the radio, all twitched nerves of consciousness, but could not retain his attention for longer than a few seconds, so that it was difficult to bother to distinguish between things which were happening inside his head, and things which were happening in the Sands Ward, where he had been placed. Wars and revolutions, the march of young American troops through jungles, the fizzling out of the youth movement in Europe, the Pope's encyclical condemning birth control (*Humanae Vitae*), the resultant crisis in the Roman Catholic Church – these were all regularly discussed and debated, sometimes by the visitors, sometimes by the voices which he heard. The discussion made a smaller impression than the flickering of shadows on a wall. They had brought him here, not because any doctor would categorically state that he was mad – at that juncture of history it was not, apparently, a word much used – but because he did not seem quite able to bear life's burdens alone. In the weeks which followed his grandmother's death he had sunk into a deeper and deeper desolation. Even his comparatively undemanding visits to Birmingham to record episodes of 'The Mulberrys' became 'too much'. On one such occasion, not long after his return from America, he had been unable to board the train at the bright new Euston Station. On another occasion he had been unable to leave a train, and the cleaners at Birmingham New Street had called the Transport Police to persuade him. His presence in the Nolan household, sitting and sitting, sometimes in clothes which were unchanged and unwashed, placed its own strain on the tolerance of his friends. But it was not, in the event, medical Nolan but cousin Felicity, who found him in his London lodgings and who was sufficiently alarmed by their squalor to think help was needed.

'I said I was coming.'

'When? I don't remember you saying any such thing.'

'In my letter. Julian, do open the door – it's silly talking through the letter-box.'

It needed some shove, since letters and newspapers were piled on the coconut matting within, to get the door open. Julian continued to sit in the hall, on the floor, amid the heaps of unopened envelopes while Felicity made them both tea.

'Julian, how long' – sniff – 'have you had this milk?'

'Oh, don't be *mean* to me!'

'I'm not being mean, old thing!' The automatic Badminton game with words, in which they had indulged since childhood. Then, 'Oh come *on*, *dear*', while he stood up and sobbed in his cousin's arms and she was able to feel how alarmingly thin he had become.

Now – after goodness knew how long – he had become – the steroids – so fat that he did not recognise his own face in the glass, and found it hard, in any case, to get this face to centre on the glass. The others squashed it out, so often, the faces which he saw there – a lost child, a rival biographer, the quick and the dead. No wonder he made the sign of the cross when he looked into the glass. Whose face had come to press out his own, that new fat face, on the morning that he had been obliged to smash the glass? He could not explain to them – he clammed up for days, aeons, after the incident, though everyone was kind and tolerant about it. The nurses on Sands Ward derived some impression that he feared punishment and reprisal, not merely for himself but for the whole dormitory, if he breathed a word about the breakage, though Dr Houlden asked them not to take too much notice of these games. Human wit, he told them, sprang very often from our need to protect ourselves. Julian was angry with himself for breaking the mirror, so he externalised the matter and wittily treated it as if it had been an incident at his private school. He did not 'really' think he was at Seaforth Grange, in spite of his behaving as if he did, his anxiety about talking after lights out, his expressions of fear that The Binker was coming to get him. The fact that he referred to Dr Houlden, behind his back, as The Binker did not mean that he truly believed this to be so. What else – Dr Houlden asked – were novels, plays, religious rituals even, if they were not just such externalisations of experience?

Only Dr Houlden's own patients appeared to disagree. They would not have been in his care if they had been able to hold down jobs, or to master timetables or to trust themselves in shops without being overpowered with the desire to drop their pants or to clobber a passer-by with a tin of beans. Once incarcerated, and released from the quotidian need to provide for themselves, they were, many of them, momentarily cheered up by their release from the imprisonment of worldly chores and tasks. No need, in Sands, or Witts, or Robertshaw, or in any of the other wards, for shopping lists; no need to turn up to work on time; no need for tidying and mending. Here were all the advantages of the cloister or the prison with none of the drawbacks. The whole day could be devoted to sadness, talking about it to the doctors, jabbering about it to the other patients, 'sharing' it during Dr Houlden's group sessions each morning, dreaming it, when dosed and bedded down and locked up at night.

Dr Houlden's group therapy sessions, held each morning, certainly sorted out the men from the boys among his patients. None of the fifteen or so individuals who sat in that circle would have been in hospital had not self-obsession rendered their lives (or, more likely, the lives of their families or workmates) impossible. They had all made Bishop Berkeley's rather childish discovery that the lives of others are less important than the puppet-show inside our own heads, and they were all 'doing time' for the offence of allowing this priority too blatantly to show.

It followed that the fifteen assembled were all practised egotists in the premier league. To dominate in such a company required qualities of ruthlessness which could, if directed aright in different circumstances and if possessed by an individual whom the world deemed to be sane, have been sure to dominate boardrooms, Cabinets or Oval Offices. Or, so, in after time, it seemed to Julian Ramsay when he remembered his own cringing silences during these sessions and the consummate, Napoleonic grasp of tactics displayed again and again by Sargent Lampitt. Sarge's ability to weep at will (what his sister-in-

173

law Lady Starling called turning on the water-works) would have been the envy of Olivier or Hubie Power; nor were his tear-ducts the only 'water-works' which he could 'switch on' if attention seemed to be straying to one of the other fifteen star performers in the circle for more than a few seconds. He could be madder and more maddening than any of them; but, when need required it, Sargie was the *honnête homme*, the common sense man of action, stepping in where the medical authorities had failed in their duty, to impose a semblance of order on a confused scene. For example, when Mr Bharadia interrupted Joanna's tearful and repetitive explanation of why she could not sit on her chair (rats in the springs) with one of his imitations of spontaneous combustion, all would have assumed that the Indian had won the day. How could universal attention fail to concentrate on a man who let forth such convincing and agonised shrieks of –

'Burning! Burning! I'm burning all up I'm telling you!'

But what everyone remembered about the incident, even Mr Bharadia, was not so much the imaginary fire as that old Mr Lampitt was the only person in the room with sufficient self-confidence to seize control, and sufficient *gravitas* to do so convincingly.

'Let him! Let him!' was Dr Houlden's response to Mr Bharadia's need to dowse the fire, first with Joanna's coffee, then with some water from a flower vase, placed on a table in the middle of the room. When two nurses started chasing Mr Bharadia around the room, they probably excited him all the more. His progress was interrupted by Sargie's foot – clad in a frayed tartan bedroom-slipper – which he stuck out at right angles.

'Go and sit *down*, damn you!' he said firmly.

Mr Bharadia stopped calling 'Fire! Fire!'

'Sit down and *shut up*. Let Joanna continue with what she was saying. Bloody interesting as a matter of fact. Rats in her chair! We all know she's barmy, but it's better than your fire nonsense.'

He spoke as if all the contributions to the group therapy were party turns, put on for his own private entertainment. Joanna's fear of rats, and the general consternation caused by Mr Bharadia's outburst, of course left the field open for this conversational Eisenhower to sweep over already conquered villages, and the smoking ruins of bombarded towns. No need today for any sympathy bids, no need for tears. He could demonstrate to the company the qualities which had made him

174

such a trusted adviser to Attlee and to Stafford Cripps or – much earlier in the century, when he was a young New College don barely out of his teens – addressing a parliamentary committee set up by Lloyd George on the reform of the House of Lords. The rest of that morning's session became a seminar, chaired by Sargent Lampitt, about the unhelpfulness of treating very different types of mental disorder in the same group.

'Julian Ramsay over there, for example; known him since he was a child. He's not barking. He's never going to run around taking his drawers off in a bank, as Norman did over there. Julian's just depressed, that's all. Whereas, you see, Joanna, my dear, you are what could be described in the old-fashioned medical terminology as a head-case. Not a straitjacket case like Bharadia . . .'

The riot which ensued was entirely predictable, but Dr Houlden, with his mania for allowing everyone their say, had been too slow to intervene and shut up the most eloquent patient on the ward. The mad all performed their tricks like circus animals; Sargent Lampitt fixed a cigarette into his bone holder and smiled at the scene which he had created, with something of the satisfaction of a great film director.

Mr Judge, a north country man who had more than once 'shared' with the group his overweening hatred of Sargie, yelled out at one point in the affray, 'Just who the hell do you think you are, any road?'

Sargent Lampitt paused, seemingly tempted to play up to the question. (Mr Judge had bellowed so loudly that there was a momentary silence providing Mr Lampitt with his audience if he had chosen to address it.) Who did he think he was? Was he going to claim, like Henry James in an account after his stroke, dictated to Sargie's brother Jimbo, that he was Napoleon?

The question, though, sparked off one of those sudden mood swings, from cocky to crestfallen, which had been so observable a feature of Sargent Lampitt's character all his adult life.

'I am my brother's keeper,' he said, his lip trembling in that combination of rage and grief which managed to produce tears not only in himself but in those who heard him. 'Poor old Jimbo.'

Julian Ramsay found Lampitt a few days later taking what appeared to be an unwonted interest in horticulture, crouched beside one of the flower-beds.

'I say, Julie, you wouldn't have a cigarette, would you?'

'You won't find any in the herbaceous border.'

'That's just where you're wrong. Look! There! You see?'

He moved forwards on his knees and stretched out a scrawny hand into the stumps of a rose bush which had been rather brutally pruned for winter. Ramsay offered him a hand under his elbow and with some difficulty Sargent Lampitt struggled upright.

'See!' With triumph he held up the stub of some two inches.

'There's a boy, a gardener's boy, I've been watching him.'

Ramsay shuffled, afraid of some lubricious disclosure.

'Every bloody day I've had my eye on him. One of Vernon's friends the Underprivileged. So bloody underprivileged he wastes his fags and throws them away before they are smoked down. Got a light?'

Agennetos: And the light is the light of life.

'Julie? Julie? I say, my dear, do try to get a grip.'

Julian's mother in 1942: O, darling, do try not to cry so much. Everyone has to go back to school, you know.

'Sorry, Sargie. I've got a cigarette, somewhere. Bloom brought them and I haven't had one yet. Don't like the French ones. You know William Bloom? The publisher? I don't think I said anything at all to him when he came to see me the other day. Nothing. I can talk again now. Sometimes. These new pills.'

Ramsay held out a packet of Gauloise; Lampitt nimbly took six or seven and thrust them into his pocket. He fitted the newly-discovered butt into his bone lighter and, with one of Ramsay's matches, got it going.

'What's your room like?' he asked.

'Modest. A bed, a table. Ground floor, of course.'

'I'm next to the wog. He farts in the night. You can hear it. Julie, my dear, you wouldn't *believe* what I suffer, lying in there. I'm sure we can switch rooms.'

'But you're on the first floor.'

Jimbo flying, flying down; upside-down he glided, into the dustbin. Virgil

D. descended into hell. From morn to noon he fell, from noon to dewy eve. Falling, falling.

While Ramsay cowered, terrified, Lampitt continued, 'I'll ask that nurse on my corridor, Keith. Vebba clebba febba. Plays chess with me sometimes. Hello, *qui vive* – Sister Sibs on the battle-path.'

Lady Starling was indeed advancing towards them. She was considerably the youngest Lampitt sibling, but with the advance of time – she was probably now nearer seventy than sixty – her face had developed all the Lampitt features to the point of caricature, so that she might (saving his moustache) have been Sargent Lampitt in 'drag', advancing with a purposefulness and vigour in her well-cut tweeds and strapping calves which made it incomprehensible that anyone could ever have compared her with a doormat. She was accompanied or followed up the garden path by William Bloom, the donor of the cigarettes. Bloom, still less than forty, showed signs of putting a lot into life – work during office hours, and plenty to smoke and drink in the evenings. His highly intelligent monkey-face was rubicund, save for the bluish smudges at the chin and upper lip; his thick hair was already grey. The unEnglishness of his appearance was enhanced by a habit of wearing dark blue shirts and crumpled dark blue suits, giving him more the appearance of a Left Bank intellectual than a London businessman.

'No, Julian, not now!' declaimed the doormat as soon as she considered her former son-in-law to be in hailing distance. 'Sargie is simply not UP to visitors.'

Bloom adopted the conciliatory tone which might have persuaded a maniac to put down a meat cleaver or the pushier sort of literary agent to lower the pecuniary expectations of a client.

'Lady Starling,' he said gently. 'I've actually come to see Julian. I mean, *here*.' He pointed with some vigour – a real *Here I stand* – at the gravel beneath his soft black suedes.

'You mean Julian's a patient? I can see now, he looks awful. And they haven't been giving him enough exercise. Going to fat. Hallo, old thing.' She advanced on her brother and planted a smudge of lipstick on his cheek.

'This is Mr Bloom, darling, the publisher. Haven't brought him to see you, just met him here quite by chance. He's come to see – Julian.'

The withering tone suggested that there was no accounting for tastes.

'Come on, Sargie, you remember Mr Bloom. He tried to get Julian here to write a proper book about Jimbo. I'm afraid he's been pipped to the post yet again. I won't even bother you, darling, with the latest horror – my dear! I have counted forty-seven mistakes in the first chapter alone. Oh, Sargie, do speak, I'm sure you could if you tried. Mr Bloom, isn't it maddening? The doctor says he's quite chatty at their morning meetings, but when I come he loses his powers of speech altogether.'

'Jules can be a bit quiet too, can't you, my dear?'

Protect me, Alcibiades. You are a soldier, protect me from The Binker. Protect me from being put in an upstairs room. Protect me from being thrown down, down, down.

Julian Ramsay clung to Bloom's side, so close that he could smell the slight but far from unpleasant odour of his armpits.

'No stairs!'

'Not if you don't want to.'

'She's trying to get me on the roof!' Julian thrust his forefinger in the direction of Sibs Starling. 'She wants me up the fire escape.'

'I always said he was bonkers,' said Lady Starling. Perhaps she would have elaborated this psychological analysis of Julian Ramsay's character, but Bloom snatched his friend's sleeve and led him away across the lawn.

'Would you like to go indoors now or are you happier out here?'

A two-minute silence.

'I've brought you a few things. Some more cigarettes. A few books.'

Julian took his old friend's elbow and led him into the middle of the lawn before speaking to him the first words which he had addressed to Bloom in three visits to the hospital.

'I think that's the most dangerous part of the roof,' he said, pointing to a tower which a fanciful Victorian architect had designed to jut above the gables of Robertshaw.

'What's dangerous about it, my dear?'

'You'd have the furthest to fall once they'd got you up there.'

'Shall we go in?'

'They haven't put Sibs Starling in charge of the school, have they?'
'Of course not, my dear.'
'Only you know where you are with The Binker. But with her – she'd put me on the roof, I know she would . . .'

Not much more was said that day between the two friends. They sat for half an hour or so in Julian's safe, ground-floor room. Bloom accepted, and smoked a Gauloise.

'Oh good – glad to see you've smoked some. I wasn't sure if you liked them, but I see you've got through about half.'

He left Julian with another little blue packet of cigarettes and with a pile of paperbacks.

'I know you'll eventually want to read Hunter's book, but I thought you might not want it here. A bit heavy in every sense. Madge publishes it in about three months and as you can imagine she's already having orgasms. I've seen a bound proof. I thought, perhaps, you'd prefer a few detective stories. You always did enjoy a good old-fashioned murder.'

Dear William Bloom, so kind to me through forty years, and, should they see print, the publisher of these words: that was the turning-point in my illness, when you left that welcome pile of Ngaio Marsh, Julian Symons and Margery Allingham. Hitherto, in hospital, my reading had been scrappy. It increased my sense of failure that I could not finish anything, not a crossword, not a short story. Romping to the end of every single novel which Bloom had brought cleared and focused the head. The hospital library was scarcely the Codrington, but it had a plentiful supply of what I wanted.

I never did make the promised visit to St Mark's Place, but some years later Treadmill introduced me to W. H. Auden in London. We discussed detective fiction and its appeal. Auden had said that he regarded it as essentially a religious form.

'They've nearly all been High, the good ones. Have you noticed that? High and women – Dorothy L. Sayers, Agatha Christie . . .'
'I didn't know she was.'
'Oh, she is. I know a priest who saw her at Mass; she genuflected at the *et incarnatus est*. Ngaio Marsh is High, Margery Allingham is High. The ancient religious origins of drama, the idea of nemesis, that the shedding of innocent blood will be punished – these are all

contained in your average old-fashioned teccy. For myself, only those set in the English countryside can be enjoyable. I don't enjoy any realistic descriptions of the act of murder.'

'So you don't enjoy *Crime and Punishment?*'

'Since you ask,' said the poet through a cloud of cigarette smoke, 'no.'

''Ere,' Cyril said – for we were having this conversation in the Black Bottle – 'what's someone been doin' to your face?'

Bloom, who had brought me an armful of Agatha Christies when he noted my recovery, asked if I'd like to vary them with some James Bonds.

'Can't stand them,' I said. 'In my case, it isn't that crime stories fulfil a religious function as that they create a saving illusion – namely that there is an explanation for things. I've no interest in fantasies about fast cars and women.'

'Isn't Sherlock Holmes heaven for that reason – that everything in the Conan Doyle world can be explained? The most consoling of all literary creations. In his company anything could be explained if you only have the patience to wait for him to drug himself up to the eyeballs, silly old faggot.'

'Don't you think Sherlock Holmes was sexless?'

'Straights always want to blot out of their pure little minds the fact that we queens do actually function from the waist down. Their sexlessness is half the joy of the stories, I'll grant you. Watson supposed Holmes was sexless, just as all the straight readers do; nice manly Watson, with his big moustache that Holmes positively ached to get his tongue into – Watson does not understand any of the evidence which he puts before us – Holmes's frequent disappearance into those marvellously convenient pea-souper fogs; his penchant for the poorer districts of London, his reliance on the street urchins – the little ragamuffins whatever they were called. The prostitutes.'

'The Baker Street Irregulars are hardly pro – '

'My dear, he was obviously one of those queens who is at it *all the time.*'

Bloom laughed, one of those huge laughs which went on for several minutes and which, depending on his company, are either embarrassing or infectious. For the first time since my hospitalisation, I found myself laughing. As the laughter died down I lovingly fingered the books which he had brought for me – *The ABC Murders, Murder in Mesopotamia, The Hollow, The Body in the Library*. My mania for this sort of literature was at its height when I was aged about twelve. On the morning that Jimbo Lampitt died I had carefully noted the time of his death and wished, as in a Christie story, that I could have drawn up a list of obvious 'suspects'.

'Of course Hunter's latest book will sell like hot cakes,' Bloom tactlessly prophesied.

'What's this?' I asked, finding in my pile of Christies *The Quest for Corvo* by A. J. A. Symons.

For the moment ignoring my question while I turned over the blue and white Penguin, Bloom pursued 'publishers' gossip' about the second (and final) volume of Hunter's biography of James Petworth Lampitt.

'How does he handle the death?' I asked.

'Certainly not as interestingly as you would, my dear. It was actually – now you mention it – *asking* to be put into a crime story, that death, wasn't it? How much Chesterton's Father Brown would have relished the grotesqueries of Lampitt's dying upside down (like St Peter); only, rather than being crucified he died with his trousers sticking out of a dustbin.'

'There was also,' I reminded Bloom, 'the fact which emerged during the libel trial – that the railing of the fire escape came up to Jimbo's chest. Therefore he could not have fallen, as the coroner concluded that he had, by accident.'

'The stuff which came out at that Albion Pugh libel trial certainly provided lots of motives for murdering harmless old Jimbo – Cecily because she thought Jimbo had betrayed her with Hunter; Sargie, so that he could inherit the Lampitt Papers and make a small fortune selling them to Virgil D. Everett; Hunter himself . . .'

Bloom was laughing.

'So satisfying,' he said, 'in detective stories, when people do things for motives: I'm not sure I ever had a single motive for any of the significant actions of my life. I just *did* things. But let's concoct a motive for Miss Hunter. She pushes Jimbo over the battlements at Elsinore – why? because she's frightened that Jimbo will expose her as a queen, is that our current little theory? Don't get me wrong, I think that, as well as being a dear person, Agatha is actually a very good writer – much better than your supposed realists like Deborah Arnott. (*Her* latest! My dear, it's so bad. I'm afraid to say she has now become so pretentious, too – *The Spirit of the Age*. What a title, for a book which is just about bores committing adultery.) But – Agatha! There's nothing more inherently absurd in her view of things – that people commit crimes for identifiable motives – than there is in Miss Freud's theories – she was another busy little explanations merchant. There's nothing wrong with playing games; that's all Agatha does. It's when you come to believe them that you're in trouble. Look at Ronald Knox.'

'I know those who do little else. In which of his aspects do you wish me to look at him?'

'Oh, you know, she wrote those detective stories and she was also a Roman Catholic priest. She drew up all these little rules about what a detective story might or might not do – practically written the Rule of St Benedict by the time she'd finished tapping away at her little Imperial portable.'

There was nothing inherently amusing about Monsignor Knox writing crime fiction, or doing so on a typewriter, but Bloom was shaking, and dabbing the corner of each eye.

'*Ten Commandments of Detective Stories*, she called it. And she laid down such rules as that the detective may never find things out by accident – as if more or less everything in history from penicillin to the joys of oral sex hadn't in some sense been found out by accident. Anyway, my dear, *listen*.' He smacked one hand against the other as he still often does for emphasis, '*The Quest for Jimbo*'.

I looked down at the Penguin in my hands – *The Quest for Corvo*.

'Brilliant title and you are holding the model for your own book in your hands. You don't need to write a big family story of the Lampitts, and nor do you need to write a vast half-million word effort like Ruby Hunter's. You could do it all in 90,000 words max, particularly now Cecily is dead and you have read those letters.'

'So I wouldn't have to go to America again.'

'Well, given the fact that you've been twice you could probably do the whole thing at Mallington. Ernie's an awfully sweet old thing, you know – and he's perfectly willing to have you there. But, it would probably be better if you went back to New York just once more –

before they get rid of the Ann-Louise Collection. You know that, now Mr Everett is dead, they are going to disperse the collection?'

Julian Ramsay had stuck out both arms and was making a whirring noise through his nose to simulate the engine of a Spitfire, maybe of a Lancaster.

'Calling control. Come in control. Roger.'

'Don't be an ass, my dear, you were perfectly all right a minute ago. This is just an act. I think when you are afraid of doing something, you retreat into this crazy behaviour as a sort of safety de– '

But it was a soliloquy, this speech of William Bloom's. Julian Ramsay taxied off down the garden path, without saying goodbye to his friend, but with *The Quest for Corvo* conspicuously sticking out of his pocket. He rounded the corner of the laurels and pulled an unseen joystick, poised for take-off.

EIGHT
(Christmas 1969)

What are the sins against hope?
The sins against hope are despair and presumption.

A pale Christmas sun shone on the piazza in Monreale, a tiny cathedral town perched high in the mountains above the capital of Sicily. No celebration of the festival would have been possible without the presence of at least one or two Lame Ducks. On this occasion the Nolans had decided to make the location a novelty. Given their changed circumstances, Fergus and Margaret Mary would actually have preferred to be alone. They knew that this was not their lot in life. Having issued the suggestion – directive – invitation – as far back as October, they had felt released from any obligation to those Lame Ducks who could not themselves contrive to fly to – Palermo!

Almost as many, Fergus jokingly opined, at the dressing-table of their hotel bedroom that morning, as might have called at Wiseman Road on an average Sunday: and the ones who might have seemed least able to make the journey doggedly made themselves of the party. But of course he exaggerated. There were only two Lame Ducks; the only surprise occasioned by their appearance being that they were the lamest of all. Linus Quarles had booked himself on to a chartered flight as soon as he heard of the changed Christmas venue. Julian Ramsay – surely too frail, too lately released from the institution, to make such a journey – was insistent upon coming. Jim and Persy were to be his minders.

184

They had all been, if not upset, then knocked about, surprised, overexcited, by the marriage of Fergus's sister to his oldest friend. Jim and Persy had not even waited for the papers of laicisation, and the wedding had taken place in a Birmingham register office, with Fergus and Margaret Mary as witnesses. Fergus assumed that it would have been painful to break the news of the engagement to Julian, who was still in hospital, and this task had been deputed to M.M. herself. He had apparently taken the news quite calmly. That was a full six months ago. Once the plan had been settled upon, Jim had left the Dominicans and managed to get himself a job as the Vatican correspondent for a liberal newspaper, and married Persy Nolan all within a space of weeks. They had a small flat in the Trastevere district and sounded, from their postcards, jolly and self-confident. They had volunteered to be Julian's minders. He had flown out to Rome to meet them, and they had brought him down by another flight to Sicily.

One might have expected Linus Quarles to have been outraged by 'Father Bon' abandoning his orders, and forsaking his vows; but, if this was the case, the Jesuit kept his own counsel. He evidently had never liked Father Bonaventure very much; but that should not prevent him being civil to Mr and Mrs Reilly, even though they were both, glaringly, not Father Quarles's type of person. Though the breaking of vows could not but shock the Jesuit, there was a hint in his manner of relief, that the club had lost, through discreet resignation, one of its less desirable members.

So – the strange little lunch party was assembled: Julian, M.M., Fergus, the Reillys and Father Linus Quarles, SJ. Having explored the *duomo*, they now sat over a Christmas dinner which worked as hard as it could to dispel memories of England and Xmas Fayre. They ate a very good risotto, in which were found prawns, clams and mussels in their shells. Roast veal was to follow. With each course, a good, unexportable, Sicilian wine.

The cathedral had delighted them, and surprised everyone but Father Quarles, who reckoned on knowing all the great art works of the Western world intimately. Told, like most reasonably well-informed people, that the cathedral of Monreale had 'lovely mosaics', the four had prepared themselves for five or ten minutes of delight as they gazed through shadowy aisles up to the stylised, gilded figures

185

above their heads. They had not been prepared for the cohesiveness of the design, nor for the fact that the workmanship, the expressions on the faces of prophets and saints, the folds of garments and foliage and feathers should have been so exuberantly designed and executed.

'I'm sorry if I offended you,' said Father Quarles. He pushed a mussel-shell to the edge of his soup plate, and did not look sorry at all. He had just made a disobliging remark about modern psychoanalytical technique. Persy, now Julian's staunchest friend, had protested. Since getting married, Persy's whole mode of presenting herself (presumably, of perceiving herself) had altered. She no longer cropped her hair – it was shoulder length. Instead of the inevitable trousers, she wore a loosely-fitting smock. Bare, unshaven legs ended in sandalled feet which were amazingly sexy. When I first met her, Persy looked like a cabin boy in the Hornblower stories. Now her appearance suggested (appropriately for one married to a friar) a delinquent Sister of Mercy.

'I am not criticising you,' proceeded the priest, unabashed by the embarrassingness of mental illness as a topic of general conversation, 'my dear fellow – you know me better than that, by now. But the modern cult of self is surely one of the most dangerous inventions of the Evil One?'

'As you know, Linus, I don't really have any beliefs.'

'That can't, logically, be true,' said Jim Reilly. 'You might have beliefs which differed from Linus, but you can't . . .'

Mr Reilly, formerly Father Bon, wore a grubby white suit, brown sandals, red socks which had holes in them. His hair was a bit longer and he did not seem any more interested in personal hygiene than when he had been a Dominican.

The Jesuit ignored the interjection.

'But think of the cathedral we have just seen, all of us,' Father Linus Quarles pursued. 'A myth in mosaic, one of the great monuments of Christendom. I often tell students . . .'

The wine had been flowing for an hour now. It enabled Jim Reilly to butt in and say, 'Often? Linus, when did you last speak to a student?'

'A real one – yes – as opposed to some old boy of Stonyhurst or Ampleforth,' contributed Fergus, who was laughing inordinately.

'Oftener than you would think, dear boy. I often have told them that the best possible way of telling the difference between Islam and

186

Christianity is to come to this building. Here you have William II, recapturing Sicily from the Muslims, and erecting a cathedral . . .'

'He built it because his bishop, an Englishman called Gualterio Offamiglio – well, it's just Italian for Walter Miller, isn't it? – was a man whom he had decided he hated; and Miller had just built a huge cathedral five miles down the hill in Palermo,' said Jim Reilly. 'William II wasn't trying to make a theological point. It was purely political.'

'Dear boy, I don't know how much of the faith you've retained.'

'Why do you assume,' asked a furious Persy, 'that because Jim's left the Dominicans he isn't a Catholic any more? We're both more Catholic than ever. It was having the same view of the Church which brought us together . . .'

'I thank God for it,' said Father Quarles. 'But you must know that the Almighty uses grit in an oyster to make a pearl. Out of William's vain desire to *épater* a bishop, there arose this wonderful monument – the whole saving story from Adam and Eve to the Day of Judgement all set out in visual terms. It's all before St Dominic and St Thomas Aquinas ever arose, you see.' He smiled at his own wit.

'It antedates the Dominican order by about twenty years,' said Jim, still loyal to the old firm. 'It antedates the Jesuits by three and a half centuries. So what?'

'Very well,' said Father Linus. 'But, you see, it isn't asking us to believe in a set of notions, nor even, particularly, is it asking the faithful to subscribe to an opinion. It awakens the idea that to see the past in a certain way is the beginning of faith. The beginning, not the whole of it. Even the events of the sacred Passion itself seemed unremarkable to the original witnesses. To the Roman soldiers it was no more than one extra sordid execution. If one may say so without profanity, it needed genius, or the inspiration of the Holy Spirit as theology would say, to see it all whole – and there we've just had it – all the stories fitting together – Noë's flood, the Holy Patriarchs and Prophets all leading up to one supreme event. Yes, Hal Fisher, dear man – if you please to think it so, History is just one damned thing after another, or if you prefer to see a *shape* in the sequence . . .'

While Jim hit back with some scathing references to Toynbee,

M.M. turned to Julian and said, 'It was lovely, wasn't it, the cathedral? What was your favourite mosaic?'

'I think, the angel rescuing Isaac from being sacrificed by his father. The one with really huge wings which filled the whole corner-bit – whatever you call it.'

'Weren't they fantastic?'

'Angel is a nice name for a baby,' said Persy – who was already ample in her large floral smock. 'I like Angel Reilly, or Gabriel Reilly. Not Michael. Mick Reilly's like Fergus Nolan – it's too much of a Paddy name.'

'There are plenty of other angel names . . .' Jim broke off from his contest with the Jesuit to put them right on the subject of angelic nomenclature. 'Ithuriel, Zephon, Uzziel – they're all good names. Or there's Raphael.'

A silence fell on the table. For the first time since the meal began, the friends could listen to the scraping of forks and spoons. The happy roar of a large Italian party at the next table seemed to have stolen all their merriment. It was a momentary stillness, perhaps noticed more vividly by some than by others.

'One misses one's parents at Christmas,' Julian suddenly said. 'Forgive me, Linus. I am not going to be an embarrassing mental patient and talk about my own problems all through the meal, but I believe I thought myself into becoming mad – if I was mad. I thought there was something so odd about not being able to come to terms with the death of my mother. I should have been able to see that – if that's the way things are, so be it. If I go on missing her thirty years after she'd died . . .'

'Ronnie Knox was in hospital towards the end of his life.'

'A mental hospital? I'd never heard that.'

Ramsay for the first time in his life seemed deeply fascinated by this oft-quoted Catholic wit.

'Of course not!' Linus Quarles's dismissal of the very suggestion revealed his old-fashioned belief that there was something demeaning about mental illness.

'A nurse came in to see Ronnie – and he was dying, poor dear man, and she said, "You'll soon be feeling your normal healthy self", and he replied, "What makes you think health is normal?"'

The momentary silence which followed any of Linus's apothegms

188

or anecdotes suggested that an outbreak of applause, or at the very least a murmur of appreciation, would be in order, before he dropped another name or recited another *bon mot*. In this, his monologic approach to conversation differed from that of the Reverend Roy Ramsay, comparable as the two were. Father Quarles, SJ, very definitely wanted to be part of the act and to take his bow when the show was over, with Martin D'Arcy, Evelyn Waugh, Douglas Woodruff, Mr Belloc and the rest. He paused in his speeches not merely that the audience should see the great ones behind the curtain which he had lifted but that the audience should believe in some manner that the wit of the great ones, their social or intellectual grandeur, had somehow brushed off on their apostle and messenger. Roy Ramsay was perhaps a more religious person, for his unstoppable flow of Lampittry poured forth like the prayers of a mystic, whether he had an audience or not. When others happened to overhear his ceaseless meditation on the theme of themes, he was not showing off. The spontaneous overflow of his obsession was involuntary.

Beneath the table-cloth, Julian Ramsay's skinny fingers clutched at his huge white table-napkin. He tried to concentrate very hard on what was being said and to prevent his mind from playing one of the games which, at the beginning of his illness, had been his undoing. He tried to distinguish between what was being said around the table and what was being said inside his head. Dr Houlden had told him that we all have daydreams, and that if they come, they come – let them happen, but try to concentrate with half of the brain by playing a few little games. For example, repeat the last few words which have just been said to you, and use your interlocutor's name as often as possible, to remind you of their identity.

Persy had noticed that Julian had become one of those people who peppered conversation with vocatives. In her experience it was usually a sign of being an American, being homosexual or having got religion – sometimes a heady mixture of all three. Fergus and Linus both found the habit annoying, and Fat-gut Reilly did not notice it.

'It is interesting, Linus, that you should mention Ronald Knox because he of course laid down the Ten Commandments.'

There was a distinct unease at the table when Julian said this. Strait-jacket time?

Inside his head, M. Poirot, played by Julian himself, had assembled

189

all the suspects in the library – or, as it happened, around that very table in Sicily. The little grey cells had been working overtime and, after several solitary sessions, building ze house of cards, M. Poirot – ah yes! – had come up with ze solution, how you say, to zees leetle *difficulté*.

'I've the highest admiration for Ronnie,' said Father Quarles carefully, 'and I've heard many great works attributed to him, but the Ten Commandments . . .'

'Cecil B. De Mille, eh?' Persy the friend rescued Julian.

Julian, clutching and unclutching the napkin, did not realise that everyone else round the table had formed the impression that he believed the original Ten Commandments had been framed by Monsignor Knox on Mount Sinai. (Protestants are notoriously hazy where matters of religion are concerned.) He was too busy concentrating on Poirot's extraordinary deductions.

'One of the Ten Commandments, Persy,' said Julian slowly, 'oh, sorry, have I said that before?'

'Said what?' asked M.M. slowly, and calmly. 'Julian, are you all right?'

'Well, in "The Ten Commandments of Detective Fiction" one of the rules is that the detective must arrive at his conclusion by logical means; he can't just be led to it by intuition. Most of our ideas about life are intuitive, aren't they, Margaret Mary?'

The others began to talk with some desperation to avoid any more of Julian Ramsay's embarrassing interjections, and this had the unfortunate effect of giving Poirot and his companions a greater control of Julian's attention.

'I'm about half way through my Christmas present already,' said Linus Quarles. 'Absolutely fascinating. He has done a first-rate job.' He referred to the second volume of Hunter's *Life of Lampitt* which had at long last been published.

Hunter was there. Dorset was there, coolly smoking a cigarette. Mr Ramsay was there, in spite of the fact that he was also acting the role of Hercule Poirot, the great detective. The Ahrlichs and Ol Pitman and At and Wilmie. And Christopher, smoking a joint. And large Jim Reilly, who, as Father Bon in the dream sequence, was still wearing his Thomas Aquinas outfit. The butler John was, similarly, wearing the uniform of a Regimental Sergeant-Major – in the Norfolk Regiment.

'When one thinks of the amount of effort, of sheer effort, which goes into a book like that,' said Margaret Mary appreciatively; it was not clear whether she referred to the effort of writing such a doorstopper or the more mundane effort of lifting it up, for Linus Quarles had been carrying the masterpiece about and had now produced it from under his chair.

'I haven't seen any reviews,' said Jim.

'I got advance copies,' said Margaret Mary winsomely. 'I don't think the book is quite out yet.'

'We come,' said Poirot, 'to the factor in this crime which has always interested me – the throwing, or the falling from ze window. It has a certain symmetry, does it not, M. 'unter? M. Lampitt, ze great subject of your book, 'e fall from the window; and Mr Everett, he also, twenty-three years later, he suffers the same fate!'

'This is preposterous!' Hunter interjects.

'Preposterous, maybe, Monsieur, but let us consider the evidence. All of you had the motive to kill Mr Everett. You, Mr Ahrlich, because he had the power to ruin your political career – yes, and you too, Mr Birk. And what of Father Reilly? Did he not too have ze motive . . .'

'Me?' Father Bon spluttered. 'Me? You think that just because Lixabrite was promoting the Pill? Haven't you followed my career? Don't you know that I came out on the side of the liberals on this one? That I was in favour of Catholic women being given the right to choose . . .'

'Ah yes, mon père, but forgive me; it was not the fact that you held this or that view on the issue of – how you say? – la Pilule. Ah, non! It was that you could not bear to see unhappy the woman with whom you were in love – and that woman, was Mme Nolan, was it not?'

'It won't affect your book, Julian,' said M.M. briskly.

'If anything, Margaret Mary, it will help it,' said Julian doggedly. It was like trying to talk to someone when there was a very loud radio play, or an episode of 'The Mulberrys', blaring in the background.

'I never really knew Petworth,' said Father Quarles, 'but he was very amusing, you know. I remember Father D'Arcy bringing him to dinner on a number of occasions at Campion Hall. I love the travel writings. There was a lovely book called On Tiber's Bank which I often read during my years as a scholastic in Rome; and what was the one about Venice called?'

'Lagoon Loungings, Linus.'

'But – though you all – yes all – were happier when Mr Everett was dead, there was only one of you who was desperate to have him out of the way – out of the way before his book had appeared. Was this not so, M. Le Chasseur? Mr Lampitt, he threatened, did he not, to telephone the police when he discovered that you had stolen from his bureau? Perhaps, too, he had discovered your true proclivities, at that date illegal, hein? And zen, after twenty-three years, your crimes come back to haunt you? Mr Everett, he has discovered, we do not know how, that all your so-called research in his library is a fraud; that you have persuaded him – how we say – to purchase the puppy, hein? So, you take the only means in your power, you push him back towards the balcony – you force zee old man to fly through the air, just as you make Mr Lampitt to fly through the air of London all zose years ago. Is that not so?'

'No, no, no!' sobbed Hunter.

'One day,' said Linus Quarles, 'the club must reassemble in Venice.'

'What club?' asked Fergus.

'You were surely aware that a certain young woman was on the committee; even if you did not know of her penchant for the older members of the Club,' said Orlando Lampitt.

The priest looked pityingly at the scientist, and waving his hand in a gesture which was halfway to being a benediction, he indicated his company.

'I think this idea of our meeting in different settings is charming,' said the priest.

'It just seems extraordinary,' said Persy, 'that Julian and I actually met the man who murdered old Mr Everett. We met him – well, you did, too, M.M. You know, the black chap who gave Julian that funny drug?'

'It's too awful to think about,' said M.M. quietly.

'Aha! Meesis Nolan, you at last fit for us ze last piece of the jigsaw together, perhaps? Non? For who else was able to persuade her brother, ze high-ranking diplomat, to call Mr Everett back to his apartment alone zat night? Who else had ze motive for protecting the killer – except ze woman who was herself in love with ze murderer?'

'Eef,' said M. Poirot aloud, 'he was ze true murderer. For there were many ozzers, were there not, who might have wished Mr Everett to be pushed, 'ow you say, over ze edge?'

M.M. laughed, in spite of the bad taste of Ramsay adopting one of his 'funny voices', but Fergus felt it was out of order. He seized control of the conversation.

'It is the most ghastly story. I mean, now that young man – what was he called, poor soul?'

'Christopher Johnson, Fergus.'

'Johnson, that's right – now he's died in police custody before so much as coming to trial, there is probably no one in the world who will ever know what happened.'

'But, Fergus . . .' Thank the powers, M. Poirot and his friends had either vanished or turned down the volume control inside Julian's head, so that he could speak again, 'no one really wants to know what happened. That's the difference between life and detective stories. Old Virgil D. had his finger in so many pies. We happen to know about a few of them.'

This was the point of the meal when Margaret Mary would always have lit up her first cigarette of the day.

'Shall we have desserts?'

Father Linus peered very hard at his napkin while this request was made, as if torn between an unwillingness to sit at a table where such an expression was used, and a simple hunger for pudding. He knew that she only said it to humour her husband – that no Mount-Smith would have naturally used the word *dessert*, unless of course referring to port and Sauternes and nuts at Peterhouse or All Souls'. This willingness to be *déclassé* – would a Protestant ever understand the little, daily martyrdom of it? ('Tea' in the novice house meant the evening meal!)

'I could be tempted by Tiramisu,' he said quietly.

There was, however, more than one reason for the priest suddenly falling quiet. There is no logical cause why a woman who is two months pregnant might be more or less likely to say that she does not want pudding. Her refusal of a cigarette, habitual at this stage of a meal, was what alerted them both, Julian Ramsay and Linus Quarles, SJ, to a simultaneous knowledge that Margaret Mary was expecting a child. They both looked up and stared at their beloved with pained shock.

In Ramsay's face there was the expression of a bereaved child. In Linus Quarles could be seen an immediate, self-protecting fear. This was going to spell the end, was it not, of those leisurely, Edgbaston

Sundays? Oh those hours, those long, beautiful hours, drinking the Nolans' wine and feeling the warmth of the Nolans' fire! Now, they would be too busy for him. The house would become much less comfortable as houses inevitably did when they became cluttered with prams, toys, chamber-pots, food-stained high chairs, and all the distasteful paraphernalia of early childhood. Father Quarles was seized with a dread of Sundays in the novice house – with water to drink, and no one to talk to except the novices, some too earnest, some too pert, all with body odour and many with provincial accents. Our fastidious priest shuddered.

'Isn't it wonderful news?' Fergus said, grinning, first at his pregnant sister, and then at his friends. He tried to derive, either from Julian or Father Quarles's disappointed expressions, some glimmer of pleasure; or, if pleasure were too much to seek, then of good manners which might at least make these two Lame Ducks pretend to be pleased in the moment of M.M.'s joy.

'Oh, darling!' Persy leant forward to kiss her sister-in-law.

'It's like St Elisabeth and Our Lady,' said Father Quarles bitterly. 'I am so very, very pleased for you both. It is what I have been praying for – indeed, I have said a Votive Marce of St Joseph for that intention on countless occasions.'

Paradoxically, little as he liked the prospect of M.M.'s pregnancy, this happened to be true.

I am your child, your unborn child. A baby of Reilly's is now in my mother's womb where, a couple of years ago, I once lay, curled up and ready to wake into life. Father! Yes, you – you are my father – Julian! No one else is my father! No one else could call me into being! Persy is with child, and Margaret Mary is with child, and only you are without issue. In Rama was there a voice heard, lamentation and weeping and great mourning, Rachel weeping for her children, and would not be comforted, because they are not.

After lunch was over, I felt more than ever nostalgic for my months in hospital. I wanted the release of solitude, and the cheering possibility of being as mad as I chose. (And I use that word in the English sense to contain the American sense – behaving like a nutter would have been a good way of releasing some of my anger.) Instead, I told them that I was going down to the centre of Palermo by myself.

The catacombs at the friary of the Capuchins had long been a subject of poor-taste jest between William Bloom (O mighty one who publishes these words!) and myself. You, William, had visited it as a sophisticated undergraduate, and come away fascinated by the rows of human corpses, imperfectly embalmed, which line the corridors. They date chiefly from the last two centuries, forming in their dusty fashion a little history of costume – here a bride hangs, seemingly from a coat-hanger, in much the same outfit which could have been worn by Miss Havisham or Mrs Rochester. There an old sea captain in smart nankeen trousers recalls the sturdier figures in Thackeray or even Jane Austen.

I had bought my ticket at the door from a straggly-bearded adolescent whose brown smock and sandals would not have been wholly out of place had he chosen to hang out with Treadmill's hippy pupils. Perhaps it was a strange impulse, on Christmas Day, to wish to visit this place of the dead; the young Capuchin certainly seemed quietly amused by my presence and I think (though I have no Italian) that he was telling me that I was the solitary visitor that day.

Bloom – your camp jokes about this place had delighted to people a catacomb of our own with our friends and acquaintances. 'Instead of a funeral in some ghastly suburban crematorium, what could be nicer than to be kitted out in one's *gladdest* of rags and shoved in a niche next to some attractive young stiff in military uniform? Something between *Psycho* and Madame Tussaud's.'

We had imagined whole corridors in which the visitor could, in after years, have seen us displayed. You placed me, not wholly to my delight, in the corridor of the actors, and with the cast for 'The Mulberrys'. Fenella Kempe, my old landlady, had, you averred, been affecting the painted scarecrow 'look' for years in readiness for taking her place in this Pantheon. Hubie Power will be there beside me, too.

'And it will do that bitch good to get some of the weight off her.'

Nothing in your hilarity prepared me for the awesome seriousness of this place. As I recall it, the catacombs are a subterranean square of corridors, interlaced and joined by subsquares, and entirely lined with the dead. Corpses are classified. One extraordinary chantry houses the virgins, now shrunken and tiny, some appearing to lean forward and retch in their shrouds of yellowing lace. Another corridor is lined

195

with the clergy. Birettas and mitres which once had perched proudly on prelatial heads have now sunk over the grinning skulls to jaunty angles suggestive of paper hats at a Christmas party. Capuchin friars themselves in untold number line spare walls, the only skeletons who seem appropriately dressed in their long brown cowls.

Inevitably, perhaps, it is those who fall into no obvious category who attract the most pensive observation – the strange angle and grin of a woman in a silken dress still bright green after a hundred and forty years; a man who could be Mr Dombey, with a frock-coat and a top hat falling down over his gaping eye sockets; children in sailors' caps and Kate Greenaway bonnets.

Sargie, who wept easily, used to be made to 'blub' on a fairly regular basis each year, gin tears streaming as he sang along to 'O valiant hearts', watching the Armistice on the telly and heard again the Lawrence Binyon tribute to the slain. I had quite often wept too, watching with him, half-conscious that it was not the truth but the untruth of the words which made us gulp and catch our breaths. For the dead will grow old as we that are left grow old; the notion that they are frozen in perpetual youth is immediately belied by the Capuchin catacombs of Palermo. There, even the babies stoop and leer like geriatric patients. Everyone is coated in the dust to which we all return. Of course, I always apply the words to Mummy: 'They shall grow not old, as we that are left grow old.' You are perpetually fixed, a young, smiling woman with thin arms and springy hair, waving at me as the train pulls out, forcing me to wave you out of my life; allowing my emotional life to churn in an endless repetition of a search for you. Age shall not weary you, nor the years condemn; and so, in each new young woman, I set out to find the protective combination of tomboy chum and maternal breast who could keep me safe in the air raid shelter. And none of them could fulfil this role, and that was no one's fault. Your darling body was blown to bits by the *fucking* Germans (whom God damn and whom I shall never forgive) and so it would never have been possible for me to visit you in a catacomb like this; but, if only I could have done so, how much saner I should be. This is a safer place than Barking in which to store our ghosts; for we see that even our dead can age and even our dead can change.

I paused to have some such thoughts by a particularly harrowing pair, a woman in a long dress with her skeletal arm through that of her husband's black frock-coat. They had the resigned but by no means cheerful air of a couple huddled by a bus-stop, at the agonisingly ambiguous point in the evening when they might, or might not, have missed the last bus home. Like so much in that underground place, they seemed archetypical: the crumbling embodiment of the married state, of the male-female relationship, never to be resolved, never to find its fulfilment; a dusty monument to the truism that happiness can be found neither with, nor without, a life-companion.

The sound of footsteps in some other part of the tombs broke the reverie and awoke selfish rage. I had wanted to be here alone; five minutes more of the place and I should indeed have transformed these silent companions into my own Persons in Barking – into my lost child, my lost parents, and the friends, known and unknown, who already, though I was but in my thirties, had trudged forward into the dust: Granny, Cecily, Day Muckley, Virgil D. Everett and Jimbo among many others.

Clonk, clonk, clonk of shoe on flagstones. Turning the corner, I saw Persephone and for the first time thought of the significance of her name, for the first time appropriate in this subterranean kingdom of the dead.

Surrounded by the silence of the departed, the Newnham Norn's voice was for once audible.

'I thought I'd find you here.'

'Why?'

'Because Margaret Mary says you have talked of nothing else ever since they told you they were having Christmas in Palermo.'

In every sense of the phrase full of life, and unwontedly plump, Persy took my arm, and we stood for a moment, contemplating the pair waiting forever by the eternal bus-stop. Comparisons were too obvious to voice. We waited until we had walked back to the Corridoio Sacerdoti before taking refuge in inevitable banter.

'All these old priests in birettas look as if they should be at the Oratory.'

'Urra-tree. Only a bit too lively, some of them.'

'I agree,' she said.

'I think some of them look like Vatican II men. Before long one of them will be leaving the priesthood and marrying.'

She squeezed my arm by way of allusion to her own recent marriage to a priest.

'Are you happy, Perse?'

'Yes, Julian. I really, really am happy. God – it's funny to hear myself saying those words.'

'Well, in that case, I'm happy for you.'

She put a hand on each of my shoulders and kissed me. Down among the dead men, we had our last kiss – not the consoling kiss of a married woman for a mental patient, but the last parting of lovers, a full and erotic kiss, long and intense.

'It would never have worked, you and I,' she said, when, hand in hand, we had left the friary and walked back towards the city.

Our Child – our unborn one – cried out, *But let me live! You have let her live!* By 'her' the Floating babe, who was the Resurrection and the Life, intended the child in Persephone's womb; and Agennetos who knew of the First and the Last, the Beginning and the End, foretold rightly that Persy was carrying a girl-child.

The voice of the Unborn drowned out the voice of the living mother, enabling me to avoid rage with her, and to blot out the fact that, by patronising me, she was rescuing herself from the intensity of our last embrace. Just as the last wisp of it evaporated, like the final puff of steam from a departing train, my love for the Newnham Norn seemed painfully full and perfect.

'Some of the sex was good, wasn't it?' I asked. A hot palm squeezed mine in noiseless reply.

She was right, I did not mind her marrying a fat old Friar Tuck if she thought that would make her happy. Probably it made her happier than if she had married me, though, when I reflect on the optimism of her early married days, I am amused to think that Persy believed Friar Tuck could cure her evilly angry temperament. (Oh, the rows I've heard since between them! The smashing of crockery, the hurling of books, glasses and even saucepans, the navvy-language – but this lay ahead when, obedient to the Almighty if not to his Father Provincial, Friar Reilly had increased himself and multiplied.)

A couple of days later, the newly-weds accompanied the rest of us to Rome on our return flight. Waves, kisses, even hugs on parting when they went towards passports and custom control, and we four

– Fergus, M.M., Father Quarles and I – towards the departure lounge for Heathrow.

The jockeying for place on the plane reflected the oddness of our idea that we might all have wished to spend Christmas together. All three men wished to sit beside Margaret Mary, but all felt a powerful aversion to the notion of sitting beside one another. Strength of character will out, however. Father Quarles sat next to Margaret Mary (on his left) with the window on his right. Fergus got to sit next to me.

'I suppose,' he said gamely to me, as we soared twenty thousand feet above the snowy Appenines, 'that you are looking forward to getting back to work – to radio work.'

It was a fair supposition. Rodney, the producer of 'The Mulberrys', had been nothing if not kind, and the script-writer had arranged that Jason Grainger, at the wheel of a sports car, was to make his raffish return to the fictitious village of Barleybrook as soon as recording started in the New Year. Once again, in quarter-hour dollops, Jason's adventures and bad behaviour would be artificially used to enliven the tedious quotidian of foot-and-mouth scares, poaching, and quarrels between the Swills and the Mulberrys.

Over by the windows, I knew that Linus Quarles was making his own strange version of a sexual advance; unable to claim that he was the father of the child, he had now frequently repeated the boast that he had magicked it into existence by saying the right kind of votive Marce and by praying to St Joseph. Thus, although the forthcoming birth gave no comfort to the priest, by threatening to banish him on some Sundays at least to the company of the lower-class novices, he could at any rate get in on the act of regeneration. Nature is redeemed by grace: that is the Catholic religion. In spite of the misfortune of its Irish surname, the new child could be a Mount-Smith in spirit. If male, it could undo its suburban origins by going to Stonyhurst and Oxford; if female, it might acquire an altogether more illustrious name, by marrying into one of the better Catholic families. As a poor mad Protestant once wrote, God moves in a mysterious way, his wonders to perform.

My voices helped to blot out the dark, bleak consciousness of Margaret Mary's treachery. I could not prove that she had become Hunter's lover; any more than I could prove that Hunter had murdered

Mr Everett; or they could prove that the bread on their altars became the Body of Christ. The certainties which guide us through life – whether consolatory or agonising – seldom admit of laboratory-verifications. All the things which had, as I supposed, made me love Margaret Mary were qualities which I had superimposed upon her beautiful features – her calmness, her spirituality, her tangible goodness. Did the clever-as-anything egghead ninny beside me, her husband, have enough common sense to recognise that he had been cuckolded; or was it easier to believe that St Joseph and Father Quarles had between them managed what years of copulation and medical treatment had failed to achieve? Not for the first time, I felt incorrigibly Protestant, unable to imagine why anyone could believe that the Almighty had given such power to the clergy or why, if he had done so, one should find the fact consoling. (In the Church of England, we too have the Catholic doctrine that *the unworthiness of ministers hindereth not the effect of the sacrament*; but how strange to inhabit a moral universe in which the clergy have the authority to withhold or grant the forgiveness of sin; and how odd it must be to believe that Father Linus Quarles, SJ, by virtue of his priesthood, has a special licence to absolve a human soul from guilt, to blot out the eternal consequences of moral responsibility. To the Catholic, the character or qualifications of the priest are absolutely unimportant, and there is no contradiction – barely even a paradox – in the fact that Father Quarles, virtually unemployable even by the Society of Jesus, should have been granted this august privilege by the power which rules the universe.)

Inevitably conversation with Fergus petered out by the time we were zooming over the Alps, and peering at the unappetising food which had been set before us. Abandoning the effort to eat the main course (some chicken) with miniature plastic cutlery, I negotiated the apparently unopenable cellophone which encased the cheese, and ate. It managed to be both sweaty and cold. Over coffee, I read the papers.

Hunter's face smiled out of all the book reviews – Madge Cruden's eccentric decision to publish his book in the quiet week just after Christmas had paid dividends, in terms of lavish reviewing space being devoted to his Volume Two. I suspect that the size of the book deterred most of the reviewers; it being an almost sure way of avoiding censure, to write books which can not conveniently be read in the week or so which reviewers would normally allow themselves for their task. Few writers dare to condemn what they have not read. The three reviews which I read on the aeroplane concentrated more on Jimbo than on Hunter. Malcolm Muggeridge suggested that Jimbo was an essentially meretricious talent, justly forgotten; a belettrist of the silver age, one tiny symptom among many that civilisation had finally come to an end some time after the First World War. In another paper, Philip Hope Wallace compared Jimbo unfavourably with Lytton Strachey – which in my opinion slightly missed the point of the kind of author Jimbo actually was. One review did surprise me. This was by Deborah Arnott, who had never in my experience suggested much sympathy for James Petworth Lampitt and his works.

This, she declared, *will surely rank as one of the great literary biographies of the century . . . a clear case of the biographer being a greater man than his subject . . . absorbing . . . delicacy of touch . . . humour.*

Either Debbie had her own perverse reasons for praising Hunter's book, or Volume Two was radically different from its predecessor which, for all his claims to a wide readership through salacious suggestion, was a decidedly lumpen product. And then, in the middle of so much trivial stuff – for who *cared* what Debbie Arnott made of Hunter's book, who really cared? – I saw the obituary.

It should not have been a surprise, but it was. Sargie was full of years – seventy-nine according to *The Times*. I read the obituary without taking in any details, and then, gradually, I seized bits of it here and there, reading the piece backwards.

I gather it was written by an old Oxford colleague of Sargie's. These were the days when obituaries were still framed in the politest of codes and newspapers observed the courtesy of *de mortuis nil nisi bonum*.

Readers of *The Times* were therefore informed that Sargie, though reclusive by temperament, was capable of high conviviality – obituarese for the sad fact that Sargie was an old man who lived on his own and drank too much. There were a number of biographical facts in the obituary notice which were certainly news to me. I never knew that he had won the MC at Ypres. His comments on trench warfare – and I had heard him make many – had been limited to denunciations of the 'I.P.', and in particular their urinary habits in relation to army boots. I had no idea, either, that until his débâcle – described here as a breakdown in health – Sargie had been destined for a parliamentary career. The House of Lords book was praised, and the obituarist suggested that, in his younger days as an academic, Sargent Lampitt had been not just the best, but in some ways the only original, thinker after the 'collapse of idealism'. R. G. Collingwood's high views of Sargie were quoted; and Hugh Gaitskell's. His marriage to Cecily was said to be based much on their mutual intellectual regard (obituary-language for the fact that they were physically incompatible and that they did not live together for the last forty-five years of their married lives).

The news of this death shook me with feelings of loneliness. The Nolans were probably very sweet in their way, but suddenly I felt as if I were among strangers. I did not even wish to allude to Sargie's death when speaking to M.M. because I did not want her heedless 'Poor Julian'. I knew somehow, after this journey, that the Nolan phase of things was over. I still had my 'crush' on M.M., but I found that, as well as hating Hunter, I also hated her, just a little, for the pregnancy.

'I see here that Sargent Lampitt has died. Now I wonder if he is any relation to Petworth – to Raphael Hunter's Petworth Lampitt,' called out Father Linus Quarles over the roar of the engine.

I shrugged. The priest was just far enough away for it to have been possible for me not to have heard him. The Lampitts were about the last thing that Fergus Nolan would have wished to discuss. I looked at Fergus's face, so close beside me, sitting in the plane. He had a high colour and he never shaved very well. Had things gone differently, he would have been my brother-in-law. I felt extremely glad that he was not.

'Change of plan,' I said, at the airport, when they assumed I was going to bundle with them into the bus for Reading. 'I've decided to go straight home.'

Sargie belonged to Timplingham. It was appropriate that the family decided to have the funeral there, even though – thanks to Sargie – there was nothing left of Timplingham Place. He had asked to be buried in his mother's grave and, with typical selfishness, he had asked for my uncle to conduct the obsequies. I wonder if the Lampitts knew what a burden they placed upon my uncle's shoulders when they relayed this part of Sargie's will, and asked him to take the funeral service. 'Sargie's tame parson' had been Jimbo's own description of Uncle Roy.

He had been so much more in Sargie's life than that; and Sargie so much more in his. Even my aunt, who had always deplored Sargie, and the disruptive effects of the friendship on vicarage life, had recognised its importance. When I had gone home – and I did not even telephone to tell them I was coming – I went straight to Liverpool Street and got the first Norwich train, I had been moved by the kindness, the solicitude of Aunt Deirdre to her husband. Abrasiveness was her natural mode, particularly in the marital relationship. Now, as she touched her husband's shoulder – by her lights this was being very demonstrative – I was reminded of her behaviour towards me when a return to boarding-school was in prospect. One could not doubt her deep sympathy; at the same time she did not wish to provoke a flood of tears by being too kind.

An unwonted silence had fallen on the Rectory. Only when I had been there for a couple of days did I realise what it was: no anecdotes, no Lampitt-lore, no Sargie-stories. Stunned into grief, Uncle Roy had nothing much to say. This was all the more painful since my aunt had arranged that the mourners would come back to us after the funeral for baked meats – there being no other house in the village that was suitable. It was a real reversal of rôles. My aunt took telephone calls, rang up Vernon at Mallington, and Sibs in Chelsea. The airy way in which she suggested that it would be 'no trouble at all' to give ham and tea and whisky to anyone hardy enough to attend the funeral in January might have suggested to the uninitiated that she was the sort of parson's wife who was forever giving parties or opening her doors to parishioners. Nothing could have been further from the truth; in fact I do not remember her ever offering hospitality to anyone except to her old school-friend Bunty. If only some minor member of the Lampitt tribe were being buried in Timplingham, so that Uncle Roy could *enjoy* it! The thought of the Blood Royal coming back afterwards for refreshments would in normal circumstances have had him jibbering with excitement for days in advance, and yelling at her for not providing suitable food or drink. He did not so much as polish a glass in readiness for their coming.

'Roy – are you sure you ought to take this funeral?' It was the first time I had ever heard my aunt use her husband's name, or indeed any form of vocative when addressing him.

'Oh, I must,' was all he said.

'I could always ring up Biggle – ' Canon Biggle being a neighbouring incumbent roughly speaking sympathetic to my uncle's liturgical requirements.

'No, no; that would be quite impossible,' was all Uncle Roy would say.

He spoke with his pipe in his mouth, his eyes unfocused. He sucked on the pipe vigorously. Most unusually for him, he had not changed from his clericals after the business of morning church was over; and he had been sitting around in a cassock all morning.

'I've got to take this funeral,' he added. And then he said the two impossible words, the words which he had, presumably, been unable to envisage through all his years of besotted devotion. 'Sargie's asked.'

My aunt and I could both see that he was weeping when he left the kitchen. She, too, seemed very much moved, which made her voice seem crosser when she said, 'I want Ron to help me tie back the winter-flowering jasmine at the front door before all the guests arrive.'

It is the Barking effect – the strength of the voices inside our heads: I never ceased to think of Uncle Roy and Sargie as a double-act, even though they had been estranged (so pointlessly and so stupidly) for the last fifteen years of Sargie's life. My uncle alluded to his friend, not merely every day of his life, but for most hours of his day. Even when he was not speaking of Sargie, it was not hard to guess where his thoughts were, as he sat with the *Daily Telegraph* half-read on his tweedy knee, with a smile of pleasure suddenly wreathing his gentle features.

Throughout my childhood in the Rectory, I had found it so boring, Uncle Roy's obsession with Sargie and All the Lampitts. Now, as one came to realise that youth was past, I saw much more vividly what a rare thing their friendship had been. Happy are those whose love lasts. Hunter's 'Petworth' was a cardboard figure determined entirely, in youth, by the number of people he had supposedly bedded, and in later life by the number of famous people he had met. In both cases,

Hunter had doctored the evidence or simply made it up. Even if he had not done so, however, he would not have been painting a portrait of a human being. Hunter had nothing to say about the real engagement of Jimbo's emotions – with his family, with his young protégés such as Albion Pugh and, above all, with his sister-in-law Cecily.

How lucky we are, most of us, not to merit a biography commissioned by some London publisher who is only interested in Sunday newspaper values and who would probably think the two volumes of Hunter's 'Petworth' a thoroughly creditable piece of work. These travesties of human life – these lists of beds and names – tell us nothing. Those deadly anecdotes of Uncle Roy's, crushing in their tedium for me as a child, said so much more; particularly the truly trivial ones.

'I leant forward and whispered, "Sargie, you can't ask a waiter to change the *carrots* at this stage of the meal."

' "Whyever not? I'm something paying. They'd change them at Clabbage's."

' "In all likelihood, but this is a very modest establishment at . . ." '

He did not often manage to say 'Sheringham' without spluttering and giggling at this peculiar vignette. The hours they had spent, motoring about Norfolk together, or taking off to the south coast, or going up to London, killing time because that was all there was to do with it. Early thoughts about their friendship had made me see Uncle Roy as the ever-patient partner, prepared to put up with the absurd tedium of these expeditions because he was always willing to pander to Sargie's whims. I had always assumed that it was Sargie's time they were killing and not Uncle Roy's. Middle age made me less sure of that. There wasn't much to do at Timplingham. Church passed a bit of time but, since he broke with Sargie, my uncle had spent most of his days doing absolutely nothing, staring out of windows. Items in the *Daily Telegraph* which had the smallest bearing on Lampitt-lore could be cut out, or copied out; and might be the occasion for letters to members of that family.

'Had an extraordinarily nice letter back from Ursula about that thing I sent her the other day.'

'What thing?' My aunt's abrupt tone would not have been too sharp if the thing in question had been a pornographic magazine.

'A very small item about the numbers of Rawlinson *alumnae* who have been awarded the DBE. I think she was pleased to see it, even though it transpired that it was she who had given it to the newspaper in the first place. A small world!'

One scribbled line from Dame Ursula Lampitt was a poor substitute for whole days with Sargie. During the mercifully brief period when they took up golf together, I remember going with them up to Brancaster to caddy for them and watch them play. I must have been about twelve. The day had started so brightly. After a picnic luncheon, and a good game, we would, Sargie said, all drive over to Mallington to tea and look up old Vernon – at that stage a very junior member of Attlee's Cabinet. One never saw him so happy.

Sargie's change of mood on the links probably crept up on him, but I did not notice it coming. Perhaps this was because I was going through my brief 'Hornblower' phase and was scanning the maritime horizon of that great five-mile straight stretch of pebble and water for tall sailing ships and French men o' war. No one thinks it's mad to indulge in such mental doodles during childhood – presumably one of the reasons sentimentalists say that childhood is the happiest time of life. Caddying is a crushingly boring experience, so it is no wonder that I allowed my thoughts to roam.

'Please, Sargie! Please!'

And there he was *sitting down* in the fairway, crying and refusing to move. He had hurled one of his irons into a bush, and some of the others were scattered over the mown surface of the links.

The tantrum was not brought on because he was losing the game. He had in fact been winning; my uncle was a moderately hopeless golfer. Sargie just wanted the whole thing to stop, couldn't bear it to go on.

When the funeral came, there were pathetically few mourners: Felicity (his god-daughter); Sibs and my ex-wife Anne (with whom I got on perfectly well these days); Vernon and Pat; Ursula, and Aunt Deirdre. At the last moment, the church door creaked open and Miss Dare slipped in. She had recently moved back into the neighbourhood from Birmingham, and she now attended all services conducted by her hero.

Hardly enough people, as my aunt observed later with a sniff, to make much of a showing with the hymns. Sargie, however, though no churchgoer, had specified in a written note that he wanted 'O valiant hearts' and 'Eternal father, strong to save'. The tunes were rousing enough, and it did not seem the moment to be wondering what possible significance the words might have in this particular case.

It was certainly the most harrowing funeral I have ever attended apart from Mummy's and Daddy's. Since, like theirs, it was conducted by Uncle Roy, distraught with grief, the one sorrow inevitably opened the old wounds of the other. I tried to keep a check on my tears by recalling adolescent states of fury with my uncle. He could still awaken these in me from time to time; and, though I no longer felt the old surges of rage with him, he could be relied upon to provoke an automatic desire to contradict, whatever the words coming from his mouth. Thus, though with tears streaming, I could mutter, 'No you're not', when Uncle Roy led Sargie's coffin into the church and announced, in a high-pitched sob, 'I am the resurrection and the life.'

A List of Characters Mentioned in the Story

If a character has made a first appearance in some other volume of *The Lampitt Papers*, this is indicated in brackets. IH is an abbreviation for *Incline Our Hearts*, BS for *A Bottle in the Smoke*, DA for *Daughters of Albion*.

CORAL AHRLICH   Married to Newt Ahrlich, *née* Birk.

NEWT AHRLICH   A partner in Virgil D. Everett's law firm, Everett, Everett, Klein, Ahrlich and Kavanagh.

DEBORAH ARNOTT   A popular novelist. As Mrs Maddock (IH) she had lived in Timplingham during Julian's childhood. She and Julian had a brief affair in the late 1950s. (BS, DA)

ATLAS BIRK   A Congressman in the United States' Democratic Party. Newt Ahrlich's brother-in-law.

WILMIE BIRK   Sister of Atlas Birk and Coral Ahrlich. Coral's and Wilmie's family were old diplomatic friends of the Mount-Smiths.

WILLIAM BLOOM   Army friend of Julian (IH), subsequently his publisher. (BS, DA)

MADGE CRUDEN   Publisher at Rosen and Starmer, whose authors include Raphael Hunter and Vernon Lampitt. (BS, DA)

MISS DARE	A recent convert to Catholicism, previously devoted to the Sarum Rite and the Rev. Roy Ramsay. (DA)
MILES DARNLEY	School friend of Julian Ramsay. (DA)
FATHER DELMAR	A retired Anglican priest living in Timplingham village when Julian Ramsay was a child.
VIRGIL D. EVERETT, JNR	Wealthy American businessman who purchased the Lampitt Papers. (BS, DA)
RAPHAEL HUNTER	The biographer of James Petworth Lampitt. Newspaper columnist and television broadcaster and man about literary London. (IH, BS, DA)
CHRISTOPHER JOHNSON	A friend of Wilmie Birk in New York and an acquaintance of Virgil D. Everett.
MONSIGNOR RONALD KNOX	Old friend of the Nolan family.
MRS LAMPITT	She lived at Timplingham Place in Norfolk. The mother of Martin, James Petworth, Michael (who was killed at Mons), Vivian, Sargent and Sybil. (IH, DA)
CECILY LAMPITT	She was married to Sargent Lampitt (IH) and was the close companion of James Petworth Lampitt. (DA)
JAMES PETWORTH LAMPITT	Son of Mrs Lampitt of Timplingham. A belletrist historian in the early to mid-twentieth century. The subject of a two-volume biography by Raphael Hunter. (IH, DA)
JOSEPH LAMPITT I	A late-eighteenth-century brewer of

radical political leanings. Purchased Mallington Hall with his fortune.

THE HON. KIRSTY LAMPITT — Daughter of Vernon Lampitt. (DA)

ORLANDO LAMPITT — An actor, the son of Vivian Lampitt and rather a black-sheep of the family.

PAT LAMPITT — Lady Lampitt, married to Vernon Lampitt of Mallington Hall. A former Wren officer. (DA)

SARGENT LAMPITT — The fifth child of Mrs Lampitt of Timplingham, he was a Fellow of New College, Oxford, and regarded by many as the best political theorist of the age. Nervous disabilities compelled him to lead a retired life in the country where he relied heavily on the friendship of the Rev. Roy Ramsay. After an irreconcilable quarrel Julian Ramsay became his companion and factotum. He now resides in a nursing home. (IH, BS, DA)

URSULA LAMPITT — Dame Ursula Lampitt, Principal of Rawlinson College, Oxford. Sargent Lampitt's cousin. (BS, DA)

VERNON LAMPITT — Lord Lampitt, of Mallington Hall. An extreme left-winger, known popularly as Ernie Lampitt. (IH, BS, DA)

CHANTAL MOUNT-SMITH — Married to Henry Mount-Smith.

HENRY MOUNT-SMITH — Margaret Mary Nolan's brother, the husband of Chantal. They have three children, Magdalen, Kitty and Patrick.

WILLIAM MOUNT-SMITH — Margaret Mary Nolan's 'Uncle Bill', a university friend of Linus Quarles.

211

DAY MUCKLEY	Old friend of Julian Ramsay. As a writer he received financial support from James Petworth Lampitt.
'THE MULBERRYS'	A radio drama series of great popularity. Julian Ramsay plays 'Jason Grainger' in this series. (IH, BS, DA)
DOMINIC NOLAN	A diplomat at the UN, the son of Fergus and Margaret Mary.
FERGUS NOLAN	Persy Nolan's brother. A strict Catholic and research scientist, he has been called upon to advise the Pope on the moral admissibility of the contraceptive pill.
JOYCE NOLAN	Persy Nolan's sister.
MARGARET MARY NOLAN	Married to Fergus Nolan, _née_ Mount-Smith.
PERSY NOLAN	Julian Ramsay's girlfriend and the lead singer in 'The Newnham Norns' while a Cambridge undergraduate. (DA)
MME DE NORMANDIN	Julian Ramsay's French hostess at Les Mouettes during summer holidays from school. (IH, DA)
P. J. PILBRIGHT	A colleague of Julian Ramsay and of Julian's father at Tempest and Holmes, the shirt factory. He subsequently became a famous painter. (BS, DA)
LINUS QUARLES, SJ	A Jesuit priest and old friend of the Mount-Smith family. Now based in Birmingham.
DAVID RAMSAY	Julian Ramsay's father. Killed during the Second World War. (IH, DA)
DEIRDRE RAMSAY	Married to the Rev. Roy Ramsay. (IH, BS, DA)

FELICITY RAMSAY	Daughter of Roy and Deirdre Ramsay, a philosopher, Julian Ramsay's cousin, they were brought up together at Timplingham Rectory. (IH, DA)
JILL RAMSAY	Julian Ramsay's mother, killed during the Second World War. (IH, DA)
JULIAN RAMSAY	The narrator. A freelance actor ('Jason Grainger' in 'The Mulberrys'), he is writing a book about the Lampitts. (IH, BS, DA)
ROY RAMSAY	The rector of Timplingham, in whose house Julian Ramsay was brought up after the death of his parents. His life-long obsession with the Lampitts stems from his close friendship with Sargent Lampitt. (IH, BS, DA)
THORA RAMSAY	The mother of David and Roy Ramsay and the grandmother of Felicity and Julian Ramsay. (IH, DA)
BONAVENTURE REILLY, OP	A Dominican priest. As Jim Reilly, Fergus Nolan's oldest school and university friend.
RICE ROBEY	A novelist, he wrote novels during his twenties under the pseudonym 'Albion Pugh'. (DA)
RODNEY SMITH	The producer of 'The Mulberrys'. (BS, DA)
ANNE STARLING	Art historian, formerly married to Julian Ramsay. The daughter of Rupert and Sybil Starling. (BS, DA)
SYBIL STARLING	Married to Sir Rupert Starling, née Lampitt. The mother of Anne. (BS, DA)
TIMPSON	Head boy of Seaforth Grange during

	Julian Ramsay's time in the school, now a bishop. (IH, DA)
VAL TREADMILL	Julian Ramsay's English teacher at public school, now teaching at a college in the United States. (IH, DA)
MRS WEBB	The best friend of Julian Ramsay's grandmother. (IH, DA)
PROFESSOR TOMMY WIMBISH	Oxford historian and friend of Julian Ramsay. (DA)